THE **KRAKEN** OF **CAPE MADRE**

LORESTALKER - Book 2

J.P. BARNETT

THE KRAKEN OF CAPE MADRE
Lorestalker – 2
Copyright © 2019 by J.P. Barnett
Cover Art Copyright © 2019 by Richard Tran

FIRST EDITION SOFTCOVER
ISBN: 1622530756
ISBN-13: 978-1-62253-075-5

Editor: Mike Robinson
Interior Designer: Lane Diamond

EVOLVED PUBLISHING™
www.EvolvedPub.com
Butler, Wisconsin, USA

Printed in Book Antiqua font.

Praise for *The Beast of Rose Valley*

The first book in this "Lorestalker" series received some amazing reviews, including these from three separate reviewers at Readers' Favorite Book Reviews:

"...a marvelous romp into the little-known world of cryptozoology... Barnett's plot is clever and irresistible, and his book is a sheer pleasure to read. Horror, thriller and mystery fans alike will find much to their liking in this intriguing story about the unknown. ...most highly recommended."
~ *Jack Magnus (5 STARS)*

"Intrigue, curiosity, surprises, and the depth of the plot will keep you on the edge of your seat, wondering if they [the characters] will understand all they need to, and be able to use it in order to save those they care for. As the first book in the Lorestalker series, *The Beast of Rose Valley* certainly sets a high bar for those to follow, and I look forward to future adventures."
~ *K.J. Simmill (5 STARS)*

"The well fleshed out characters are one of the strengths of the story. The relationships between the protagonists are deftly developed without overwhelming the intriguing pursuit of the elusive beast. The narrative is simple yet engaging and the gory scenes are not too extreme or disturbing. ... On the whole, Barnett is a fluent storyteller and I found myself gripped to the last page."
~ *Lit Amri (5 STARS)*

BOOKS BY J.P. BARNETT

The LORESTALKER Series
The Beast of Rose Valley
The Kraken of Cape Madre
The Witch of Gray's Point (Coming December 2019)

CHAPTER 1

Miriam Brooks stared across the beach and tried to focus on the waves calmly creeping up the sand. Her stomach fluttered with anxiety. Social anxiety, she guessed, though she hadn't been to therapy. Whatever the problem, it had gotten much worse since the death of her brother—at the hands of a vicious government experiment, no less.

It felt weird to think of it that way. But it was the truth. The terrifying, surreal truth.

She did love the ocean. If the beach were empty, and she hadn't reluctantly agreed to wear such a ridiculously revealing swimsuit, she might have actually enjoyed it. She hadn't had access to an ocean growing up in Missouri, but she'd spent her high school years lifeguarding at the local pool.

Miriam felt a tug at her hand, followed by the voice of her friend Macy, who urged her toward the surf. "You look fine!"

Maybe she did. Miriam couldn't really tell when she looked in the mirror, but she did know that she regretted giving in to Macy's flattery and encouragement. The fact that she showed more skin than she would have liked wasn't her problem, though. No. The problem centered squarely on the silly purpose of it all—to meet boys. Macy's Number One pastime, and Miriam's Number One fear. Miriam didn't want to talk to any boys about anything, ever, but certainly not when she was half-naked.

Another tug on her hand — this one more forceful — finally pried Miriam's arms away from her midriff. Macy interlaced her slender fingers with Miriam's and jerked her along the sand, leaving no choice but for Miriam to follow. The wind whipped across her belly button and Miriam felt the briefest jolt of exhilaration.

This whole thing seemed so much easier for Macy. The simple blue bikini she wore looked amazing, hugging her skin, showing off her curves, and dutifully ignoring any flaws. Macy didn't have knobby knees, or a pear-shaped figure, and though her skin may have been even paler than Miriam's, somehow Macy carried it better, exuding a beautiful porcelain glow as opposed to Miriam's more sickly pallor. Miriam insisted on wearing a wet-suit. Macy would have none of it.

As they moved closer to the water, Miriam spotted relief in the sizable form of Tanner. The only family she had left. He waved when he saw them, beckoning them to a slice of beach he'd staked out earlier.

Once they closed in, Tanner exclaimed, "Holy crap, Mir. Put some clothes on!"

Macy punched Tanner playfully on the arm. "Leave her alone. She looks pretty."

"I'll have to take your word for it," Tanner replied, massaging his bicep. "No offense, Mir, but you know..."

He left the rest unsaid, but Miriam knew what he meant. Though Tanner was only her cousin, the two of them had grown up together under the oppressive regime of Miriam's abusive father. For all intents and purposes, Tanner Brooks had earned the title of brother.

Macy scanned the beach. "So, what's the sitch?"

"The jocks are over there," Tanner said as he pointed up the shoreline. "They staked out the volleyball court, of course." Then he motioned the opposite direction, toward the array of toned, glistening bodies lying on towels. "Sunbathers over there."

Macy nodded towards the large mountain of sand between them and the water, then shot Tanner a derisive look. "And you put us with the sandcastles?!"

Tanner shrugged. "Sure. Why not? Didn't figure Mir would want to be in the thick of things."

Exactly. She didn't. At all. This location presented the perfect place to avoid everyone. Except the sand castle people, of course. Even though Miriam hadn't built a sand castle since before her mother died, she felt like the kind souls carefully attending to their sculptures would keep to themselves. No flirting. No awkward conversations.

Yes. The sand castle people were her people.

"Fine," Macy sighed. "You ready, Mir? Let's go meet some guys."

Tanner interjected on Miriam's behalf. "Maybe hit the waves first. Water looks great."

Macy cast a sideways glance at Tanner before slumping her shoulders at Miriam. "Ok. Ok. Go swim. But I'm not letting you leave this beach without meeting at least one new person!"

Miriam nodded solemnly, not really intending to agree to anything, then dashed off towards the water, rushing in up to her waist. She enjoyed the enveloping comfort of the warm salt water, and, her favorite aspect, the endless stretch of horizon. She liked to think of the world like this: an infinite expanse. A world that didn't end meant a world of endless possibility, where the laws of culture and society and even science didn't have to matter.

Her dad had honed her into a monster-hunting robot. She had finally rebelled against it, but part of her still believed. How could she not, after what she'd seen?

In her youth, Miriam dreamed about being a marine biologist, or deep-sea diver. She loved the documentaries where people folded themselves up into tiny little submarines and charted the unknown. Alas, her father never let her pursue that dream, but she could feel the very earliest vestiges of choice coming back to her. Maybe she could one day spend her time out in the water. In a wet-suit, though, not a bikini.

The splish-splash behind her alerted Miriam to Macy's approach, causing her to lament the loss of her perfect, lonely moment. Macy—usually one to chatter—didn't say anything. She just stood silently, comfortably close and seemingly as enthralled by the horizon as Miriam.

The ocean waves muted the sounds of people up the beach. A seagull squawked overhead, then swooped down into the water, coming up with a fish that it would never be able to swallow.

"You know," Miriam said. "There's a parasite that lives in snails. Gets eaten by the fish. Then it burrows up to their eyeballs and—"

"Ew, Mir! You're ruining the moment." Macy giggled, nudging Miriam with her shoulder.

"No this is totally cool," Miriam continued. "Once it takes root, it basically controls the fish! When the parasite is young, it makes the fish move more slowly and stay in deep waters. Then, when it wants to reproduce, it makes the fish swim near the surface and jerk around. Causes the birds to eat it."

Macy narrowed her eyes. "So, help me, girl, if you say something about poop, I'm gonna drown you."

"Well," Miriam said as her cheeks flushed. "Yeah. Then the snails eat it. Then the fish eat the snails and it goes on and on. Super awesome."

Macy shook her head. "You and I have very different definitions of awesome."

"It's called *Diplostomum pseudopathaceum*." Miriam beamed, now intentionally trying to goad Macy on.

Macy didn't take the bait. Instead she turned toward Miriam and changed the subject. "I know it's been a hard coupla years, Mir. Losing Cornelius and all. I know you'd rather be studying, but thanks for coming with me on my spring break adventure."

Miriam felt a surge of emotion flow through her, threatening to open a floodgate of tears, but she batted the thoughts away. She refused to cry anymore for Cornelius. He wouldn't want that.

"Come on," Macy said. "Let's go meet someone. Anyone. Doesn't have to be a guy."

Miriam took a deep breath and gazed over the horizon again. Macy only wanted to help, Miriam realized, but being normal was so agonizingly difficult.

As Miriam relented and turned back to the shore, she heard shouting. Off to their left, a young female swimmer hurtled through the air from twenty feet up. With nothing that she could have launched herself from, it seemed impossible—as if something threw her from the water.

Adrenaline flooded through Miriam. Though she couldn't tell how the teenaged girl got so high in the air, she knew the impact on the water would certainly be jarring. Might even knock her unconscious.

The girl seemed to fall back to the waves in slow motion, her black hair tumbling and flailing. By the time she plunged through the surface, Miriam took off toward her, throwing arm over arm as she kicked forward with expert grace.

Dumbfounded, Macy shouted after her. "Mir! What are you doing?"

The sloshing against Miriam's ears prevented her from hearing anything else. Only when she'd crossed an appropriate distance did she pop back up to tread water and look around. Her head turned in every direction, looking for any sign of the girl's pink bikini or raven hair.

Miriam took a deep breath and held it to try to steady her vision. The girl might be unconscious, face-down in the water. If so, Miriam didn't have much time.

There!

She saw a spot of pink pop up in the trough of a wave, barely visible. Miriam threw herself back into the waves and swam to her target. In a matter of seconds, she pulled up next to the swimmer and quickly flipped her limp body, so that she faced up out of the water. Scrutinizing the girl for any injuries, Miriam winced when she saw deep purple bruises around the girl's midsection.

With no pier or boat in sight, Miriam worked through the possibilities of what could have caused this girl to fall out of the sky. And maybe more importantly, what could have possibly done this to her stomach?

Miriam sucked air in, working to calm herself before the long trek back. Tanner would have seen this from the shore. He would come. Miriam knew he would.

Something ran into her leg, hard enough to knock her sideways. A fish, maybe? She kicked at it, forcing it to scuttle away. A splash to her left caused her to turn her head. Something floated in the water.

Not floated. Writhed.

Its purple, slimy skin moved along the surface, skimming towards her. A wave caused it to twist, revealing a lighter pink underside and the outline of huge suction cups. An octopus? A squid? It seemed far too large for either.

A slideshow of legendary creatures flipped through her head; stories from the age of pirates and Greek sailors. She needed a second set of eyes, but they were far from shore. Too far for anyone else to possibly see this.

Miriam shook her head to try to make sense of it, but as the ominous tentacle moved closer, she hooked the girl under one of her arms. Kicking as hard as she could, Miriam moved towards the shoreline, desperate to put distance between them and the monster below.

Sploosh!

Something deep and loud. She twisted her head but kept kicking. She didn't see it anymore. Her lungs burned. Her legs ached. Too much time studying. Not enough time training. She pushed away the pain and swam. Like her life — and the life of this girl — depended on it.

The shore seemed forever away, but another form swam towards her, causing her to slow to meet them. Tanner? Or a lifeguard maybe?

Tanner's head popped up a few feet away. "Mir. Are you okay?"

Miriam nodded and transferred the unconscious swimmer to Tanner's stronger arms. "Something was out there. Something—" She shook her head. "Go. Let's just *go!*"

Together, they swam until they could stand. Tanner lifted the girl in his arms, trudged through the remaining water, and laid her down on the sandy beach. Miriam collapsed next to the girl and rested an ear against her chest, listening carefully. The girl's chest rose and fell. Faintly. She coughed and convulsed, her eyelids flitting wildly.

Miriam registered cheers behind her, but they seemed distant. The fact that this girl remained unconscious was bad. Very bad. Miriam worried that there might be internal bleeding. Didn't this damn beach have any lifeguards?

Mesmerized by the injuries, Miriam grazed the tips of her fingers along the bruises around the girl's midsection. It looked painful, possibly life-threatening. That tentacle. It must have grabbed her. And threw her? That didn't seem possible. She pushed away her fascination and stood up.

"Someone get help!" she pleaded.

No one budged.

"Emma!" another teenaged girl screamed from the throng, pushing through and throwing herself on the sand. She turned her tearful eyes to Miriam. "Is she okay? Is she going to be okay?"

"I don't—I'm not sure," Miriam stammered. "Hopefully."

A rumble echoed across the beach, and the crowd parted for a red four-wheeler with a stretcher on the back. Finally!

Miriam backed away, tapping Tanner on the shoulder to encourage him to do the same. The lifeguards took over, rushing to secure Emma to the stretcher before zooming her down the beach along with her friend. They paid no attention to Miriam and Tanner.

Miriam collapsed to the sand, dropping her head between her legs to catch her breath.

Tanner sat beside her, his hand on her back. "Nice job, Mir."

She didn't want adulation. Not for this. Maybe she had saved a life today, but if she could believe her own eyes, something dangerous lurked beneath the waves. Her body begged her to relax. To let the adrenaline fade away. But her mind used it to fuel a fire that burned inside of her. Her father had trained her to hunt monsters.

Maybe she'd just found one.

"Mir!" Macy cried, tumbling over toward her. "Holy crap. Don't do stuff like that! Are you ok?"

Macy wrapped her arms around Miriam's shoulders and squeezed.

"I'm fine." Miriam nodded, the salt water dripping off her mousy brown hair. "But I'm counting that as meeting someone new."

CHAPTER 2

Emma Lynn Chu. 20 years old. Student at the University of North Texas in Denton. Her parents had flown in from DFW as quickly as they could. In only his second spring break as a detective, Tommy Wallace was already over it. The town of Cape Madre had gone eleven months without any action, then turned into a circus overnight. He had gobs of interviews to do, including with Emma herself — assuming she woke up — but the signs all pointed to the same place. The same thing. The same inexplicable phenomenon that got swept under the rug the first time.

Tommy regretted becoming a cop. He'd felt bad ticketing spring breakers for arbitrary infractions. Not to mention his numbers were always low, his car was always dirty, and his clothes were always disheveled. He thought moving to detective would make things better, but he was wrong. It had made it worse. Now he had more responsibility, seemingly less power, and had added about twenty more pounds to his gut. He went from svelte, wide-eyed rookie to overweight jaded detective in record time. At least he held a record in something.

He crinkled up yet another burger wrapper and tossed it into the backseat of his car. The old Crown Vic could hold an impressive amount of trash in its backseat, so he didn't have to empty it that often. Usually someone remarked on his slovenly ways before it ever got full, which would occasionally shame him into doing something about it. Depending on who was making the comment, of course.

Full up on fast food carbs, Tommy stepped out of his car into the parking lot of Emergency Plus. When he grew up, hospitals boasted impressive-sounding names like Metro Central and Harris Research Center. Now they just sounded like discount clubs where you could go and stock up on all your medical needs — in bulk. He imagined stepping up to the counter, ordering a box of syringes, then being told that he could only pay with Discover.

He banged through the dirty glass doors of the hospital and landed immediately into an overflowing waiting room. A quick glance showed largely minor injuries. Mostly kids. Well, college kids, really, who were only his junior by a few years, but he still called them kids, because they acted like children. Whenever spring break rolled around, they lost all their damn marbles. They'd jump off piers into a rocky jetty, or maybe try to dance in the burning embers of a hot fire. Some animals strutted their brightly-colored feathers to attract a mate, but humans had evolved—or devolved— down a much more embarrassing path.

The desk staff knew him, but didn't put themselves in any hurry to attend to him once he stepped up to the counter. They all clicked away on computers, conveniently protected from any judgment. Maybe they were working. Maybe they were playing Tetris. Maybe they were swiping right and planning their evenings.

After what felt like an eternity, one of the receptionists looked up from her computer, didn't bother standing, and finally acknowledged Tommy's presence. Tommy could have forced his hand. He considered throwing around the weight of his badge, but why bother? Emma Chu wasn't going anywhere.

"Hey, Detective. Here to see the Chu family I assume?"

Tommy nodded as the receptionist pointed down one of the long hallways. "Room 166. Her parents hardly ever leave, so I'm sure they're in there."

Each hallway had a color associated with it to help patients find their way. Tommy took off down the purple path. He didn't rush down the hallway, but took his time, dodging the carts and gurneys and noticing every staff member to see if maybe they had hired somebody new. It didn't look like it today. One of the friendlier nurses smiled at him as he walked past. Alice. No, Anna. Something with an A. He made a mental note to remember next time.

Room 166 waited for him with its door slightly ajar. He listened for a few seconds to get a sense of who might be inside, but heard nothing. He rapped lightly at the door as he let himself in.

Darkness enveloped the room. Emma stretched out, nestled in the bed, looking fairly healthy with the exception of the bandages around her midsection. On a small, cheap couch against the wall sat two people that Tommy could only assume were her parents. They both looked up from their phone screens, and immediately stood up to greet him. At least someone had some manners around here.

Tommy offered a hand to the father first, and then the mother, "Mr. Chu? Mrs. Chu? I'm Detective Wallace. I've been assigned to Emma's case."

It was hardly a case. There was no crime here. A girl had gone out swimming in the vastness of the Gulf of Mexico and had a run in with the local fauna. If it wasn't for the previous incident, the police department probably wouldn't have dispatched a detective at all. This case wasn't of interest to the law. It was of interest to the Chamber of Commerce. No one wanted to visit a potentially deadly beach.

As an afterthought, Tommy fished into the pocket of his jacket for his badge, only to find it missing. Did he leave it in the car again? He searched his back pockets and then his front, only to come up empty. He did find a stack of business cards, though, so he held one out to Mr. Chu as if that had been the plan all along.

Mr. Chu took the card and lowered his head slightly, revealing a shiny bald pate. He looked like the type of man who had weathered a stressful life; judging by Mrs. Chu's ageless beauty, though, Tommy suspected the stress had been something Mr. Chu shouldered alone. Tommy could respect that — protecting loved ones from the harsh realities of life.

Unfortunately, there was no protecting them from this.

Tommy motioned over to Emma. "I didn't get a chance to talk to the doctor. How is she?"

Mr. Chu walked over to his daughter's side before answering, pausing to run his hand over her forehead. "Some internal bleeding. They did the surgeries already. They've just got her on sedatives. She should be okay."

Mrs. Chu sniffled a bit and reached for a tissue from the box next to the couch. It was empty. Tommy carried a handkerchief for occasions like this. He handed it over to Mrs. Chu without skipping a beat. She took it and murmured a "thank you" before using it. Carrying a handkerchief was a tradition way too archaic for someone his age, but as a detective, he ran into a lot of crying people. He was an old soul anyway. Possibly ancient.

Sedatives meant that Emma would be awake soon. "That's great to hear. When she's well enough to talk to me, I'd love to hear what she has to say."

Mr. Chu nodded. "Of course. Do you know what did this to her? The doctor doesn't seem to know."

Tommy had his suspicions, and although he made a habit of disobeying orders, the ones on this case were extremely clear and unbreakable, so instead of the truth, Tommy offered up what he could. "No, sir. I'm afraid not. Some sort of sea life, I suppose. Sometimes injuries can seem weird and inexplicable, but they usually have mundane causes. Emma just got unlucky is all. Even though this isn't a crime, I've been assigned to figure it out. For the public safety."

"Of course," Mr. Chu responded.

"There's not really a lot for me to do here until Emma wakes up, but I just wanted to meet you two and let you know that I'm on the case. If you need something, you've got my card. It would help me if I could talk to anyone who might have been with Emma at the time. Do you know who she came here with?"

The two exchanged a glance. More tears trickled down Mrs. Chu's face. Tommy had clearly hit a nerve. He didn't press the issue, choosing to just stand awkwardly while Mr. and Mrs. Chu shared a silent conversation.

Mr. Chu finally settled his gaze on his daughter's peaceful face before answering quietly, "We don't know. She didn't tell us she was coming. She was, um, supposed to be studying. Her grades haven't been ideal."

This revelation didn't surprise Tommy. Most parents wanted to promote themselves as having total control over their children. College kids were all too eager to escape the bonds of their parents, though. They had minds of their own. Though Tommy felt bad for stereotyping, he suspected that the academic pressure on Emma Chu was high.

"No one's come to see her? Who came into the hospital with her?"

For the first time, Mrs. Chu spoke up. "Not since we've been here. I think one of her friends came with her, but she was gone when we arrived. Maybe one of the nurses would know?"

Tommy nodded. "I'll check with them. Thanks. I'll be in touch."

Both parents murmured their gratitude as Tommy slipped out of the room back into the hallway and toward the nurses' station. The friendly one manned it now. Amy. No, Amber, maybe? She flashed him a genuine smile as he approached.

"Well, howdy, detective," she said, not really with as much of a drawl as one would expect of someone using the word *howdy* unironically.

"Hi there, A —" he paused, flustered. "I'm sorry. What was your name again?"

She pointed to the tag on her ample chest. "Kristine. But you can call me Krissy."

Kristine. That very clearly did not start with an A.

"Krissy. Right. I was wondering if you could answer a few questions about Emma Chu in Room 166?"

"Of course, of course. Shall we find a private room, or is here fine?"

Tommy spent a half-second parsing the inflection in her voice when she said the word 'private' but then decided that he might be reading into things. Maybe he was lonelier than he knew.

"Here's fine. Mostly, I just need a lead on someone I can talk to. Someone, you know, conscious. Who might have seen what happened to Emma."

Krissy leaned over the desk between them, propping up her chin with one hand, and searching the ceiling for an answer. Tommy fought with himself to avoid looking down her top. Luckily, she zoned back in before he lost the fight.

"A girl did come in with her," she said. "Another Asian girl. I don't know if we kept notes on that since she wasn't a relative. I think her name was Hannah, maybe? That sounds right. You got a card? I could call you if I remember anything else."

Tommy detected the slightest hint of mischief in her eyes.

Ok. This couldn't be an accident. Krissy was definitely flirting with him, right? It had been a while since Tommy had even dipped his toes into the dating pool, so he was a bit rusty, but there were just too many signs here. Then again, until five minutes ago, he thought her name had started with A, so he hardly knew her.

He glanced down to his gut, considered the possibility that someone might find him attractive, and then dismissed the entire idea. No way. Couldn't be.

Tommy fished a card out of his front pocket and slid it across the desk to her. She took it, studied it, and, in a move that Tommy was not anticipating, slipped it under her top into what he could only assume was her bra strap.

"Okay, Detective Tommy. I'll let you know if I hear something. Or if she drops by."

Tommy instinctively rapped his knuckles on the desk and willed his heart to slow down just a smidge. "Sounds great. I look forward to hearing from you."

He turned and shambled back down the purple hallway. Look forward to hearing from her? Seriously? That wasn't a very professional answer.

Work. He needed to work. He picked up his pace, snaked his way through the waiting room, and collapsed back into his Crown Vic, inadvertently glancing into his rearview mirror as he did so. What kind of slob left his car like this? With no leads, and time to spare, Tommy put the car in drive and pointed it towards the local car wash.

CHAPTER 3

Miriam's face dropped as her eyes beheld the Cape Madre City Library. Tucked into the corner of the town square, its width barely accommodated the dirty glass of the front door granting access to its tomes. She should have known that a tiny tourist trap like Cape Madre wouldn't have an extensive collection of literary and scientific books. Still, it was the best she had at her disposal for the moment, so she marched over, and gently pushed open the door. A bell rang as she did, which she thought wholly inappropriate for the quiet sanctity of a library.

An old, cantankerous-looking woman sat behind the counter, making no move to acknowledge her entrance. No matter. Miriam could find her way around.

She could have done all of this from her phone, or Macy's laptop, but she enjoyed the thrill of the hunt more when there were physical objects. It was old-fashioned, sure, but also more reliable and tangible. Besides, sometimes the greatest finds were in books and records that no one had ever bothered digitizing.

As she snaked through the claustrophobic shelves, her fingertips grazed the spines. She loved books. Not so much fiction, but she could curl up for hours studying anything that taught her something new about the world. Cornelius had loved books even more than she, though. He had a gift for remembering things, and his careful analytical approach to all problems made him invaluable for correlation and collation. Her heart fluttered as she allowed herself to picture him. She owed it to him. In this place. The library would have been one of the first places he visited if he were still alive to go on this trip with them.

The tears for Cornelius had mostly run themselves dry, but it didn't stop Miriam from feeling every day that she had lost a part of herself. A full third of herself, she supposed. She, Tanner, and Cornelius had always operated as a unit, but she never appreciated Cornelius' particular talents until she no longer had access to them. She wished she would have. She loved him and needed him. Of course, it was his death that finally opened her eyes to a lifetime of brainwashing and gave her the strength to walk away from her father, but she would have enjoyed taking that walk with Cornelius at her side.

As she reminisced, her feet and eyes guided her automatically to the non-fiction section, where she landed very near the beginning of the Dewey Decimal System at 001.944 - *Monsters and related phenomena / Cryptozoology.*

Yes! There was a section specifically dedicated to her craft. Most people would have filed such pages under the occult, or maybe even under fiction, but Cryptozoology was real, and monsters *did* lurk in the deepest shadows of the earth. They often deviated from the more fantastical elements of the folktales, but the stories always hid a kernel of truth. Usually, the monster was merely a misidentified animal, but sometimes it was more, and those were the times for which Miriam had spent her life training.

She had a hard time separating her love of Cryptozoology from the hatred of her father, but she was drawn to it, nonetheless, and this Emma girl deserved to have someone looking into the real culprit of her near-drowning. Whatever caused the injuries to Emma's stomach wasn't natural, and Miriam intended to prove it.

Miriam eyed the entire section, able to take it in all at once. This was where she would begin unraveling the mystery. Her skin tingled with excitement. She needed this. She had to know whether this was something she could still do on her own. Without her father.

And, more importantly, without Cornelius.

***

The library sported only one table. Yet Cape Madre was small, and books were the last thing Spring Breakers were looking for, so Miriam took the liberty of commandeering the entire thing. The selection was lacking, but there were a couple of good general reference books, and of course those had led her into other sections so she could study the geography and oceanography of the Texas Gulf Coast.

Yet another path had her studying pirates, not necessarily for their swashbuckling stories, but for their legends of the sea. From there, she took a gentle turn to the free nation of the pirates of Nassau, and then to the mythical creatures of the Bahamian waters. Every place on earth had a monster somewhere in its history.

So focused on flipping from book to book, Miriam didn't notice the librarian approaching her table. She jumped as the old lady cleared her throat.

The lady didn't fit with the image of her job, with a flowered sundress that stretched down to her ankles, and skin more leathery than Miriam's chair. Her gray hair was pulled up into a bun, tightening her facial features. Tiny spectacles hung on a chain around her neck that jingled when she spoke.

"Trying to catch up on some homework?" she asked.

"Something like that, yeah. Hope you don't mind."

The librarian eyed the books strewn about the table, making no effort to hide the fact that she was snooping into the investigation. "Library closes at four."

Was is that late? How could she have spent so much time pouring over so few tomes? Miriam didn't wear a watch, so she slipped her phone out of her pocket and saw that she only had a little over an hour to complete her search. She wouldn't be done by then. Cornelius would have been. And he would have taken notes so that they could refer to them later. Miriam hadn't written down a single thing, instead allowing the facts to swim and mingle in her head, trusting that all the information would cook itself together into some palatable soup of truth. This was no way to run an investigation at all.

Miriam nodded at the librarian. "Yes, ma'am. I'll be done. I just have some friends meeting me here to go over our project."

The librarian pursed her lips and emitted a low *mmhmm* before shambling back to her desk. Miriam realized she'd been holding a breath, and exhaled. She had never been much of a people person, and she hated having to lie. But it was a project, of sorts, and even though she hadn't texted them yet, she really did intend to have her friends meet her. Time was wasting, though, so she used the phone in her hand to summon Macy and Tanner to the library.

***

"This is what you've been doing all afternoon?" Macy shouted in a hushed whisper. "This is a vay-cay-shun. Let the police take care of it."

Macy wore a bikini top, worn out jean shorts, and sandals. Her normally pearlescent skin was approaching the color of boiled lobster, save for the strips of white skin protected by yesterday's top. She looked beautiful, of course, but it was hardly appropriate attire for the library.

Miriam shook her head, gave Macy the best *shh* look she could, and then whispered, "They won't be looking from this angle. And, besides, it's fun."

Macy rolled her eyes. "You're hopeless, girl." And then, motioning to Tanner. "Are you gonna talk some sense into her?"

Tanner looked towards the ground sheepishly, choosing not to answer the question. Surely, he was as interested. Or maybe he just knew that he couldn't dissuade Miriam from her quest.

Macy sighed and folded her arms across her chest. "Fine."

It was only a matter of time, Miriam calculated, until Tanner and Macy coupled off. They were both attractive and fun-loving, and their time together was only increasing. Miriam had caught Macy's eyes trailing down Tanner's sinewy muscles more than once, and Tanner, though always a gentleman, had stolen a few glances as well, sometimes at the more unmentionable areas of Macy's body. Neither of them knew it consciously yet. But it was inevitable, and Miriam worried what their coupling would do to the social dynamics of their group.

There was no time for that now, though. Right now, it was time to present her hypothesis and see if it held weight. Or, at least, see if Tanner thought so.

"So, we have to start in the Bahamas," Miriam said, holding up a book with a picture of clear blue water. A beach sat in the distance, but down lower in the picture was a giant circle, also blue in color, but of a much darker shade than the surrounding water.

"A blue hole?" Tanner asked, arching an eyebrow and leaning forward on the table.

Miriam nodded. "Right. Huge depression in the sand, leading down to a network of underwater caverns."

Macy wasn't quite onboard yet, but she was paying attention. "Looks dangerous."

Miriam felt a surge of excitement shoot through her. "Exactly. They are. People go missing in and around them all the time. There's a lot of theories as to why. Undercurrents and maelstroms caused by the differences in elevation and temperature, et cetera."

Macy seemed confused. "So, you think Emma got sucked down into a blue hole? That doesn't make sense. She was flying through the air like Superman."

Miriam pushed on. "Well, there's no evidence that the Gulf of Mexico even has blue holes. But, in the Bahamas, there's a creature said to live in them. A creature that attacks and eats humans on occasion, if the reports are to be believed."

Tanner's lips curled up just barely, a look that Miriam instantly recognized from years of presentations exactly like this. Of course, usually it was Cornelius doing the presenting while Miriam sat on Tanner's side of the table making the exact same faces. Would Cornelius be proud of her for putting this all together on her own? She liked to think so.

Tanner jumped in, forgetting entirely to whisper. "Right. Right. Lumba. Or something?"

Miriam smiled and pulled up another book with an artist's rendering in it. "Lusca."

Macy laughed. That outburst coupled with Tanner's excitement warranted a shushing noise from the cranky librarian, who turned in her old rickety chair to give them a look of warning. Tanner held up his hands as if to apologize, and Macy cupped her mouth to contain the giggles. Miriam believed in the traditions of library etiquette as much as the next girl, but the librarian's insistence on quiet seemed absurd given that they were the only patrons.

Once she had gotten control of herself, Macy uncovered her mouth and whispered, "That looks like a sharktopus."

Miriam and Tanner both turned to her, asking for more information without actually saying anything at all. Macy looked at them both like they were stupid.

"The movie?" said Macy. "There's like three of them. About a giant half-shark, half-octopus. Like the one in your picture there." Macy looked to each of them and didn't seem impressed with their reaction. "Whatever. It's a funny movie. You should watch it."

Miriam studied the picture again and felt the slightest tinges of humor well up inside of her. It did look a little like a half-shark/half-octopus. Sharktopus. Clever. But no, this thing was not something out of a bad science fiction movie.

Miriam flipped the page to another drawing, this one grounded more to reality. "This is from another eyewitness report."

The picture took up the entire page of the book, and, despite the absurdity, was quite well drawn. Miriam could almost feel the sliminess of its skin. The bulbous, saggy, body stood in the center of the illustration, with its terrifying sharp-toothed beak open towards a boat on the surface of the water. Four tentacles anchored it to the bottom, three were wrapped around the boat, and one waved a person just above the water.

This was what happened to Emma. Miriam was sure of it.

Miriam said, "Some reports say it's up to 200 feet. Others closer to forty. But either way, it's big. And dangerous."

Tanner filled in the rest. "And capable of picking up a hundred-pound girl like a sack of potatoes."

Miriam nodded. "Exactly."

Macy remained quiet, studying the picture. If not for the sunburn, she might have gone white. Her big eyes looked wet and fearful, and a bit incredulous, framed in by wisps of red hair. After a lifetime of chasing monsters just like this, Miriam had long forgotten what it felt like to fear the unknown.

Miriam sat the book down as if to rest her case. She felt confident in her hypothesis. There were still unknowns. Without blue holes, where could this thing possibly even live? And if it existed outside of the Caribbean, why had it not been reported before in the Gulf of Mexico?

She needed more library time, but for now, the book research would have to be over. She needed to get out into her element, studying the environment, looking for clues, and hunting the great big kraken that lived in the waters. But how? She had no resources. Her father had cut her off, or rather she had cut herself off. She no longer had access to his equipment, or research, or (though she was loathed to admit it) experience.

Tanner said, "This is really cool, Mir, but you can't go chasing this thing. We don't have the resources. Promise me you won't."

Surprised, Miriam averted her eyes away from Tanner. She thought for sure that he would be on board. She thought he'd feel the same pull to discover whatever it was out there in the waters.

Across the library, the librarian rose from her seat. Was it four already? Miriam tapped her phone to check. They still had ten minutes. That would be enough time to put all the books away, especially with Tanner's help. He knew the Dewey Decimal System as well as she did.

As the librarian approached, she did so almost cautiously, glancing around as if someone else had snuck into the library when she wasn't paying attention. Miriam noted something different about her now, less dangerous and more inviting. The old lady leaned on the table and looked at each of them slowly, seeming to gauge their worth. Before the librarian even uttered a word, Miriam had a strong premonition of what would come next.

When the librarian talked this time, she didn't whisper, but her voice cracked just slightly as she began. She stopped and started over. "Last year. October. Joe Hampton. That's all I can say."

The librarian spun quickly and rushed past her desk and into a room marked "Employees Only," as if she would get in trouble if someone saw her talking to the patrons. Miriam turned the information over in her head.

There was only one explanation. This had happened before. Here. In Cape Madre. It wasn't reported in the news, though. Miriam could be sure of that. Cryptid sightings did not escape her; not with the internet at her disposal, set to email her whenever a news article popped up anywhere in the world. That could only mean that the attack was covered up, by someone, for some reason.

Miriam shot a glance to Tanner, trying to gauge whether he felt as intrigued as her.

Macy sighed, whirled a finger around, and deadpanned. "Woo. Let's hunt monsters instead of boys."

CHAPTER 4

The sun danced across the water, almost blinding Miriam with its brightness. The horizon looked different now. Full of promise, still, but also infinitely menacing. Her legs dangled off the end of the pier, far above the crashing waves. It wasn't often that she took the time to reflect, which was fine with her: she found it tiresome.

She heard Tanner coming before he said anything, instantly recognizing her cousin's gait. He slid down beside her, joining in her reflection. Of everyone in her life, he surely understood the emotions roiling inside of her; the inexplicable drive and terrifying uncertainty in constant tension.

Tanner spoke first. "Lusca, huh?"

Miriam only nodded.

He continued, "How many expeditions do you think your dad dragged us on over the years?"

"Too many."

"Remember that ranch out in West Texas? I think Uncle Skylar still owns it. We spent, what, three weeks out there looking for skinwalkers? Didn't find a damn thing."

"We found a coyote pup under the porch," she reminded him.

"You wanted to take it home. Uncle Skylar wouldn't let you."

Miriam shrugged. "That's what you get when you take a twelve-year-old on a monster hunting expedition."

"Yeah..." His sentence trailed off as he took his own turn silently staring across the water.

She sensed that Tanner was probing at some deeper point. The two of them didn't talk much, confidently relying on unspoken bonds. The last time they'd talked about their feelings had been after Cornelius died.

Eventually, Tanner spoke again. "Does it ever haunt you? The things we've done?"

His question immediately conjured memories of the giant science experiment in Rose Valley; a man who had lost his humanity long ago. Did the memories of putting a bullet through its head haunt her? She'd taken a life, sure, but did she have any other choice?

"Not really," she replied. "We just do what we have to. So much of it was out of our control."

Tanner shook his head and breathed deeply. "I don't know. I still feel bad. That cheetah in Rose Valley. The rare eagle up in Minnesota. I know it's what we got hired to do, but sometimes I just got tired of killing things."

Miriam didn't answer. Should she also be tired of killing things? Though she had no interest in taking random lives, she also didn't feel the same remorse that Tanner did about it. Maybe she'd cared about such things at some point in her life, but her dad had ironed that out of her.

Changing the subject, Tanner quietly asked, "Do you remember your mom?"

Miriam squirmed, adjusting her position and rocking her legs back and forth before answering. "Not really. Just flashes. We were so young when it happened."

"Same."

"Do you miss them?" she asked.

She felt Tanner look at her, but she faced forward with her question, staring toward the horizon, terrified to share a moment more intimate than she could handle. She regretted asking the question almost immediately.

"I don't know. I guess? We were young, like you said, so I don't know if I miss them exactly. But I wonder sometimes. What things might have been like if they hadn't all died. If we didn't have to live with Uncle Skylar."

"They were a team," Miriam said. "It would have been this life either way."

"Maybe," he admitted. "But I think Skylar had a lot to prove after that. I think it made him scared that he'd lose us, too."

Miriam wanted to run. Literally stand up and run away. She'd spent the last two years pushing her father out of her life, and part of that process, rightly or wrongly, was to dehumanize him. To only focus on the bad things. The training. The expeditions. The constant criticism. She refused to believe her father did all of that out of fear.

"He didn't seem very scared when Cornelius died," she blurted out, using the anger and defiance to shield herself from the threat of tears.

Tanner didn't answer right away, choosing to remain silent and calm, the light breeze tussling his close-cropped blond hair. His serenity irked her, even though she knew she was being irrational. She hated being irrational.

"He would've loved this," Tanner finally said.

At first, Miriam angrily assumed that Tanner referred to her father, before realizing he meant Cornelius.

She replied evenly, "He would've hated the beach. But the two-hundred-foot octopus out there? Yeah. He would've loved that."

"Well, he would have loved telling us how to catch it, anyway," said Tanner. "That kid had two left feet."

"Yeah," she said with a chuckle.

She'd left the library in a flurry of excitement, but with the adrenaline dying down and the reality of her situation settling in, Miriam began to question her course. Why did she have this insatiable need to hunt down this creature?

"I don't know if I can do this without Cornelius," she said.

"Mir," Tanner said, flipping one leg up on the pier to face her. "You don't have to do this at all. That life is over."

"But I need to. I want to?" She was surprised to hear the last statement come out a question.

Did she want to? She struggled to separate her own desires from her upbringing and conditioning. She equally hated and yearned for everything her father gave her.

Tanner popped to his feet in an instant, surprising Miriam. He seemed bothered. Annoyed, maybe? She didn't have the strength to question him, instead trusting that whatever his reasons, he wouldn't abandon her. Not when she needed him the most.

"Good talk," he said, bounding away from her, his feet heavier on the pier than when he approached.

Alone again, Miriam breathed deeper to try and center herself and find the resolve that had started to fracture. As she exhaled, tears came, and the blood rose hot to her cheeks. Facing the possibility of going against everything she knew felt too overwhelming. Impossible, even.

So, she stared out across the water and let her mind wander back to the mysterious monster that she felt sure swam beneath the waves of Cape Madre and Joe Hampton, the man who'd encountered it. In the musings of her mind — the terror of her fantasies — Miriam found her center, felt her heartbeat returning to normal, and settled into the comfort of the hunt.

CHAPTER 5

Tommy killed the engine on his Crown Vic and threw the shifter into park in one swift motion, but didn't immediately get out of his car. He went through this same ritual every week before getting on with it and carrying through with the promises he'd made. This house, this *old* house, with its sagging once-yellow siding and drooping roof, had once meant so much. Now, it barely held itself together.

***

Joe Hampton excitedly jumped out of the front seat of his rusted-out truck and motioned for Tommy to follow. Tommy tumbled out and stretched his back, taking in the tiny craftsman before him. Given its distance from the water, it would be cheaper than most, and its age would help keep the price down. Maybe Joe could afford this. Maybe.

"What do you think?" Joe asked.

Tommy shrugged. "Looks well-maintained. Good house. But can you really afford this?"

Out of high school, Joe had decided to stay in Cape Madre and work odd jobs down at the docks. It barely kept Joe fed, so it was hard to imagine how he might afford this kind of purchase.

"I can get the money," Joe said. "The bank'll give it to me."

That's exactly what Tommy was afraid of. The banks were giving money to anyone with a pulse, and an inconsistently paid dockworker represented exactly the kind of schmuck they were looking for. Joe was gullible, and hopeful, and he had never accepted that the deck was stacked against him. Socially. Financially. Genetically.

"That's a lotta debt, Joe," Tommy warned.

Joe waved a dismissive hand as he bounded up the walkway to the door. "This is an investment!"

Unlikely. Tommy followed Joe into a remodeled living room with clean carpet and pristine white walls. Though not huge, the room carried a certain charm. Joe stood in the middle and spread his arms wide.

"Do you think Stacy will like it?" Joe asked.

"You know, most people just propose with a ring."

Joe laughed, not at all deterred. "She'll say yes. I want her to know that I can provide for her, ya know?"

Yeah. But could he? Stacy worked as a clerk down at the tax assessor's office. Before long, Tommy had no doubt that her more stable salary would be paying the mortgage. Joe spoke the truth, though. Stacy wouldn't say no. The two of them had made it through high school and were still together when Tommy got back from college and then the academy. They were as good as married already.

Sometimes, the best thing a friend could do was to go along with it. Support each other, even through misgivings and worry.

Tommy clapped Joe on the back and nodded. "She'll love it."

***

The walk up to the front door always felt a mile long, even though Tommy crossed it in less than ten seconds. He rapped quickly and quietly on the fading blue door, then turned to look out on the street. From here, he could almost forget that the ocean stood only a few miles away, tucked behind the rows of houses between here and there. The home across the way looked abandoned, with chest-high grass and holes in the roof. Nobody wanted houses this old anymore — if they wanted any house at all. After 2008, buyers had become a lot more skittish. If it couldn't double as a vacation rental, no one would bother paying for it.

A soft voice came from behind, saying, "Hi Tommy."

Tommy spun to see Stacy's tall lanky frame in the doorway. She wore yoga pants and a shirt that swallowed up her subtle curves, hiding them behind folds of fabric. One of Joe's old shirts. Her teeth were too big for her narrow face and small mouth, which made her look happy to see him, but Tommy knew better. Stacy Hampton didn't know how to be happy anymore.

"Hey Stacy. How are things?" Tommy asked as she moved to the side to let him in.

"Oh, you know."

Tommy did know. Bad. Things were bad. They had been bad for Stacy for over six months, and they didn't seem to be getting any better. She hadn't made it back to work yet, and though they told her she would always be welcome, Tommy expected the invitation had a looming expiration date. Frankly, Stacy was depressing to be around, but she needed help, and by extension, Joe needed help. Posthumously, maybe. But Tommy owed it to him.

"So, what's on the agenda today?" Tommy asked, forcing himself to sound helpful and upbeat.

Stacy pointed down a narrow hallway. "The guest toilet's running."

Easy enough to fix. So easy, in fact, that Tommy wondered why Stacy hadn't repaired it herself. He worried that she was becoming dependent on him.

"Yes, ma'am. I'll get right on it."

Tommy made his way to the guest bathroom which already contained a toolbox, and an unopened replacement for the assembly inside the tank. Good news. It meant Stacy had at least been out of the house. That, or she had ordered it on the internet.

As he worked, Stacy leaned against the doorway, resting her flaxen head on the splintered frame. Though never a traditional beauty, her now-extinguished spark of life could mesmerize anyone. Now, she looked almost like a drug addict. Tommy had never known her to have a drug problem, but in the wake of what happened, it was not impossible that she could've developed a habit.

"It's back isn't it?" she asked suddenly. "I heard about the girl down on the beach."

Tommy stopped his repair work and sat down on the toilet. Of course, she would have heard about it. Every townie had surely linked Emma's attack to Joe's case, and even though the powers-that-be would keep that correlation out of the papers, it wouldn't stop a population from gossiping.

Tommy studied his fingernails, trying to conjure an answer that wouldn't demolish Stacy's fragility. But Tommy couldn't lie to her.

"Maybe. I dunno yet. Still working through the witnesses."

Stacy pulled up her head and shifted her slight weight. Tommy tried to ignore her cobalt eyes bearing down on him; those angry, blaming eyes. He didn't need her reminding him how he'd been complicit in downplaying what had happened to Joe. He dealt with that guilt every damn day.

"She's gonna die, Tommy."

Tommy sighed. "We don't know that, Stacy. Joe didn't die from the attack."

"That thing changed him, Tommy. It caused him to..." Stacy's eyes moistened. She ran her hand over her nose and sniffled. "It's going to do the same to this girl. You better keep an eye on her after she wakes up."

Tommy nodded. "Of course, Stacy. I'll keep an eye on her."

***

As Joe slid into the booth across from him, Tommy couldn't help but notice the weight loss. At one time, Joe had been a burlier man, but now his giant beard looked comically large and unfit for his face. His eyes darted around the bar, manic and wild. It had only gotten worse, and Tommy didn't like it.

"How's it going?" Tommy asked.

Joe noticed the beer that Tommy had bought for him — for the first time — then drank half the mug before training his bloodshot eyes back on Tommy. "Good. Good. I think."

Tommy had his doubts. "How's Stacy?"

For the briefest of moments, it almost seemed like Joe didn't know who Tommy was even talking about, but then he dialed in. "Stacy. She's fine. Good. Same."

Stacy wasn't fine. Tommy knew that because she had called him at 3am, frantically searching for Joe. Joe barely slept anymore, always eager to get back out on the water, intent on returning to the creature that had nearly taken his leg. He still walked with a limp, and likely always would.

Tommy liked to be supportive. Tommy liked to look the other way and let people live their lives. But Tommy also liked to keep his best friend from ruining his marriage. And now he found himself staging an intervention, of sorts, causing no shortage of discomfort. How had it come to this?

"Look, Joe. I wanted to talk to you about something," Tommy said. "Since the accident, you've been acting a little strange. Stacy's worried about you."

Joe didn't respond or even acknowledge the sentiment.

Tommy continued, "Hell. I'm worried about you. You gotta come down from this. Let it go, man."

Joe shook his head. "I can't. I just. Hard to explain. I need to find it."

Tommy couldn't understand. This wasn't like Joe. Joe didn't obsess over things. Joe just stumbled through life, moving on to whatever thing caught his fancy and then to the next. There were no constants in Joe's life. That's how he liked it. That's why he never settled into a 9-to-5.

"You've got a wife, Joe. She needs you."

Joe stopped on this and appeared to be contemplating the statement. He drank the rest of his beer and fumbled with his fingers. Tommy could feel the table shaking, as Joe's good leg quivered. It also wasn't like Joe to be nervous. Bastard didn't know how to worry.

"Yeah. Stacy. She's important. I — I should..."

Tommy sipped his beer and waited for Joe to finish the thought, but it never happened. Joe just stared off in the distance, or down at the table, or anywhere but at the face of his oldest friend.

"Joe. Come on, now. You've — "

Joe held up a hand, interrupting Tommy with a finger. "Keep an eye on her for me. If anything happens."

"Joe, I don't think that's — "

"Promise me, Tommy. Promise me."

Sometimes, the best thing a friend could do was to go along with it. Support each other, even through misgivings and worry.

Tommy nodded. "Of course, Joe. I'll keep an eye on her."

***

After his promise to keep an eye on Emma, Stacy disappeared into the house to let Tommy finish up the repair-work alone. Tommy liked it better when she didn't hover. Her presence wore on his soul.

Would this thing have the same effect on Emma? Surely not. Joe was a man of the sea. He saw something he couldn't understand or explain, and needed to verify it. Curiosity overtook him. But Emma ... Emma grew up in a land-locked part of the state where water could barely be found. She'd just want to go back home. That's what Tommy would want to do in her shoes.

Stacy would have Tommy believe that this creature somehow changed Joe in ways that couldn't be seen. Altered his mind somehow. Tommy just couldn't buy into that theory. There was no evidence for it. The injuries to Joe's leg, while severe, were all physical. Repaired. Patched up. No different than what might happen in a car accident.

Finished with the toilet repair, Tommy washed his hands and found his way back to the living room. Stacy sat on the love seat, doing nothing. No television. No cell phone. Nothing.

She looked up at him. "All done?"

Tommy nodded. "Yep. Anything else?"

She stood up, across from him, and glanced around before shaking her head. "No. Not this week."

Now came the hug. She wrapped her arms around his midsection and rested her head on his shoulder. Tommy squeezed her in, as he did every week. This week, though, she didn't let go, so Tommy just kept holding her, becoming aware of her bony frame against him. She had become dangerously thin since Joe's death.

When Stacy finally pulled herself away from him, she had to wipe tears from her face. She blubbered, "Sorry. I might have gotten your shirt wet."

"Not a problem," Tommy said without a second thought. "Listen. I'll keep stopping by every week like this, but you can call me. When you need help. Or if you just wanna talk. I'm always available."

She nodded and wrapped her arms around herself. "Thanks, Tommy."

Tommy made his way back to the car, emotionally exhausted. He had to keep doing this. His promise to keep an eye on Stacy was the last promise he'd ever made to Joe. But it was taking a toll on him. He didn't know how to help, and it bothered him that fixing toilets and painting fences wasn't doing the job.

A buzz in his pocket interrupted his melancholy mood, pulling him back into the real world. The reports had come back from Emma's credit card. With any luck, it would tell Tommy where she had been staying, then lead him straight to her mysterious friend.

Eager to put Stacy and Joe out of his mind for at least a little bit, Tommy put the Crown Vic in drive and headed back to the station.

CHAPTER 6

Miriam collapsed to the floor and lifted Macy's backpack into her lap, rummaging through for the laptop charger. Instead she found makeup, sunglasses, sunblock, and all other manner of beach paraphernalia.

"Where's your laptop charger?" Miriam yelled, hopefully loud enough to be heard over the hum of the hair dryer in the bathroom.

Macy stopped the dryer and stepped out in only a towel, her hair frizzier than straight. Miriam would have just put hers up in a ponytail, but Macy tamed her hair down every time she left the house — or hotel room, in this case. Tonight, Macy planned to hit the clubs even though she was almost two years shy of twenty-one. To Miriam, that didn't seem worth the risk.

"Should be in the bottom pocket," Macy said as she crossed the room.

Bottom pocket? Miriam turned the backpack over and found a zipper running along the bottom. *Huh.* A bottom pocket. Macy squatted beside Miriam and undid the zipper, pulling out the long white cable that went with the laptop.

"There ya go," Macy offered before coming all the way down to sit next to Miriam on the floor. "You sure you don't want to come out tonight?"

Miriam nodded. "I'm sure. I just really want to figure out this Joe Hampton thing. But you and Tanner should go have fun."

Miriam said the last bit with a little bit of reservation, even if she felt it was the most appropriate thing to say. The two of them needed some time alone, and Miriam didn't want to be a third wheel in case tonight was the night the two of them paired off. Macy insisted that she intended to meet new boys. Surely, though, that would be difficult with Tanner playing wingman.

Macy sighed, putting a hand on Miriam's shoulder. "I don't know what I'm going to do with you."

Miriam smirked back. "I feel the same about you."

Macy laughed, jumped back to her feet and continued taming her hair. Oftentimes she felt like the sister Miriam never had, and Miriam surmised that her friendly duty was to act like seeing her walking around in a towel was no big deal, even though it felt like a big deal.

The hair dryer *whooshed* back on. Miriam plugged the laptop in and got it situated on the tiny desk in the corner of the room. Macy had carted her computer all the way from Dobie without turning it off, leaving it completely drained. Miriam found that to be irresponsible, but then she was starting to learn that she could be a bit of a stick in the mud, and that bothered her, so she tried to keep it cool. It proved a very challenging goal.

The laptop booted up to the password screen, ready for her input, which she keyed in quickly. Back at school, Miriam only had a desktop, so Macy frequently let her use the laptop. A child of divorce, Macy seemed to have two parents fighting to take care of her college expenses, while Miriam had barely scraped by on scholarships and work-study programs. Miriam's father had taken her laptop back after the falling out. Petty, sure, but not entirely unexpected.

Miriam minimized all Macy's homework; lines upon lines of computer code that Miriam didn't understand at all, but she admired this nerdier side of Macy.

With her view unfettered, Miriam scanned down the launch bar until she found the browser, then launched into her search. Cape Madre hid a secret from her, and she intended to bring the power of the Internet to bear on uncovering it. Her first task would be to find official sources. Newspaper articles, mainly, but maybe a live news report had found its way to YouTube. After that, she would lean into some of her more exotic sources.

A search of "Joe Hampton Cape Madre" turned up two news articles from the local paper, one about an attack and another about his death. The dates of the two articles differed by a month. Miriam clicked the first article.

Local man Joe Hampton was admitted to Emergency Plus hospital this past Thursday for an injury related to a shark attack. Mr. Hampton was working on a fishing boat at the time.

Mr. Hampton sustained significant bruising on his leg, in addition to perforated skin and substantial blood loss. Though doctors warn that he may have permanent damage to his leg, he is expected to be released from the hospital within a few days.

"I am just so grateful that he got to the hospital in time," said Mr. Hampton's wife, Stacy. "We appreciate all of the many well-wishes from the community."

Shark attacks off the coast of Cape Madre are rare, and generally only lead to minor abrasions. Sharks rarely exceed four feet, and most commonly enter shallow waters to feed on stingrays.

A shark attack? Possible, but unlikely. Miriam had a hard time believing that a shark in the coastal waters of Cape Madre could be capable of doing that much damage. And if it had only been a shark attack, then why would the librarian have mentioned Joe Hampton at all? Miriam clicked over to the second article.

Local man Joe Hampton has been pronounced dead following a tragic drowning accident. His death comes almost one month after suffering a shark attack.

"We are heartbroken to hear of Joe's death," Detective Tommy Wallace of the Cape Madre police department said. "Joe was a wonderful man and a personal friend. His death will weigh heavily on the community."

Mr. Hampton's body was found in the waters off Cape Madre after a tourist reported seeing a man swimming out to sea, past the buoys that separate the beach area from the fishing lanes. It is unclear why Mr. Hampton was swimming out so far.

Those who wish to offer condolences are invited to send flowers to the Manchester Funeral Home on Palm Street. Mr. Hampton is survived by his wife, Stacy.

Miriam sat back in her chair, so absorbed in her reading that she didn't notice Macy pop back into the room, now with perfectly straightened hair and expertly-applied makeup.

"Earth to Mir. You ok?" Macy said, jolting Miriam's attention away from the screen.

"Uh. Yeah. Fine. Just reading about this guy. He got attacked by a shark, recovered, and then drowned a month later."

Macy rummaged around in her poorly organized suitcase that sat open on her bed, pulling out a matching set of underwear. Miriam had no matching sets of underwear.

"Weird. Are shark attacks common around here?" Macy asked.

Miriam shook her head. "No. Not at all. And then to drown a month later?"

Macy stopped dressing and shrugged. "It's a beach town. I'm sure people drown all the time."

Miriam nodded. "Yeah. That's true. But the librarian. There's gotta be more to this story, right?"

Macy held up two dresses in front of her, swapping them back and forth in front of the floor length mirror bolted to the wall, making faces at each of them before turning to Miriam.

Macy swapped them back and forth a few more times for Miriam's benefit. "Which one?"

Miriam didn't want to pick out dresses. She wanted to talk about Joe Hampton, and mysterious sea creatures. Macy kept moving the dresses back and forth, though, expectantly waiting for an answer.

Miriam forced herself to be a good friend and consider the dresses. One was the typical "tiny black dress," coming down to mid-thigh with spaghetti straps and a deep neckline. The other, a shiny green number with cap sleeves and a V-neck. They both looked great, Miriam supposed, but the green of the dress, paired with Macy's big green eyes and red hair, would be a phenomenal look.

"The green one," Miriam said.

Macy turned back to the mirror and considered the green one again, smiling at herself in the mirror as if to see whether the dress would look good when she showed teeth.

While admiring herself, Macy asked, "You think he was attacked by something else? The thing you saw?"

She tossed the black dress on the bed and removed the green one from the hanger.

Miriam answered, "I don't know. Maybe? Seems likely, right? Given what we know."

Macy stepped into her dress and pulled it up snugly across her hips and onto her shoulders, then walked over and presented her back to Miriam for zipping, all before replying, "Yeah, I guess so. But what are you gonna do?"

That was a good question that Miriam didn't have the full answer to just yet. It felt natural for her to be investigating this, and she found it a lot more engaging than typical spring break shenanigans, but could she really expect to hunt this thing? Before the split with her father, Miriam had had access to weapons and equipment she could use to hunt and maybe even kill it, but now she had only a borrowed laptop and a cheap cell phone. Where would she get the support needed to carry through with this?

After one last look in the mirror, Macy turned towards Miriam again and curtsied, a playful laugh echoing into the room as she raised her eyebrows and silently asked for Miriam's approval. The dress looked amazing, of course, as Miriam had predicted. With some heels to boost Macy's height, Miriam doubted that anyone would be able to resist her.

"Looks good. Really good. Tanner'll like it."

Macy scrunched up her nose in disgust. "Ew. This isn't for Tanner."

Before Miriam could offer her doubts about that statement, someone knocked on the door. Macy, already standing in front of the mirror in the hallway, leaned over and pulled the door open to reveal Tanner, standing with one hand snug in a pocket of his well-fit chinos.

"Ready to go?" he asked.

Macy turned back into the room, causing Tanner to catch the door and step inside. "Yeah. Just gotta get some shoes."

Miriam watched as Macy stepped into a pair of three-inch heels, bending over to get the straps pulled onto her feet. Her look complete, Macy was ready for action.

Before leaving Miriam alone with her research, Macy turned back one last time. "We'll miss you tonight. Have fun!"

Macy's effervescent smile felt genuine and honest, giving Miriam the briefest pause about her night's plans. No— she wanted to keep digging. "Thanks. You too!"

Tanner gave a small wave and the door slammed shut, leaving the room silent. Miriam lingered on the idea of spending time having fun. Would she even be able to *have* fun? She had no ability to dance whatsoever. Her life had always been so driven, and even without the whip of her father behind her, she still wanted to accomplish things. Meaningful things.

Pushing Tanner and Macy out of her mind, Miriam went back to searching. She didn't find any long-form information, but within a few minutes she found herself staring at the link for a cryptid forum. It might have information about what really happened to Joe, but that link would take her somewhere she had tried so hard to avoid.

She took a deep breath and clicked the link that took her to *SkylarBrooks.com*.

Ignoring her father's smug headshot in the top left-hand corner, she focused on the thread. A person claiming to be a junior medical examiner for the Cape Madre coroner's office had written up a long description of the injuries that Joe had sustained, as witnessed after the retrieval of his body a month after the attack. The content of the description starkly opposed the idea of a shark attack. Instead of jagged, tooth-rendered wounds, the lacerations were more consistent with cuts. Joe had also, allegedly, suffered significant bruising, which the coroner attributed to being squeezed with extreme force.

And then, at the end, the strangest description of all — perfectly circular bruising up and down Joe's leg.

Miriam's heart jumped in her chest as everything clicked together. Emma had also suffered bruising, and though Miriam hadn't noticed any circles, it was possible that the immediate trauma was covering it up, hiding it among the more generalized discoloration of her skin. Circles meant suction cups. Suction cups meant tentacles. Like an octopus. Or a squid.

Or Lusca.

Miriam scrolled down, fearing what she may find next. She passed by random comments from enthusiasts offering up possible cryptids, alternate theories by skeptics, and then the one reply she didn't want to see. Skylar Brooks himself had responded, indicating that he was eager to learn more about this attack.

Had her father already investigated this? Had he been here? In Cape Madre? She quickly clicked over to his main page and scrolled through the news section, looking for any indication of an expedition to Cape Madre.

She found nothing. The latest post indicated that he and his research team were on a safari in Papua New Guinea looking for pterodactyls. Miriam exhaled and melted back into her chair, pondering on the curious fear that her father might be drawn to Cape Madre.

She clicked on the link to his research team, a team that less than two years ago had consisted of herself, Tanner, and Cornelius. Now she had been replaced. All of them had. Miriam was now Brynn, a short-haired blonde girl with a crooked smile. Tanner was

Gabriel, a burly bearded man with tiny eyes and huge biceps. And Cornelius had become Kent, a scrawny, bespectacled biologist. The new team so closely mirrored Miriam's family that it flushed her cheeks with anger. How could he do this? His son had died, and he'd just replaced him with a nerdy college graduate?

Miriam slammed the laptop shut. Perhaps there was more to find on Joe Hampton, but she couldn't do it right now. Not when every search would inevitably lead back to her past. She hated him. She tried to avoid admitting that to herself, but she did. He had ruined her entire life. He'd made her into the anti-social weirdo that she had become. Because of him, she now sat alone in a hotel room instead of partying with her friends. She didn't know who she was anymore. Was she obsessed with this creature because she had a genuine interest, or because Skylar Brooks had taught her to be? Did she even have any real interests of her own?

Miriam threw herself onto the bed, desperately trying to sort through it all. Her mind tugged at a new idea. An idea that she could be something else. That she could change herself to whatever she wanted. Maybe she could dig deep enough and find out who Miriam Brooks was really meant to be.

Or she could beat him. She could show him that she had surpassed him. Skylar Brooks was a con-man, traveling from place to place and convincing people that he could save them from a monster that often never existed. Cryptozoology had a hard enough time being taken seriously, and Skylar Brooks did it no favors. If she could find this thing, she could legitimize the industry. She could amass more power than him and crowd him out.

She felt petty and vindictive as she stared at the worn walls of her hotel room. Maybe it was a bad idea. She couldn't suppress echoes of her father's voice telling her to work harder, to be less awkward. She conjured memories of traveling the country, never sleeping, waiting on him hand and foot. Always doing what he told her. Always striving to be the best at everything that he taught her. And she was the best at those things. Those unusual, completely useless-to-the-real-world things.

It was all she had. All she was. She could do nothing but excel at it.

CHAPTER 7

The old part of town smelled like fish. Not like a nice seafood restaurant. More like a rotting pile of carcasses mixed with garbage. It felt like home, though. Before all the money poured into rejuvenating Cape Madre, this was all the charm the city could muster.

Credit card receipts implied that Emma Chu had rented a room on this side of the cape from the Shady Shark motel. If her friend hadn't skipped town, this was Tommy's best bet for finding her. He couldn't be sure that they'd shared a room, but it was a reasonable guess.

Tommy pushed through the grimy glass door and stepped into a mildew crucible straight out of the seventies. A ripe-smelling, elderly woman named Bea sat behind the counter, as she had for as long as Tommy could remember. Always behind the counter. Always watching soap operas. Always in need of a shower.

Tommy rapped his knuckles on the desk next to the rusted bell. "Hey, Bea."

Bea looked up from her ancient television and gave Tommy a toothless smile. He couldn't remember her with teeth, but surely she'd had them when he was a kid, right?

"Detective Wallace. What brings you to the bad part of town?" Despite not having many teeth, her eyes still twinkled with the mischief of troublemaker. He thought maybe she was proud to live in the part of town without any police presence.

"I'm looking for info on a girl. Checked out a room here. Emma Chu."

Bea rolled over to the other side of her cubby hole and flipped through an old logbook. There wasn't a computer in sight, which seemed impossible with the volume of people that must have come through. Bea pulled some reading glasses from around her neck as she scanned the pages, running a wrinkled finger over the paper as she read, shaking her head with each miss.

"Ah!" she said, at last. "Here it is. Emma Chu. Room 223. She checked out this morning."

Checked out? That didn't make sense. Emma was unconscious in a hospital bed. "That can't be right, Bea. She's in the hospital."

Bea shrugged. "I dunno. Didn't talk to her. Maids must've found the keys in the room. That's how they all check out these days."

"Did she leave anything behind? Her clothes, bags? Anything?" Tommy asked.

"Not that I know of. Maids didn't bring anything in to lost and found this morning."

Tommy nodded and drummed his fingers on the counter, trying to figure out his next move. Clearly, he had found Emma's friend, but why the sudden check out? And why take Emma's stuff?

"Thanks, Bea. Do you know if she had anyone staying with her?"

Bea laughed. "Of course she did. These college kids never get a room for themselves. Can't afford it."

"Let me guess. You don't take the names of roommates, do you?"

"Of course not. Not enough paper in the world for that. Sometimes they bunk up three to a bed." Bea twisted her mouth up in thought, then took off her reading glasses. "Chu. Asian, right? I remember her checking in. Had another Asian girl with her. Cute little things."

"Don't suppose you caught a name?" Tommy asked even though he already knew the answer.

"Nah. I wouldn't remember if they'd told me. You can try asking around. The kids like to mingle."

The old door to door. Tommy hated bothering people on their vacation, but that was the job. The best he could do was start at the room next to Emma's, hopefully cutting his search time down by zeroing in on the people most likely to have met her. With any luck, he could get the name of her friend and then hunt her down. Make sure she made it safely back to college.

"Thanks, Bea."

Bea grunted and turned back to her soaps.

***

No one answered at room 221. The kids in room 222 had checked in late last night and hadn't met any of their neighbors. Now Tommy stood in front of room 224. He said a silent prayer that this one would be the one, though prayer was a strong word. Tommy hadn't been to church in decades, much to his mother's chagrin.

He knocked on the door and immediately heard a commotion inside. The words were muffled but frantic as drawers slammed and beds creaked. Before long, a boy answered the door in only his boxers, long sandy hair covering one of his eyes.

"Hey, dude. What's up?" he mumbled, clearly drunk or stoned. The smell of marijuana, latex, and ineffective air freshener wafted out of the room.

Tommy flashed his badge, which he'd thankfully remembered to bring this time. "Detective Wallace. Cape Madre police. I'm looking for someone and thought you might be able to help."

The kid's eyes widened as he glanced back behind him and started making hand gestures to someone else in the room. He turned back and opened the door wide. "Of course, officer. Come on in."

Tommy tucked his badge away as he stepped inside and made the correction. "Detective."

The boy looked down. "Right. Sorry. Detective."

Tommy took in the room. The wood-paneled walls were old, the art was cheap, and the shag carpet had been worn bare in places. Two queen beds took up the bulk of the room. One of them hadn't been slept in. A pretty, brown-haired girl sat in the other, wearing a t-shirt far too big for her with the covers pulled up to her waist. The boy grabbed a pair of shorts from the floor and stepped into them.

"This won't take long." Tommy had no interest in ruining their vacation. They could smoke MJ and bang the whole day away for all he cared. "Did either of you know the girls staying next door?"

"The Asian chicks?" the boy asked.

Tommy nodded. "Yep. Those are the ones."

"Dude. Those girls are freaks, man."

The timbre of his voice, and the curl of his lips, made it clear that *freaks* was a compliment. Tommy had finally found his room.

The girl from the bed turned towards Tommy, careful to keep herself covered. "Emma and Hannah.

That's their names. Brady and Justin have been hanging out with them a lot. With Hannah just last night."

Tommy looked to the shirtless boy and wondered whether he was Brady or Justin. "Which one are you?"

The boy in the shorts laughed. "Oh, I'm Frank."

The bathroom door creaked open and another guy walked into the room, stark naked, his man bits dangling.

"Oh crap. Sorry," the naked boy said before quickly ducking back into the bathroom, returning moments later with a towel around his waist.

The bed girl motioned to the naked man. "That's Brady."

Tommy nodded. "Brady. I'm Detective Wallace. Wanted to ask you some questions about Emma and Hannah."

A smile spread across his face briefly before he wiped it away. "Sucks what happened to Emma. Hannah was pretty beat up about it."

"Do you know where Hannah is?" Tommy asked.

"She's not in the room? When I came back here, her and Justin were headed out for food."

"And what time was that?"

Brady shrugged. "I dunno. Three or so?"

The bed girl jumped in. "Closer to four."

Tommy nodded, then brought out a notepad from his breast pocket and jotted down some notes. "And Justin's staying here?"

Frank rejoined the conversation. "Yeah. I mean, not last night, obviously."

Ok. So, Hannah checked out and Justin didn't come back? Something seemed off, and Tommy's instincts went into overdrive. If Hannah disappeared, his cop brain told him, then maybe Justin and Brady had done something to her. That was a leap, though. None of the evidence pointed to that yet, and it wasn't even the reason he was there to begin with.

"I don't suppose you know Hannah's last name?"

"Hung," Brady answered. Frank snickered.

The girl in the bed rolled her eyes. "It's pronounced Wong, you dickhead. H-U-A-N-G."

Tommy wrote it down, glad to finally have a name. With this, he could track her down in Dallas and find her parents if he needed to. Only once he'd confirmed that she hadn't gone back home could he allow himself to worry about her whereabouts. Maybe Hannah was scared she would get in trouble, and so had skipped town. It didn't explain Justin, but maybe he'd just met someone new at a pancake joint in the middle of the night. Cape Madre never slept during spring break.

He took a few more minutes to gather contact information for Brady, Frank, and bed girl — just in case he had any more questions for them later. They complied readily. Tommy wanted to believe that he had made them comfortable enough that they weren't worried about the pot, but likely they were just too stupid to realize that he knew about it. Either way, he didn't care.

Tommy handed a card over to Frank. "If you hear from Justin, have him give me a call."

"Sure, dude."

Tommy helped himself out of the room, his mind racing to put the pieces together. He was trying to solve a crime that hadn't even been committed and reminded himself that the assignment was just to look into what had happened to Emma. There was no foul play. Just an unfortunate accident.

***

As Tommy walked across the parking lot of the Shady Shark, he scanned his eyes over the boats dotting the adjacent piers. Most prominent was the nearest ship, where a cat watched him lazily from the bow. *Madre's Mayhem* it was called. The ship was old, rusted, and worn, well past its prime. Though large compared to its competitors, it was still a modest ship, capable of being manned by a crew of only one. On a hunch, Tommy changed his course and headed toward it.

Tommy had a lot of fond memories of this area. It was one of his favorite places to hang out as a teenager. He'd stolen his first kiss hiding behind the *Mayhem*, and might have made it further if they hadn't been caught. Of course, the *Mayhem* was prettier back then, with a clean white hull and ropes that didn't look like they were about to snap.

He strode up to the wooden ramp to the ship and hollered, "Hey, Bark. You up there?"

A different cat, this one black as night, snaked around Tommy's legs, rubbing dirty matted fur all over his suit pants. Tommy shook his leg in an attempt to shoo it away, but it persisted.

"He just wants some love, Detective," came a gruff voice from above. "Won't hurt you."

Tommy's allergies disagreed. "Got a few minutes?"

He went by "Bark" — a shortening of his last name— but one would be forgiven for thinking the name came from his wrinkled, leathery skin. Bark was bigger in Tommy's head, but the old man had slimmed down over the years, slowly giving in to age and likely undiagnosed health issues. Still intimidating, though, just like he always had been. Tommy hadn't forgiven him for interrupting that make-out session all those years ago.

Bark smiled and motioned up the ramp. "Of course, detective. Always time for the law."

Tommy took that as permission to come aboard and trudged up the creaky ramp. On the main deck, he looked in horror at dozens of cats and reminded himself to double up on the allergy meds later. Bark hobbled over to a pair of folding chairs near the bow of the ship and motioned for Tommy to sit. Tommy chose to stand. Bark didn't protest.

"I'm investigating the accident with that girl yesterday and wondered if you might be able to help me."

"The Asian girl?" Bark asked rhetorically. "I heard about that. No one seemed to care when it happened to Joe."

Shots fired. Tommy really couldn't blame him. The locals always got short shrift around Cape Madre. Local taxes were nothing compared to the considerable influx of wealth that came from the tourists. It was a damn shame what had happened to Joe, and Tommy would have liked to have taken it more seriously, but his hands were tied. He couldn't expect Bark to understand.

Without allowing Tommy to comment, Bark continued, "I was out at sea when that happened. I don't know nothin' about it."

"Right." Tommy motioned behind him towards the motel. "My question is actually about her friend. They were staying over there at the Shady Shark. Thought you might have seen them coming and going from up here."

An emaciated, mangy cat jumped into Bark's lap, begging for attention. Bark obliged before answering, "Yeah. I seen her. Whoring around with those boys. Saw her take two of'em into her room last night. Kids these days."

"What about this morning?" Tommy asked, ignoring Bark's social judgement. "Bea says she checked out. Did you see her leave?"

Bark stopped petting the cat to stroke the stubble on his chin. "That sounds right. Took her suitcases and left really early. Earlier than people should be awake, but I don't sleep much these days."

"Was a boy with her?" Tommy asked.

"Hmmm. I don't think so. She either left'em there or they went back to their own rooms when I wasn't lookin', I reckon."

At least the facts were aligning. For whatever the reason, Hannah had taken off. Tommy's fears of foul play were clearly misplaced. Just a college kid reacting to a stressful situation. Most of the beach-goers hadn't been paying attention when Emma had been attacked, but if the handful of eyewitnesses Tommy scrounged up were to be believed, it was no wonder that Hannah might be spooked. She probably wouldn't even have new information.

"And what kind of car did she drive away in?" Tommy asked.

Bark looked towards the parking lot of the Shady Shark, taking a curiously long time to answer. He smiled. "You know, I don't remember. This old brain, detective. It's not what it used to be."

Switching gears, Tommy asked, "What do you think this thing is, Bark? The thing that attacked Joe and this girl?"

Bark turned his gaze to the sea now, absent-mindedly stroking the bony feline in his lap. Tommy also shifted his own gaze, watching the waves gently roll in, wishing he could peer beneath the murky waters of the gulf coast to see what bizarre creatures lived below. Despite growing up on the beach, Tommy didn't care much for the ocean. He knew how to swim, of course, but the depths disturbed him on a fundamental level. He preferred a swimming pool.

Bark's gravelly voice rumbled a slow answer. "Something ancient, Detective. Something unbelievable."

CHAPTER 8

Though Tanner and Macy weren't completely dismissing her crusade, Miriam could tell by their tepid support that she wasn't going to convince them to forgo their entire spring break on a lark. They just didn't understand. This creature of the deep presented a curiosity to be studied, yes, but it also meant so much more. She'd been on an uncountable number of monster hunts, but all they'd ever found were pranksters and out-of-place animals, with the lone exception being a government experiment that didn't quite qualify as a cryptid. This was her chance to do something her father never could. Her chance to prove that she could be better than he. Her chance to make Cornelius' death mean something.

When she parked in the public lot next to a seedy motel, Miriam felt alive with purpose, but after stepping outside and taking one deep breath, she almost lost her lunch. The stench was overwhelming. Missouri had fishing, of course, but nothing like this. The boats lined the piers so closely that she couldn't fathom how they managed to park. Burly men (and a few equally burly women) went about their business working nets and tossing around dead fish. It looked like thankless work.

If Miriam intended to change the world by discovering something new, she would have to do it on a shoestring budget. Macy had only reluctantly handed over one third of what she called their *clubbing* money so that Miriam could try to turn it into *boating* money instead. The marinas charged too much for charters, so this jumble of fishing boats represented her next best option. On the plus side, Miriam suspected that they'd know the waters better anyway.

She took off toward the dock, eying each boat and trying to get a sense of which she'd have the best luck with. There were newer boats, older boats, scary boats, and happy boats, but none of that told her which one would have the most amenable captain. She chose a small boat nearest her with only one person onboard. The curly blue script on the side read *Mama Jean*.

Awkwardly, Miriam waved at the man on the deck. "Hi. I'm Miriam."

The man smiled and started toward her with a youthful exuberance. He was lean and tall with dark skin and well-defined muscles beneath his ratty clothes, and he wore a pair of cheap plastic sunglasses. When he got to her side of the boat, the man planted one hand on the side and landed firmly with a creaky *thud* onto the wooden planks stretching before her.

"Hi there, pretty lady. Lost?"

Miriam bristled slightly at being called "pretty lady" but didn't take it as a threat.

"No. Not lost. Um. I'm looking for a charter. I have a..." She paused to find the least alerting words. "School project. Uh. For my oceanography class."

"I see there," he said with a solemn nod. "That's quite a project. Me and *Mama Jean* might be able to help you. Providing you're able to go out tonight. That's when *Mama Jean* helps me find all the fishes."

He seemed trustworthy enough. Friendly. She'd bring Tanner along just in case. This man was strong and sure, but Tanner was bigger and better-trained. She hated having to rely on him like that, but she needed to ensure that *Mama Jean*'s captain wouldn't pose a threat.

"It'll be me and a friend," she said. "Maybe two friends. How much?"

"Oh, let me think," he said, counting off fingers on his hands. "Three people means less fish. I could take ya out for a coupla hours. Hundred bucks."

Miriam swallowed hard. More people and less fish made sense mathematically, but she doubted *Mama Jean* ever reached capacity. There'd be plenty of room for three more people. She hated negotiating, but her third of the clubbing money was just barely a hundred dollars, and she couldn't spend it all on one charter.

She fought back. "You're telling me you fill *Mama Jean* up to the brim with fish every night?"

He nodded. "Yes'm. Of course."

She wished she could see his eyes. Then, she'd know for sure whether he spoke the truth. The *Mama Jean* was the first boat she checked. There were dozens of others. Her gut told her to comparison shop.

"Let me talk to a few other captains here. Make sure your rate's competitive," she said, drawing up her courage and forcing herself to turn away.

He hollered after her, "You won't find no better deal, pretty lady. You'll come back to Ol' Newt."

Indeed, she might, but she kept walking, putting more distance between them and fighting the urge to look back. She wondered whether he waited beside his boat, expecting her to change her mind. She hoped he would chase her and offer her a better deal, but she heard no footsteps other than her own.

***

Miriam walked past numerous boats that didn't quite look right. Too gnarly. Too old. Most of the crews looked considerably less friendly than Ol' Newt. She took a shot on a few of the boats that looked less imposing, but no one had time for a little girl with a science project. They all had deadlines and quotas, and routines they were unwilling to break. Some laughed at her, while others showed some sympathy, but none of them wanted to take a risk on her.

There weren't many ships left on the dock, and most of what remained looked uninviting and dilapidated. Miriam had never had to be the front man. Her father had always taken on that role, confidently glad-handing everyone he met and using his God-given charisma to win people over to a crackpot cause. Getting people to cooperate was harder than Miriam imagined. She wondered if Macy might have had better luck.

Closing the distance between them, a man walked intently toward her, looking almost out of place as she did in his disheveled suit.

"Mornin'," he said as they crossed paths, never slowing from clomping across the wooden planks in his scuffed-up dress shoes.

She mumbled a hello, but he was already crossing a nearby parking lot to a shiny black car. How embarrassing. She needed to work on her social skills.

Walking forward, she spotted a black cat sunbathing ahead of her, meticulously cleaning its paws. Her eyes scanned the docks in front of her, quickly losing count of all the cats. As a distraction, Miriam bent down to pet the one near her, causing it to roll onto its back and stretch its long legs. She liked animals. They never made her feel weird or uncomfortable. Or embarrassed.

"Popeye likes you," a voice echoed from somewhere above.

She stood and looked up to a gaunt old man with tanned, leathery skin. He wore a newsie cap from another era, patchy overalls, and a smile full of rotten teeth. His boat, *Madre's Mayhem*, stood taller than the others along the docks, and, based on the worn paint and sagging deck above, Miriam imagined that it had also seen the most years.

"Well, he's a very pretty cat. Is he yours?" she asked.

The man nodded. "Aye. No one else'll look after'em if I don't."

Her eyes searched across the man's boat, noticing even more cats lying along the bow and hidden amongst the ropes of the docks. A bigger boat would surely be more expensive, but Miriam felt safe with a man who would go out of his way to take care of so many animals.

"Can I come up?"

The man looked up and down his deck, to places that she couldn't see, before answering, "Don't trouble yourself. I'll come down."

He started immediately, but slowly. Miriam had been standing next to the bottom of his ramp for what felt like an eternity before he finally hobbled down. He offered her a scarred hand, devoid of jewelry.

She took it, shaking firmly. "Hi. I'm Miriam. I'm looking for a charter. Uh. For a school project. Wondering if you might take a stowaway or two."

The man's droopy eyes considered her, looked her up and down, and landed back to meet her gaze. "You look fit enough, but it's dangerous out there on the seas. Fishing boats aren't for tourists."

Miriam responded quickly, "Yessir, of course. I'm not a tourist. Well, I am. I mean. I'm not from here. But I don't want to go sightseeing."

The old man shook his head. "Mmhmm. I'm Fred Barker, by the way. People call me Bark."

"Nice to meet you, Bark. I'm Miriam," she forced out, eager to get on with the negotiations. "I won't be any trouble. We can help. My cousin and I have a lot of experience."

This caused Bark to cock an eyebrow. "Experience? On a deep-sea fishing boat?"

"Well, not exactly," Miriam stuttered. "But with boats. Our dad was super outdoorsy and taught us how to drive them when we were young."

"You and your cousin have the same dad?" he asked with a laugh.

Miriam felt the heat rising in her cheeks. "It's complicated. We were raised together by my father, though, yes."

"I see. Well, it is always nice to have a hand. I do most of the work myself these days. Ain't none of these boys wanna work for Bark anymore. They say my bite is worse."

He laughed mirthfully at his own play on words, tilting his head back and wrapping one hand around his belly. This man was old, odd, and mysterious, but also interesting. Less slimy than Newt on the *Mama Jean*, but also much rougher.

After coming down from his laugh, he continued, "I could take ya on. You can go out on my run this evenin'. If you're willin' to work for it, won't even be no charge."

Miriam felt her entire body relax. "That would be so great. Thank you!"

Bark smiled and nodded. "I'd like to know a little more about your project, though. You won't be needin' to take me too far outta my way, will ya?"

Of course. What was she thinking? He wasn't going to drive her around like a chauffeur when he had a route to run and wasn't getting paid.

She considered her answer carefully. "I'm looking for the deepest part of the waters around here."

"For a school project, you say?"

Miriam nodded solemnly, doing her best not to give away the fact that she really intended to find a giant sea monster — or at least, the probable hiding place for it. Surely, he wouldn't understand that motivation. Few would.

"The deepest part's the vortex. But we ain't goin' anywhere near there. It's not safe."

The vortex? Did this mean there was a blue hole somewhere in the waters of Cape Madre? Well, likely not a blue one. The waters here were murky and green, but if there was an exceptionally deep hole on the ocean floor, then that could be exactly where she needed to go. She just had to convince this old man to take her.

Without anything else to offer, Miriam decided on the truth. "I think that the monster that attacked that Emma girl might live there."

Bark laughed harshly, and for the first time Miriam felt uncomfortable. He looked different now, no longer like a kooky old man. He turned and moved up his ramp, faster than she otherwise would've guessed when she met him just moments ago. He seemed to suddenly have a purpose.

"Wait! I'm serious!"

Bark waved a dismissive hand on his walk up. Reaching the top, he turned to look at her. When he spoke, his voice was gruffer. Almost angry.

"Stay out of things you don't understand, girl. The seas are dangerous. Any captain crazy enough to take you to the vortex is someone you shouldn't trust."

With that, Bark disappeared into the bowels of his ship, leaving Miriam confused and flustered. She hadn't been thinking terribly far ahead. Even getting to the vortex wouldn't solve her problem. It's not like the sea monster would just pop up for a cup of tea once she got there. But she wanted to see the vortex anyway. Get an idea of its depth, its width. Assuming she could even tell that from the boat. She had hoped her charter would at least have a depth finder.

As she worked on regaining her composure, and deciding her next move, a charismatic voice came from behind. "I'll do it for fifty."

She spun around to see Newt flashing his bright smile. Had he heard her conversation with Bark? Surely, he wouldn't lower his price once he knew the danger she would be asking of him.

"To take me to the vortex?" she asked hesitantly.

Newt nodded and extended a narrow hand with long fingers. "Sure, pretty lady. *Mama Jean* likes ya."

Miriam crossed the few feet between them and shook his hand without even considering it. Apparently, Ol' Newt was exactly the kind of crazy she was looking for.

CHAPTER 9

Bark banged around his hold, trying to get things in proper order so that he could get out on the seas. He paused when he picked up a brightly colored backpack, making a mental note to dispose of it next time he had the chance. He could feel his heart pounding hard, and wondered how many beats it had left.

He could handle Tommy. That boy was scared of him and wouldn't push things too far. But now this girl? What did she know? She looked fit and capable, and that made her a sight more troublesome than the Asian girl. He didn't want it to go down this way. That was never the intent. But now he had tracks to cover and obligations to meet. Damn tourists always mucked things up.

It hurt so much when Joe had died. Bark hadn't known real pain until that day. Since then, he hadn't felt like himself. He just skated through existence in a murky haze. No one deserved what happened to Joe, and Bark did his damnedest to make sure it wouldn't happen again, but he'd failed. And this time was worse. There were too many people asking too many questions.

A cat meowed from the entryway up to the deck, giving Bark pause. He could tell it was Popeye. They all sounded different if you paid enough attention to the timbre of their mews. Poor fella hated coming down into the hold, and though he'd wander off like any cat, eventually he would frantically come searching for Bark. Bark had never seen a cat act so much like a dog.

Bark was, at his heart, a caretaker. He loved caring for his cats, just like he loved fishing to provide food for people. And even though it would be easy to think he ignored its well-being, he loved keeping *Madre's Mayhem* afloat.

He had been taking care of Cape Madre for far too long, and no one ever cared. When they'd regulated the fishing and taken away some of his routes, he had complied. He just wanted to keep the town strong. When they moved the docks and told him to keep away from the teenagers, again he listened, though it meant giving up swaths of beach that he had always enjoyed. He just didn't know how much longer he could do it.

Nothing felt right anymore. Bark felt like someone had flipped a switch and put him on auto-pilot. He wanted to get back to the person he had always been, but it was out of reach. Impossible to find. And so, he moved to the next task. To the next thing that would hopefully keep Cape Madre together for one more day.

CHAPTER 10

Tanner didn't want to go. Miriam could tell. After their conversation on the pier, she wondered whether he had any curiosity left in him at all. Macy, of course, had no trouble flat out refusing, but it was more complicated with Tanner. He hadn't said no, exactly, or even resisted. He had just sighed, dropped his shoulders, and told Macy to have fun. Miriam felt bad. A little. But she needed him.

The *Mama Jean* skipped over rough waters, the crisp sea-winds blowing Miriam's hair into a frenzy until she managed to tame it in a ponytail. Newt sat on a higher level, behind a plexiglass shield, smiling at nothing, still wearing his sunglasses despite the waning sun.

Tanner sat across from her on a padded bench with frayed stitches. He was making a point not to look at her.

"Thanks for coming with me," she shouted, hoping to be loud enough for Tanner to hear without Newt being able to eavesdrop.

Tanner just nodded, so Miriam moved across to sit next to him. He briefly acknowledged her. From here, they could have something more like a regular conversation. Neither of them liked to talk. Most of the time, they didn't even need to. She would know when Tanner needed a gun, or a knife, or a light. She would know if she should follow closely or hang back. But for all the little nuances of their communication, she couldn't quite figure out why he was so resistant to this endeavor.

"Aren't you excited?" she asked.

Tanner looked at her this time, his blue eyes considering her. He looked like he wanted to say something, but then reconsidered, nodded once again, and faced back out to the ocean. Miriam knew what Excited Tanner looked like, and this wasn't it. The Tanner beside her seemed worried, frustrated, and maybe a little bit angry.

She wanted to ask him to explain his feelings, but she didn't really know how. It wasn't something either of them had ever done. They shared respect and love, but, just as they'd been taught, it remained unspoken. Miriam felt the heat rising in her cheeks, along with a wave of indignation. She wanted to be excited. She wanted to share it with him. Why wouldn't he engage?

"We might be able to do something Dad never could," she said, hoping to stoke a fire within him. "There might really be something out here. And we could find it."

Tanner looked at her again, poised to say something until he choked down his words. There was something new and different going on. Something she had never considered Tanner was capable of.

Fear.

"What? Say it," Miriam pleaded.

He sighed, "You just don't get it. What are we even doing?"

Miriam didn't understand. They were doing what they trained to do for their entire lives.

"What do you mean?"

The boat hit a particularly big wave, causing them both to bounce. Miriam braced herself against the back of the bench. When the ride smoothed out again, Tanner pursed his lips, and Miriam felt certain he would clam up and never answer her question. Then he exploded.

"Cornelius is dead, Miriam! *Dead*!" he shouted, surely loud enough for Newt to hear.

Tanner's words winded her. Miriam gasped, fought back stinging tears, and crossed her arms over her chest. Of course Cornelius was dead. She knew that. She didn't need reminding.

"I know that, Tanner. That's why I'm here. That's why I have to find this thing. To show that he didn't lose his life for nothing." She tried to explain it calmly, but it came out too fast, her words falling over one another and threatening to become gibberish.

Tanner shook his head. The fear, frustration and worry all disappeared. Unlike the tears that Miriam fought back, Tanner's eyes burned with anger.

"Why? So, you can die too!?"

The engine on the *Mama Jean* grew quieter, and the boat slowed down until it was coasting over the water at a smooth, hurried pace. Tanner's words hung over them, piercing into the quiet ocean air. Newt most certainly heard the last part.

Miriam took deep, long breaths, trying to center herself, but her heart beat too fast for her to slow it down. Anger-fueled adrenaline coursed through her. She shot to her feet, where she wobbled, almost slipped, then fell back onto her bench.

Newt took the stairs down from the Captain's perch two at a time, his long legs planting his feet surely on the wet deck of *Mama Jean*. Newt's face no longer wore a smile.

Miriam felt certain Newt would comment on the argument, making the tense situation even worse, but he didn't. Instead, he walked to the bow of the ship, between Tanner and Miriam, and slipped off his glasses to stare out onto the ocean.

"Here she is. The vortex."

Miriam ran her eyes over the horizon in front of them and saw only water, calmer than what they had just navigated through, but otherwise nothing special. If there was a color difference, she couldn't see it. She wondered whether Newt had even taken them to the right place.

As if he could sense Miriam's distrust, Newt offered a steady hand to pull her up. "Come with me, pretty lady. I wanna show you something."

She took his hand and floated to her feet, surprised at the strength in his wiry frame, then followed him up to his perch. Tanner stayed behind.

Once they were behind the plexiglass shield, Newt dusted off a small screen with his hand and pointed at it. "That's the depth."

It read just over two hundred feet. Deep, sure, but nothing out of the ordinary. A depth that Miriam expected in the gulf water this far from the coast. Unimpressed, she looked back out to the waters in front of them.

"No, no," Newt said. "Wait for it. Keep looking. We're almost there."

Miriam looked back down. The depth remained relatively steady, moving only a few feet in either direction, but then the number shot up, from two hundred to just under six hundred.

Six hundred feet? Dean's Blue Hole in the Bahamas came in at almost seven hundred. How could this exist without being cataloged alongside all the other holes?

Any anger Miriam held for Tanner evaporated with excitement. "Tanner! Come here. Look at this. This thing is huge."

Tanner was slow to get up, but he started to make his way to them.

"How wide is it?" she asked Newt.

Newt tilted his head back and forth. "Not sure, exactly. Twenty, Thirty yards maybe. Never measured. It's big, though. And there ain't no fish here. Never is. Never was."

Tanner joined them in the cockpit, his eyes finding the depth finder without assistance. Miriam watched his face, hoping for a spark of excitement. Maybe it was there. The smallest glimmer.

A radio crackled to life. "*Mama Jean*. Come back to me. Over."

Tanner tapped her on the shoulder and pointed out in front of them to the silhouette of another ship. It was too far away to make out, but Miriam knew from the voice on the radio exactly who it was.

Newt cocked an eyebrow. "Excuse me a second." Picking up the worn CB handset, Newt pressed in the button. "This is Mama Jean. What you need, Bark? Over."

"Turn around, Newt. Those kids shouldn't be out here!" Bark's voice reverberated.

Miriam took offense at being called a kid, but, moreover, even though Bark had made it very clear that he wouldn't go near the vortex, there he was, a few hundred feet away. The hair on the back of Miriam's neck prickled. Something strange was afoot.

"They ain't hurtin' nothin', Bark. Go back to your fishin'."

Fishing. Bark's job. And something he couldn't do here. Newt said there were no fish. Miriam's heart sunk deep into the bowels of her gut. Every one of her honed senses started going off. Maybe it wasn't a kraken, per se. But something bad.

"I think he's right," Miriam suggested, "We should probably turn back. It's almost dark."

"Newt, don't do this to them," Bark's voice came back over the radio.

Out of the corner of her eye, Miriam sensed Tanner's body stiffen, instantly alerting her to an impending move.

Tanner pushed Newt against the back of the cockpit and stood menacingly in front of him. "What's he talking about?"

Newt shrugged, his eyes wide. "I don't know, man. Honestly. Bark's crazy."

The boat shook, knocking Miriam to the ground. Newt slumped against the wall but held his footing while Tanner managed to plant his hands on either side of Newt to keep his balance. Miriam tried to scramble back to her feet but once she got to her knees the boat reeled, spinning around. She tumbled against the floor, her body jolting towards the doorway. She looked down the wet metal stairs leading to the deck, then past the bow of the ship where something writhed in the water, thick tendrils of muscle shifting in and out of the waves. It could only be one thing.

Miriam gasped and grabbed at the railing to haul herself back up. After pulling herself half way, she felt two strong arms lift her by the armpits, planting her back on her feet.

Tanner shouted into the cockpit, "Get us out of here. Now!"

Miriam couldn't see inside, but she heard the engine of the *Mama Jean* start. The boat surged forward.

"Get inside!" Tanner shouted as he pushed Miriam into the cockpit with Newt.

She watched as one of his feet stepped into the cockpit with her, but then Tanner disappeared, backward and over the railing. Breathing hard, Miriam ran to the door, careful to hold on to the frame. Tanner held on to the railing, his biceps pushed to their limits, veins popping out down his arms. Miriam lunged toward him and grabbed one of his hands.

"Newt! Help me!" she shouted behind her.

Miriam looked down Tanner's body to see a slimy, wet tentacle snaking out of the water and wrapping his legs together at the ankles.

She planted her feet under the bottom rail and held tight to Tanner. The force of his weight pulled hard against her, shooting hot pain up her legs. She gripped Tanner's wrist with her other hand and pulled as hard as she could, locking her eyes onto his.

"Hold on! Hold *on!*"

He inched towards her and she pulled harder. The motor of the *Mama Jean* sputtered and whined, pulling against the force of the tentacle. She wanted Newt's help to pry Tanner free, but she needed him at the wheel even more. The boat started to dip towards Tanner. Surely this thing couldn't capsize them. Not a boat this size.

Miriam's ankles and shoulders screamed for relief, but she refused to let go. The tension slacked and as the boat tilted upright his head slammed into the railing with a *thud*. Miriam held on, but with Tanner's weight pulling down on her arm, she wouldn't be able to hold on for long.

Then, Tanner's handhold on the rail relaxed, and fell. Miriam tried to grab his wrist, but she was too late. The blow to his head had knocked Tanner unconscious and she wouldn't be able to reel him back in. He slipped further down, as Miriam folded herself over the railing, the hard metal digging deep into her ribs.

"No!" she protested, but it was too late. Tanner slipped from her grip and into the water.

He was right there. At the base of the ship. She could see him. She could save him. Miriam yanked off her shirt and shimmied her jean shorts down to the floor, stripping down to the one-piece bathing suit she wore underneath. As she dove into the water, Newt shouted after her. She didn't know or care what he said.

She popped up to the surface and coughed out warm, salty water. He should be right here. Miriam stretched her arms around her in every direction and scanned the dimly lit surface for any sign of Tanner. He had to be here. Dammit. Where was he?

Water splashed onto her face just as his body popped up ahead of her. She swam — hard — but he was moving through the water, not floating. She couldn't catch him. That thing had him. It was the only explanation. She pushed hard, throwing her hands over into the water and kicking as fast as she could. With each breath, she made sure that she could still see Tanner's body gliding away from her.

Tanner stopped suddenly, and Miriam almost bowled him over with her frantic stroke. She had him. She could see his chest rising.

"You're gonna be okay," she promised through ragged breaths. "I got ya. I got ya."

His eyes fluttered, and then snapped open. "Miriam?"

Miriam felt hot tears push their way onto her face. "Yeah. I'm here. Can you swim?"

Tanner wriggled out from her grip and pushed himself upright to tread water. He winced. "I don't know. My ankles."

Miriam nodded and offered a relieved, blubbering laugh. "It's okay. I can get you back."

At least she hoped she could. Miriam was unsure how far she'd swum from the *Mama Jean*. A quick scan of the horizon showed that it wasn't far, steadily puttering toward them with a searchlight brightly shining their direction. They were still too far away to be fully illuminated, but Newt had the right track. It would only be a couple of minutes.

Miriam held Tanner close to her, one arm hooked under his so that he could float on his back. They needed to get out of the water, but she was so tired. She couldn't catch her breath, and Tanner's dense, muscular frame was too much for her to pull. She tried to kick forward towards the boat but moved slower than she wanted.

That thing was out there. What had she been thinking? Tanner was right. This whole thing was utter madness. They didn't need to do this. They needed to live. They needed to keep each other. Tanner was the only family she had left. She wouldn't lose him. Not tonight. Not ever.

After an excruciatingly long wait, she heard Newt holler across the water, "Ahoy there!"

Only a little further now. A life preserver splashed into the water. Relieved, Miriam lunged at it and grabbed hold, then secured Tanner.

Newt pulled on the rope attached to the preserver and Tanner glided away from her. Lighter now, she ducked down and started a freestyle stroke towards the *Mama Jean*. They'd made it. They would be all right.

Her speed outpaced that of Tanner's, and before long Miriam pulled herself up on the deck, salt water rushing off her. She bent over and grabbed her knees, taking deep breaths. She didn't allow herself long before she sidled up next to Newt and took the rope behind him. She pulled as hard as her tired muscles would allow.

"Oh, Jesus!" Newt exclaimed.

Miriam peered around his frame and saw writhing in the water. Her heart sank.

"Pull, Newt. Hard!" she yelled as she heeded her own advice, ignoring the pain against the tender parts of her hands.

Newt leaned further and pulled harder, but the rope started moving the other direction, burning Miriam's hands. She couldn't grip it. She grunted and screamed and blinked away hot tears. She fell to the deck, trying to use her weight to anchor herself, but she only slid towards the railing. She shook her head. She wouldn't give up. She couldn't give up. The line went slack. Miriam wailed.

Without giving it a thought, she tossed herself back into the ocean, but saw no sign of Tanner, the life preserver, or the rope. She turned in every direction, drowning out the cries from Newt for her to get back on the boat. She would find him. He would resurface and she would be ready.

She waited, and when the waiting became too painful, she swam. She picked a direction and pushed forward, stopping periodically to catch her breath and scan the waters. There was nothing. No signs. Minutes passed by, and Miriam felt the hope draining out of her. She would not accept this. Not Tanner.

Her face burned, and she couldn't breathe. She considered diving. Not because she thought she could find him there, but because maybe then she could join him. But she didn't. She only swam and surveyed and swam some more. The *Mama Jean* caught up and trailed beside her. Newt begged her to get back on the boat.

That probably made more sense. The boat was safer and potentially faster, but no. She needed to be here. With him. As long as she stayed in the water, then she was with Tanner. He would pop back up. He had to.

But she knew he wouldn't. It had been too long. She stopped swimming and gave up, relaxing her muscles. If she drowned, she didn't care.

Newt would have none of it, though. He pulled up beside her limp silhouette floating in the ocean and reached down a huge fishing net on a pole.

"I don't know if this will work, pretty lady, but I'll scoop you out if I have to," he said, far too exuberant for Miriam to accept.

She gave in to his pleas and hoisted herself up the side of the ship and collapsed on the deck. Newt didn't stop to check on her or make sure she was okay. Instead, he rushed up to the cockpit and fired *Mama Jean's* motor for all it would take.

Miriam laid on the deck and cried.

CHAPTER 11

The whereabouts of Hannah Huang suddenly took a backseat. The call woke Tommy as he napped on the couch, passively binging a mediocre TV show. He never replayed an episode when he fell asleep. He just soldiered on in a state of perpetual confusion and convoluted plotlines. He slept through a lot of episodes.

With a tall cup of coffee in his hand and a well-rested mind, Tommy walked into the office to meet Miriam Brooks. Twenty-one. Originally from Missouri. Student at Dobie Tech University in Dobie, Texas. Most of the work had already been done by the police who met her at the docks, and the coast guard was dutifully searching for her cousin, but Tommy knew better than to expect a happy outcome.

Now the case was his. Because Miriam Brooks insisted that her brother had been attacked by a giant sea monster. Like Emma Chu. Like Joe Hampton. Tommy didn't like being the go-to guy for a case that he'd just be asked to downplay, but he wanted to help these people. If he could. Yet it felt like the only thing he could truly offer these days was toilet repair services.

When he rounded the corner into the bullpen, he peered into his window-lined office and saw only one girl inside — a knockout redhead that was way too young for Tommy to think of as a knockout. She paced back and forth in front of his desk, mascara streaking her face. He hadn't met Miriam Brooks, but a hunch told him this wasn't her.

He knocked on his own door to avoid startling the girl, but she jumped anyway, sniffled, and searched his face with big green eyes. He offered the best reassuring smile he could and set his coffee down on his desk.

"Ms. Brooks?" he asked.

The girl leaned over and shook his hand. Firmly. Like an adult. "No. She's in the bathroom. She wouldn't let me go with her."

Tommy motioned to a seat across from him and sank down in his own chair when the girl had also sat. She plucked a tissue from a box on his desk and dabbed at her eyes, but there would be no repairing the havoc the tears had done to her makeup.

"I'm Macy Donner. My dad's a cop. Or was, I guess. He's the mayor now."

Ah. A child of law enforcement. Tommy didn't care if her dad was the president of Mars, but he admired the gumption to use her father as a way to get better treatment for her — friend? Tommy couldn't be sure yet.

"And you know Ms. Brooks how?"

"Um. It's uh... We met when... We're friends. Roommates at DTech."

Tommy nodded. The police didn't mention anyone on the boat with Miriam and Newt other than the missing person. "And were you on the boat with Ms. Brooks at the time of the attack?"

"She called me," Macy said as she shook her head. "I came as fast as I could. I don't know if she'll survive this. Maybe he's still alive, right? Maybe he'll wash up somewhere? Or a fisherman — maybe a fisherman'll find him."

Tommy doubted that very much, but it was always tough deciding when to be frank with family of the deceased. For now, he decided to ignore the notion completely. Maybe not the most responsible thing to do, but the easiest. Instead, he decided to go after the idea that Miriam wouldn't survive losing him.

"People are stronger than we think, ya know. She'll pull through, I'm sure."

Fresh tears came, and Macy made no effort to catch these with the tissue. "No. You don't understand. She already lost one brother. Almost two years ago. In Rose Valley."

Rose Valley. The name rang a bell, but he couldn't place it beyond knowing it was a tiny town somewhere in the vicinity of Fort Worth.

Wait. One brother? Tommy flipped through the case file that had been conveniently left on his desk.

"This must be wrong. Says here Tanner Brooks is Miriam's cousin?"

"Technically," a strained voice interrupted from the doorway.

Tommy looked up to see a girl of average height; thin, sinewy, and strong, with wide hips and a small chest. A girl who spent time in the gym, or maybe running marathons. Water seeped through her shirt, vaguely outlining a swimsuit underneath. Stringy brown hair curtained her shoulders. Her brown eyes were bloodshot.

Macy pulled Tommy's attention back. "They were raised together."

Tommy made a note in the file and sighed. The beat cops didn't understand the first thing about detective work. He needed this sort of information to make people comfortable.

Miriam shuffled into the office and took the seat next to Macy, who immediately offered a hand for Miriam to hold. Miriam took it, looking stronger and more resolute than Tommy imagined she would. Certainly, more physically strong, but also mentally tough. A lot of times, people in this situation just withdrew. Tommy had been prepared to table this until the morning, but the police on the scene said that she insisted on talking to him tonight. But where to start?

Miriam didn't give Tommy a chance. "They're searching for him already?"

For all the good it would do. "Yes. They'll be searching all night and into the morning."

"He's strong. If that thing didn't kill him, he'll fight to live. He's a master swimmer. And survivalist."

Seemed like a lot of skills for a college kid. Tommy wondered how much of it was true. Miriam looked sporty enough, so maybe they went camping a lot as children or something. But to be a master swimmer and survivalist? Not many adults could say that, much less university students.

"Let's talk about that 'thing' as you call it. What do you think it was?" Tommy asked, deciding to ignore the survivalist comment entirely.

"Lusca," Miriam said plainly.

Macy translated, "A cryptid."

Tommy blinked again and looked back and forth between the two young faces, begging for a word that actually meant something to him. Both girls looked as if they had told him all he needed to know.

"And that is?" Tommy addressed the question to Macy, hoping to get a more coherent answer from her.

"An animal. A monster. Um. Something unknown. Something science hasn't found yet." Macy fumbled through the words, clearly trying to find the exact right terminology to get her point across.

Miriam shifted in her seat, closed her eyes, and exhaled. "Like Bigfoot."

Bigfoot? Tommy's first reaction was to laugh, but his training successfully held that off. Instead, he tried to piece it all together. What Joe told him. Tentacles. Sea monsters. Something bigger than any octopus or squid had any right to be along the gulf coast. But Bigfoot came from myth, and this monster was all too real.

"Is that why you went out there? To find this thing?"

Miriam swallowed hard and blinked her eyes to clear the wetness. "Yes. I wanted to find it. To prove that it existed."

"But why?"

The words came tumbling out, as if she wouldn't be able to say them if she didn't force them out as quickly as possible. "It's all I know how to do. That girl, Emma. At the beach. She was attacked by this thing. Something fantastical. Unbelievable. But real."

Tommy could tell more was coming, so he remained quiet as Macy squeezed Miriam's hand in an offer of extra support. Miriam squeezed back before untangling her hand and leaning on Tommy's desk.

"My father is a Cryptozoologist. Um. A scientist sort of... who hunts creatures just like this. He taught me everything he knows."

That threw Tommy for a loop. He did not expect to be sitting across the desk from a self-proclaimed monster hunter. What did that even mean? He briefly entertained the notion that maybe Miriam Brooks was the answer to his prayers. Maybe she could help him save Cape Madre. While he could only repair toilets, maybe she could kill giant sea creatures. But no. She was a kid. From Missouri. With a friend who didn't look like she'd done hard labor a day in her life. And if monster hunting was a thing, he would have heard of it.

"That's all very impressive, Ms. Brooks, but I don't under—"

"Help me, Detective," Miriam said with determination. "I don't have resources. You do. Tanner might still be out there. And even if he isn't, I will find and hunt and kill this thing."

Tommy believed it. He shouldn't have, he knew that. But the fire in her eyes was undeniable. Miriam Brooks wasn't delusional or grief-stricken. But he would need to verify. He needed to know there was at least some truth to what she said before sticking his neck out to get the sort of resources she'd ask for.

"I..." Tommy stammered and shook his head in disbelief. "Who are you?"

"Miriam Brooks. I killed Rose Valley's beast for killing my brother, and I'm going to kill this thing too."

The Beast of Rose Valley. The context brought it all flooding back. The news articles about an escaped government experiment terrorizing a small Texas town. He didn't remember the details, but he knew that it had happened. Digging up the old articles would be easy enough. If that was really her... if she was telling the truth... then, maybe...

Head swimming, Tommy said, "I'll see what I can do."

***

Tommy started feeling foolish for even entertaining the idea of using Cape Madre resources to help a college kid hunt a monster. It sounded ridiculous. Then again, getting rid of a problem that could haunt the tourism industry for years to come might warrant going to any lengths. Maybe.

The news reports on The Beast of Rose Valley mostly corroborated Miriam's claims, but there seemed to be conflicting reports on who had actually brought it down. Maybe that didn't matter. Skylar Brooks had certainly benefited the most from the whole debacle, even moving his home base from Missouri to Rose Valley. In the end, though, The Beast had been a man. Not a monster. Tommy wasn't confident that the skills necessary to hunt a man would translate to hunting a giant squid. Or Octopus. Or Kraken ... maybe? Hell. Tommy didn't even know what to call it.

Tanner Brooks had to be dead, though. Had to be. Miriam seemed resolute and clear-headed, but she had lost someone close, and that had compromised her. Like it compromised Stacy. Tommy had spent months trying to convince Stacy to live again. To move past her pain. And this Miriam kid had done it in the span of a few hours. Few people could do that. That either made her very strong or a complete sociopath. Possibly both.

Tommy needed to get back to his mission. To figure out what was attacking tourists. To... what? Neutralize it? That was never really clear. So far, his job had consisted almost entirely of covering it up and downplaying it in order to make sure that it didn't affect the bottom line. Maybe the real answer should be to clear the waters, shut down the beaches, and let Cape Madre waste away. That would save people from death-by-kraken, but it wouldn't save all the people whose livelihoods depended on the city's economy. This stuff was way the hell above his pay grade.

Tommy's desk shook with the buzz of his cell phone, relieving him with distraction. He glanced at the clock as he picked up, noting that it was almost midnight. Too late for any reasonable person to text. It came from an unknown number.

Emma Chu woke up. Thought you might want to know.
- Krissy

Krissy? It took Tommy a few seconds to place her: the nurse whose name he'd sworn had started with an 'A.'

Did it even matter whether he talked to Emma Chu anymore? Miriam Brooks had provided a more-than-adequate description of what Tommy was dealing with. A repeat of what Joe had told him months before. If only he'd taken Joe more seriously.

Tommy ticked out a response, backing up a few times to correct his mistakes. Cell phone keyboards were not meant for his giant thumbs.

I'll be by first thing in the morning.

He was exhausted, but not sleepy. He knew all of this would be turning through his head for hours still. He had a lot to do. Hannah Huang. Tanner Brooks. And now back to Emma Chu. She might not tell him anything new, but he had made a promise to keep an eye on her. A promise he couldn't break.

CHAPTER 12

Newt slammed into the deck of the *Mama Jean*, blood trickling out of his mouth. He tried to get up, but a hard kick to his abdomen sent him sprawling back down. He didn't try to get up again. Instead, he just rolled around to a sitting position before leaning against the outer wall of the cockpit. Holding his midsection, he spat blood on the deck.

"Goddammit, Newt," said the man now towering over him. "What the hell were you thinking?"

Bark had years on Newt, and by all accounts, he should have stood no chance in an altercation, but his fists were stone-hard, his boots were steel-toed, and he was mad. No. Beyond mad. Pissed.

Newt breathed out a ragged response. "I was just trying to help, Bark. Like you always do. But when she showed up, I... I didn't want that to happen."

Bark lifted a hand to the crown of his nose and rubbed. He felt a headache coming on; or, rather, worsening. His entire life had become a headache.

Newt was an idiot, so convincing him to use his brain seemed impossible. Maybe it was time to take him out of the equation. Bark didn't need any help keeping things in order. He would have never picked Newt as a partner; it just happened that way.

Newt tried to get up again, and Bark dropped his hand to glower at the wiry, stupid man below him. Newt took the hint and slid back to the deck. The moon didn't provide enough light for Bark to see how much damage he'd done, but he could see the fear reflecting in the whites of Newt's eyes. Bark had gotten his point across.

"Tommy's gonna come 'round to talk to you, Newt. What are you going to say? How are you going to get yourself out of this?"

Newt dropped his gaze. "I dunno, Bark. I didn't think that far ahead."

"Exactly. You never think for yourself. I got enough to take care of 'round here without making sure you don't screw things up."

"I'll just tell him that I chartered a boat for'em. Didn't know what would happen. Didn't know that thing was out there."

Bark considered Newt's plan. Tommy might buy it. Certainly, from Bark he would, but Newt was a slimy asshole and Tommy wouldn't hesitate to nail him to the wall if he had to. Then again, there was no reason to believe that Tommy had any inkling of what was really going on in Cape Madre, no idea how much blood, sweat, and tears went into keeping the city safe. Sometimes, the hint of a different solution weighed on Bark's old mind, but something always brought him back to this path. The only one that felt right.

As stupid as he was, Newt had become part of the plan. Bark believed him when he said that he just wanted to help, because that's all Bark wanted to do. It compelled him, and Newt as well now. Rather than an obstacle, Bark needed to start using Newt as an asset.

"You still got that abandoned house out there?" Bark asked.

Newt nodded. "Yessir. Ain't got no 'lectricity, though."

"That's fine. It don't need no 'lectricity. I need to store something there for a while. Until it's time to go back out."

Newt reached his long fingers into the front pocket of his pants and fished out a keyring. He fumbled around in the dim light for a few seconds, until he got a key off and tossed it up to Bark. Bark caught it in his meaty hand.

"All right," Bark growled. "We'll get this sorted out. It'll blow over. Stop being stupid."

Newt nodded in pain and worked his way to his feet. Bark didn't stop him this time.

Bark just needed a few days. As long as Tommy didn't turn up the heat too high on'em, he'd be able to get things back on track.

As Bark stepped off the *Mama Jean* onto the wooden planking of the boardwalk, he turned back to look up at Newt. "Well, come on now. We got work to do."

CHAPTER 13

Throughout the night, Miriam drifted in and out of sleep, but her body had given up on being hungry. At some point, Macy had joined her and now they nestled under the covers, tangled together in an attempt to fortify themselves against the grief. As the morning sun streaked through the hotel room's cheap blackout curtains, Miriam snapped fully awake. For a few seconds, Tanner and the attack stayed in the back of her mind, but soon the tears came once more.

Macy still slept, her chest softly pushing against Miriam's back. Miriam had never been held before. Not that she could remember. There was an unexpected safety in it; not so much physical as existential. Miriam curled her fingers into the crooks of Macy's hand, desperately soaking in the warmth.

Miriam's natural tendencies pointed her towards action. As grief-stricken as she was over Tanner, the only solution she could calculate was revenge. It's how she had handled Cornelius' death. And that had worked, sort of, allowing her to at least move forward. To uproot her life, switch universities, and strike out on her own. Well, not on her own. She'd had Tanner, and because of a chance encounter in a tiny Texas town, she had Macy. But now, she worried that she had only Macy.

Technically, Detective Wallace had classified Tanner as "missing." For a while, Miriam had been convinced that Tanner still clung to life out in the roiling ocean, but the reality of the situation had started to settle in, and claw at the edges of her resolve. With likely broken ankles and land too far away, what could Tanner possibly do to survive? Not even *he* was that strong.

Detective Wallace had asked Miriam whether she'd like to be the one to call her father about Tanner's disappearance, but she declined. She couldn't handle talking to her dad like this. Not when it was her own foolish fault. She wondered whether the call had been made, whether her dad was even reachable. And if he had gotten the call, how had he reacted? Would he even care?

Miriam stretched her legs as best she could without kicking Macy. How would she tackle the day? Without support, she felt shackled and ineffective. It didn't make sense to go back out on the water until she had a plan. And weapons. Lots of weapons.

Part of her begged to stay in bed. The covers were warm, and the idea of complete and utter retreat strongly enticed her to just sink into depression and accept her life of tragedy. But something urged her forward. The same something that had managed to get her this far. Maybe the one thing her father accidentally gave her: he had forged her into a survivor.

Miriam forced herself from the covers. There were things she could do. Joe Hampton had survived an attack by this creature, so maybe Tanner could, too. She sat at the tiny desk, opened the laptop and started her search with the article about Joe's death. She scanned it again and found the part she was looking for — *Mr. Hampton is survived by his wife, Stacy.*

Stacy Hampton. She would know the full story of how Joe escaped the clutches — or tentacles — of evil. Miriam would find Stacy, go to her house, and ask her about it. Though it had been over six months, she considered the possibility that Stacy wouldn't want to talk about her late husband, but the larger part of Miriam didn't care. She needed this information. It was the only way she would be able to stay sane while they waited for further developments, and until Tanner's body turned up, Miriam didn't think she could ever accept his death.

Cape Madre was small enough that there was only one Stacy Hampton. Miriam found references to her as a clerk for the county, as well as few mentions here and there of her donating her time at local high school fundraisers. None of that since Joe's death, though. Her picture still adorned the county website, but the little paragraph that described her ended with: *Mrs. Hampton is currently on an extended leave of absence.*

Had she left Cape Madre? Miriam could drive. As long as she could get back to Cape Madre quickly, she'd drive anywhere to meet this lady. Calling would work in a pinch, but Miriam suspected that it would take a little bit of elbow grease for her to get in the door.

She clicked and typed and searched and read until she finally found what she was looking for: an address for Stacy Hampton.

Miriam typed the address into her phone and stood up from the chair, filled with purpose and, perhaps, a little bit of denial about her situation. She crossed back to the bed where Macy slept and tapped one of her feet.

Macy's eyes fluttered open, bloodshot and tired. Miriam knew the feeling well; she just wouldn't let that stop her.

Macy sat up with a jolt. "Did they find him?"

Miriam sat on the end of the bed and laid a hand on Macy's covered leg. "No. I'm sorry. I didn't mean to startle you. I just... I have a lead. I want to go talk to Joe's wife, and I want you to come with me."

Macy looked confused. "Who's Joe?"

"The guy. Who got attacked before. In October."

One of Macy's eyes went narrower than the other as she tried to work it out with her fuzzy morning brain. "Isn't he dead?"

"Yeah," Miriam sighed. "But this thing didn't kill him. He escaped it. He survived it. I need to know how."

"But why? Just get back in bed. Detective Wallace will call if they find something."

Miriam slapped Macy on what she took to be Macy's shin. "No. Get up. I need to know that it can be done. If some random fisherman could escape, then Tanner might have, too. Maybe they found Joe later washed up somewhere, or maybe a boat found him. I need to know how it all happened."

"Because if you know," Macy said with defeated sympathy. "Then it gives you hope?"

Miriam looked down at the shape of Macy's legs beneath the covers. She hadn't thought of it that way, but yeah. It gave her hope, something she desperately needed right now. She nodded.

Macy threw the covers off herself, stood up, and stretched her arms above her head. "Fine. But can I take a shower?"

***

For the first time that Miriam could remember, Macy hadn't straightened out her hair, instead stuffing it into a huge frizzy ponytail. Miriam liked it this way, rugged and natural. It hinted at a Macy who could eschew public perception and dive into the nitty-gritty of a good hunt.

"This is it," Miriam said, as she pulled the car up along the curb of a sagging, yellow house.

They both studied it for a moment, with Macy breaking the silence. "Looks rundown. You sure she still lives here?"

"Only one way to find out!"

Miriam stepped out of the car and met Macy on the other side. The morning smelled like grass up here, which Miriam preferred to the fishy smells down on the beach. The house across the way looked abandoned, even though it sounded like someone was mowing the backyard. Hopefully their next project would be the weed-laden front yard. The house they were visiting, however, did have a well-manicured lawn.

Miriam knocked on the splintered blue door and steeled herself for a chilly reception. Macy hung behind, studying her surroundings.

When no one answered the door, Miriam began to do the same. A truck sat on the curb across from their car, old and rusted with a fishing pole rack in the bed. Most of the other houses looked empty, but it was the middle of the week, after all. Maybe Stacy was out running errands.

Macy shrugged. "Maybe she's not home. We can come back later?"

On cue, the door opened. Not entirely, but enough for Miriam to see the tall, slender frame of a woman.

"Can I help you?" the woman asked.

Miriam swallowed, then regurgitated the speech she had been working on in her head. "Hi. My name is

Miriam Brooks. My cousin, Tanner, was recently attacked by something out in the waters. Something scary. And big. And —" she paused here for effect. "Not a shark."

The door shimmied as the woman considered closing it, but Miriam locked her eyes onto the woman's and begged, "I really need some information. So I can save him. Please."

A moment of silence passed between them as probably-Stacy studied Miriam's face, then Macy's.

"Please?" Miriam stated again emphatically, this time choosing to make it more of a question than a statement.

The woman shifted. Miriam thought for sure the door would slam in her face, but instead it opened wide and they were motioned inside. With the door out of the way, Miriam could now see her host entirely. She was a tall, lanky woman, with big teeth and large, sunken eyes. Even as her clothes were dramatically oversized, it seemed a safe guess that Stacy Hampton was underweight.

"I'm Stacy," the woman said.

"Miriam, and this is my..." she paused. "...best friend, Macy Donner."

It was the first time Miriam had ever called Macy that aloud, not to mention the first time she had ever given anyone that label. To Miriam, though, Macy had fit that role for some time.

"Nice to meet you both," Stacy said as she led them through the small foyer and into a well-kept living room. Stacy sat on the love-seat, leaving the couch for Miriam and Macy.

The three of them sat in silence at first. Miriam spent the time sizing up the room and her host. Stacy looked sad, and Miriam wondered if Stacy thought the same about her. Miriam might have looked that way, but she had a hard time reconciling her grief with her will to push on. Sad people didn't force friends out of bed to interview random strangers, did they?

When it seemed that no one was going to talk at all, Macy took over. "Thanks for talking to us, Stacy."

Stacy flashed a sympathetic smile. "This part's hard. After the attack."

"It all seems so unbelievable." Miriam nodded. "I just want him to be okay."

Silence filled the room once again as all three women struggled to broach the topic. Miriam certainly didn't want to dredge up feelings that Stacy may have buried, so she thought hard on how to ask her questions in the most sensitive way. She didn't even know where to start. Maybe with condolences?

"First off, I want to say that I'm so sorry about your husband's accident," Miriam offered.

"Thank you." Stacy's eyes glistened. "You just need to keep an eye on your cousin right now, okay? Keep him close. Don't let him go off on his own."

Miriam glanced at Macy, who looked as confused as Miriam felt. "But he's still missing. That's why I'm here. I wanted to ask about how your husband escaped."

Stacy looked taken aback, as if she had misunderstood the entire premise of their conversation. She stood from her love-seat and walked to the mantle, turning her back to both girls as she studied a photo on the mantle. Stacy sniffled.

Macy took a tissue from the box on the end table and offered it to Stacy. Stacy mumbled appreciation as she took it, clearly enjoying Macy's comforting hand. Miriam marveled at how natural it all was for her friend.

"May I see?" Macy asked, referring to the photo.

Stacy nodded and handed Macy the frame. Macy studied it for a few seconds before walking it over to Miriam. The cheap gold frame looked like it came from a discount store, but the picture inside spoke volumes about the woman Stacy must have once been. Miriam absentmindedly ran her fingers across a picture of a man and a woman standing next to one another, each one holding on to one end of a very large fish. The man was big. Jolly. Like a lumberjack of the sea. And he was happy. They both were. It was almost hard to tell, but the woman in the photo was Stacy, with a huge smile, windswept hair, and a long neck leading down to a cute black bikini. There were curves under all those wrinkled clothes, after all.

Miriam stood and offered the photo back. "Thank you."

Stacy took the photo and carefully placed it back on the mantle, adjusting it left and right until she found the exact right spot. There were more tears, more dabbing. Macy returned to Miriam's side on the couch, and both waited in silence. Miriam's stomach swam, and she worried for a second that she might be sick, but she pushed the feeling down.

Tanner could not be dead. She would not allow him to be.

Once Stacy had collected herself, she answered, "Um. The attack. He was out on a job. On a fishing boat. Joe fell overboard when that thing rocked the boat."

"Why did the paper say it was a shark attack?" Miriam asked.

Stacy shrugged. "I don't know. No one believes that. No one who lives here anyway. Everyone here knows the truth."

Miriam shuddered. Sharks. Krakens. Both seemed like bad news for a beach that staked its livelihood on tourism.

"How did Joe get away from the kraken?" Miriam asked.

Stacy huffed, a hint of a smile turning up on her lips, before both her smile and her body sank back down onto the love-seat. "Is that what they call it? Fitting, I guess." Abruptly, she sat up. "Are either of you thirsty? I could make some tea. Or, there are sodas in the fridge, I think. Old, but do those things ever go bad, really?"

Stacy didn't want to answer these questions, and Miriam couldn't blame her. "No, I'm good. Thank you, though."

Stacy's gaze turned to Macy who smiled. "A soda would be lovely. Thank you."

Miriam wondered if accepting the drink was the appropriate thing to do in a situation like this. Probably so; if it's what Macy did. How had Miriam learned so many skills, but never how to be a normal human being? She envied Macy her normal childhood, even if it did include a divorce. At least divorce occurred in a remarkably high number of marriages. Very few children were raised to be monster hunters.

Stacy disappeared into the kitchen. Macy squeezed Miriam's hand and whispered, "It might take a while. Gotta be patient."

Miriam nodded as if she understood, but she only knew it logically. She didn't feel it in the way that Macy seemed to.

Stacy returned with a generic brand Coke and handed it to Macy, who immediately popped the tab and took a drink. Stacy sat back in her seat and nursed her own soda, sending the three women into silence once again. Miriam wanted to push forward. To pepper Stacy with questions. But she held back like Macy said.

Eventually, Stacy broke the silence. "He couldn't remember a lot of it. It pulled him under. Over and over. Joe thought he'd drown, but every time he couldn't hold his breath another second, he would pop back up to the surface. He said that it was playing with him."

Macy must have winced, causing Stacy to continue, "Yeah. Crazy, right? That it would be smart enough to do that. I don't know what it is. I've never seen it. But it's evil."

"How did Joe get out of the water?" Miriam prodded.

"Bark fished him out. Chased him for almost an hour until the thing let him go."

"Who's Bark?" Macy asked.

Miriam, of course, already knew the answer to the question, but there had been no reason to tell Macy about him. Bark. The man with the cats. The man who was too scared to go to the vortex but showed up there anyway. So, he knew more than he'd let on. Miriam made a mental note to call on him next to get a firsthand account of the kraken.

"He's a local fisherman. *The* local fisherman really. He's been doing it longer than any of the others. Really cares about people. The town."

"His cats," Miriam added.

Stacy smirked. "So, you've met him then?"

"Yeah. On the docks. Before I chartered the boat from Newt."

A wave of concern washed over Stacy's face that she quickly hid behind her can of soda. "Be careful with Newt. He'll talk you out of your last penny."

Miriam could feel the heat of Macy's gaze on her, silently asking why she didn't already know about Bark. But it didn't seem important at the time. It wasn't the boat they had chartered anyway.

"How did Bark find him in the water?" Miriam asked, trying to further the conversation along.

Stacy answered plainly, "He saw him fall in, I suppose. Joe was working for Bark when it happened. Helping him haul fish in on the *Mayhem*."

Bark had been there. Across the vortex from the *Mama Jean*, shouting words of warning across the radio. Bark knew what was going to happen, because it had happened before. But Newt said there were no fish at the vortex. Why would Bark and Joe have been fishing there?

The possibility flitted through Miriam's mind that maybe Bark had found Tanner and fished him up out of the ocean the same way he had done Joe. But, if so, surely Detective Wallace would have gotten word by now. The need to talk to Bark overwhelmed Miriam.

"I really appreciate you talking to us like this. It gives us hope, you know? That maybe it didn't kill Tanner. Maybe he's still out there."

Stacy didn't respond to that, probably to avoid telling Miriam the obvious. It wouldn't have upset her, though. Not when she had leads to follow and hope to grasp onto. Miriam stood, followed by Macy, then Stacy.

Before walking them to the door, Stacy warned, "If you do find him. Alive. Hold onto him. Don't let him out of your sight. He'll need you. Living through that changed Joe."

Miriam could only imagine. Not only did Joe have to recover from horrible injuries, he'd also had to face the fact that reality wasn't what he had always thought it to be. Having to accept that legendary monsters were real sounded hard. It just wasn't something Miriam had ever had to cope with.

Stacy escorted them to the door and ushered them out to the walkway. "Good luck finding your cousin."

"Thanks," Miriam said.

Once they made it to the car, Macy started talking. "Bark? We gotta go see Bark, right? You know where he is?"

Miriam nodded. "Yeah. He was there last night. On the water with us."

CHAPTER 14

Tommy dropped a full bag of fast food into the garbage can next to the door, followed by a Coke that he hadn't even touched. He'd already ordered when he got the call, so he dutifully paid for his food and drove off like a normal customer, knowing full well that he'd only toss it the first chance he got. It all made a satisfying thud as it hit the bottom of the empty can, reaffirming that it would have hit the bottom of his belly even harder.

The sign on the door read "Cape Madre Medical Examiner's Office," and inside waited something horrible and gruesome. The kind of gruesome that had a habit of erasing appetites.

That's all that ever waited for him through those doors. While the doctors inside seemed to have grown accustomed to dead bodies and severed limbs, Tommy hoped he never would. Still, he suspected that he visited this place with more dread than the usual detective.

***

The trash can in front of the medical examiner's office overflowed with garbage, but Tommy didn't notice. Through those doors lay the dead body of his best friend. He hadn't seen it yet, and before telling Stacy, he needed to see it for himself, but there was little doubt that the medical examiners of Cape Madre knew who Joe Hampton was, no matter how swollen his lifeless body.

This part was a matter of protocol — to have a close family member or friend positively identify the deceased. It should have been Stacy, but Tommy couldn't do that to her. No one deserved to see their spouse dead on a table, least of all Stacy. Her husband had already been taken from her once, and even though his husk had come back to sleep in her bed, she had been alone ever since Joe had returned from that attack.

Deputy medical examiner Jess Gearhart met Tommy outside examination room C, his young face looking less concerned than Tommy wanted. Jess nodded, astute enough at least to realize Tommy wasn't in a mood to chat.

Together, they stepped into the room and Tommy fought the rumbling in his stomach that threatened to hurl up his lunch.

Joe's huge form laid stretched out on a metal table, milky white, and bloated. He might look like he was only sleeping if not for the lifeless, empty expression on his face. Even though they had dragged him out of the water hours ago, he still looked wet, not on the surface, but from inside, as if he were comprised only of water now. But it was him. No doubt about it. His belly. His beard. Everything laid on that table except the part that made him truly human.

There was nothing Tommy could do from within this room that would honor the life of Joe Hampton, so he nodded to Jess, stood a few seconds to make sure Jess understood the meaning, and then busted out of there as quickly as he could. The tears didn't come, but he felt them building in the corners of his eyes. Now came the even harder part.

***

Tommy stepped into examination room A, immediately buffeted by the unique smells of the dead. His stomach lurched. On the metal table lay a disembodied leg, surreal in its cleanliness with a white tarp wrapped around the ragged edge. Jess Gearhart appeared from a small connected room and gave his familiar welcoming nod.

"What've we got here, Jess?" Tommy asked even though he already had a strong suspicion.

"Well, a leg," Jess started the list like he was reading the ingredients off a cereal box. "Obviously, I guess. It's from a white male. Again, obvious. Uh. Pretty big guy. Probably over six feet. Pretty muscular. Lots of activity or exercise or something."

Check. Check. And Check. All of those finds confirmed what Tommy loathed to admit to himself. It had to be the leg of Tanner Brooks.

"Where'd they find it?"

Jess grabbed for a clipboard on a small cart rolled up next to the table and studied it for a few seconds before answering. Tommy wondered if Jess honestly didn't know the answer or if the clipboard gave him some sort of comfort.

"A jogger found it this morning. Washed up on the beach. Near the pier. CMPD processed it, then someone decided that maybe it related to a case you've been working on?"

Unfortunately, yes. Tommy studied the leg for anything unique, and immediately noticed circular abrasions along the thigh. Faint, with the edges fading in and out of the victim's milky skin, the circles were large and evenly spaced apart. He recognized the wounds, because he'd seen the same ones on Joe's leg. No bruising, though, which surely meant something. Clearly, no shark attack.

Tommy massaged his eyes with his thumb and middle finger. They suddenly felt dry, burning, screaming for rest. If only he had that option. His entire day had now been rearranged. What should have been a pleasant chat with a newly wakened co-ed had now turned into the excruciatingly painful task of informing Miriam Brooks that her cousin looked to be more dead now than ever.

"Can you tell me anything about these cuts?" Tommy asked.

Jess put down the clipboard but kept a pen in his hand to use as a pointer. He ran it along the abrasions as he talked, careful to not actually touch the flesh. "Nearly perfectly round. Evenly spaced. No bruising, so the victim was likely dead when this happened. If it wasn't for the size? I'd say an octopus or something. That's certainly what it looks like. Though, not really possible. In the real world, they aren't this big or strong."

Next, Jess removed the tarp from the end of the leg. "This is the more interesting part, though."

Tommy steeled himself before looking up at the amputation point. Most of the blood had been washed away, so now it almost looked like this leg had been ripped from a human-sized stuffed animal. Not ripped, though. Cleaner than that. Jess must've already cleaned that up, too.

"This leg wasn't ripped off, Tommy. It was cut off. Cleanly. By something. A saw maybe?"

"What? I don't understand."

Jess shrugged and pointed out some of the signs with his pen, prompting Tommy to move around the table and examine the socket to see the white bone. Tommy tried to stay detached, fighting every instinct he had to just run away and switch professions to something that didn't involve dead bodies.

"This bone was cut smoothly," Jess said. "If the leg had been ripped off by a wild animal, we would have seen it snapped. The wounds along the skin also indicate the same. There is no doubt about it that someone cut this leg off the body."

"But why? When? Before or after the..." Tommy paused to decide what to call the creature that had left the cuts. "Kraken attacked him?"

Jess smirked. "Is that what we're calling it now?"

"I guess so," Tommy said. "I don't know what else to call it."

"Fair enough. So, yeah, like I said, almost definitely whatever left these marks did so after the victim was dead. No way to know for sure whether it was after the leg was detached, though. Maybe if I run some more tests, or do some research into this kind of amputation, I can come up with something?"

Survivalist. The word popped into Tommy's head out of nowhere, forcing him to place it in context. That's how Miriam had described Tanner, when she seemed resolute that he was still alive. Tommy's memory conveniently juxtaposed an older news story alongside his current predicament, that of a man hiking alone. Trapped.

"Could someone survive losing a leg like this?" Tommy asked.

Jess's eyes went wide, not out of shock, but as an indication that he was thinking on it. "Yeah. I mean, it happens. People lose legs in war all the time. And, of course, we can safely medically amputate them if we have to. But out in the ocean? There'd be so much blood. Predators would come from miles around —

and that's if he didn't bleed out before he was eaten alive."

"What about self-amputation?" Tommy asked.

"You mean, like if he cut his own leg off? That would be really hard. Again, it's not unheard of, but this leg is huge. That guy who did it up in Utah broke his bones first, so that he only had skin and tissue to cut through. This bone wasn't broken. I don't think anyone could stay awake to finish the job of sawing off their own leg. Where are you going with this, Tommy?"

Tommy waved a dismissive hand. "Nowhere, I don't think. Just thinking through possibilities. Silly tangent, I know."

There could be no doubt that Tanner's injuries had started with the attack. Miriam and Newt both described exactly what had happened. This all meant that someone fished his body out of the water, sawed off a leg, then threw it back into the ocean? That just didn't make any sense at all.

Jess continued, not nearly as well informed about the attack on Tanner. "Well, I don't know that there's much mystery — other than the attack by the giant octopus that we like to just ignore around here. In my professional opinion, we can assume the victim is dead. I'd rule it a homicide based on the amputation."

A homicide. As if the kraken didn't present enough problems for Tommy to deal with. But no. It just couldn't be. It had to have happened in the reverse order. There had to be a reason that Tommy just didn't see yet. He was ready to accept that Tanner Brooks was dead, but he just couldn't believe what the science was telling him.

Jess rattled on. "We should really try to get an ID if we can. Sounds like you have a suspicion of who this might belong to?"

"Yeah, I do. I can get his cousin here to identify him. Anything noteworthy about the leg? Something unique?"

Jess put his pen down and rotated the leg so that Tommy could see the back of it. This side of the thigh had more of the circular suction wounds, but farther down the calf was a tattoo: the head of a tiger roaring above a banner reading "State Champs." No date. No school. But it gave him something to go on.

"That's perfect, Jess. Thanks. I should be able to get a positive ID on it from the cousin with this. I'll get to work on that."

Tommy said his goodbyes and stepped back out into the hallway, happy to finally be able to take a deep breath without feeling nauseated by the smell. Now he had something new to be nauseated about. Both breakfast and Emma Chu would have to wait a little bit longer.

***

Though small, old, and a little worn, Joe and Stacy had managed to make their little house look happy, but on this particular day Tommy reviled the freshly painted blue door before him. He stood there unwilling to knock. Unwilling to shatter Stacy's world. He rubbed his eyes with his fingers, trying to force his countenance back to normal. His best friend had drowned, and Tommy knew that gave him some leeway to be emotional, but he didn't think he could carry through this task without at least trying to detach himself.

Stacy had been the first one to sound the alarm. Joe hadn't come home all night, and even though he had become unreliable and obsessed, it was the first time he had never come home. She knew that Tommy was on the case, looking for her husband, but likely she thought he'd turn up drunk on a boat.

Not this. No one could ever prepare for this.

Tommy knocked lightly, a small part of him hoping that she wouldn't hear, that he would have to come back later. But she was there in an instant, parting the doorway and staring at Tommy with those big sunken eyes.

He tried to form the words that he had come to tell her, but the dam broke and those withheld tears came pouring out.

Stacy wrapped him up in her arms and Tommy reached back, absorbing her warmth. He felt her tears on his neck, but that only made him squeeze harder. Tommy lost track of how long they stayed embraced like this, but he knew that he didn't want it to end. When it ended, he would have to tell her. But she already knew. Of course, she already knew.

Maybe Stacy had already started mourning for Joe. Maybe, it was Tommy who had just now come to the realization that Joe was gone. Tommy had seen Joe's body on that table, but it still didn't feel real. It didn't feel like something he could ever process.

Stacy had the courage to break their embrace first, backing up, but keeping Tommy's hands in hers. She sniffled, locking her eyes into his and nodding to let him know that he didn't have to say it out loud. The tears fell harder when he saw the pain on her face. She would never be the same. She had tried to warn Tommy that something was wrong with Joe, and Tommy ignored it. Now he had to carry the pain with her. And he always would.

***

The engine of the Crown Vic rumbled to life, mirroring the uneasiness in Tommy's stomach. He searched through his phone until he found his notes on

Miriam Brooks, then looked for the hotel where she and Macy were staying. These sorts of things had to be handled in person.

As he turned onto the main beachside road, Tommy looked out on the horizon and briefly entertained the idea of just driving. Forever. Until he hit another ocean. An ocean that didn't have a sea monster. An ocean that didn't have so much pain and misery. Somewhere he could just relax, unwind, and pretend like the world wasn't unraveling around him.

CHAPTER 15

Bark sat surrounded by darkness, a switched-off flashlight balanced on his thigh. No 'lectricity, indeed. The wall behind him creaked as he leaned his head back, sounding like it might crack and crumble against his touch. He had been trying to get some sleep for hours now, but sleeping at all was hard for him in his old age, and even moreso in an old beat-up dining room chair. He had managed to doze here and there, but something always kicked him awake.

His eyes felt heavy now, as he focused on the hum of the lawn mower running outside. He liked it better than the silence that had filled the night. Too much silence left him too much time with his thoughts, and those, more often than not, frightened him. Bark didn't wear a watch, but the light seeping through the cracks on the boarded-up windows told him that morning had come. Newt must have woken up early — to mow the lawn, apparently.

Bark's right foot hurt, as it often did. The pain started in his leg, but always settled in the arch of his foot. He flexed his toes as far as he could within his boots to try to work out the kink. It helped a little, but it never fully went away. Distraction always proved better than anything to numb the pain.

Bark mulled over his relationship with Newt and wondered whether it would work out. The two of them had been fishing in the waters of Cape Madre for years, so they had a lot in common, but Bark couldn't be sure that Newt really understood what was going on. He hadn't been through the same things that Bark had.

Bark's eyes shot open when the lawnmower's engine stopped. Seagulls cawed in the distance. The walls in Newt's old investment — a word that could only be used ironically — were paper thin. Being inside them was almost like being outside.

The screen on the back door creaked open and the light flooded into the room as Newt stepped into the house, covered in sweat. Bark could smell the grass clouding the air as Newt removed his trusty sunglasses to peer into the darkened room.

"Still got the front yard to do. Been too long," Newt said as he walked into the kitchen. He filled up a glass at the sink.

"You know I don't even pay for this stuff? I canceled the account and they just never shut the water off."

Bark grunted. "They'll come for it eventually."

Newt had no answer for that. He sat in a folding chair across the room and took a long drink. The two men sat in silence for a few minutes. Bark started to plan his day. He'd have to trust Newt to stay at the house without him eventually. There were things to get done. The cats needed to be fed.

Newt broke the silence with a quiet thoughtful question. "Mind if I ask when she got to you?"

Newt surely didn't know the gender of that thing any more than Bark, but it seemed right that they both settled on it being female. Bark tried to make out the expression on Newt's face, but he saw only the lithe outline of Newt's stringy body. Bark answered slowly, "A while ago, now. A good while."

A shadowed nod in the dark. "Sounds 'bout right. Prolly before me. I think I got lucky holding off for so long."

Lucky. Maybe. Bark had never considered the situation as lucky or unlucky. He could hardly remember the times before. His current life seemed natural. Like he was born to it. It had gotten worse in recent months, though. She was never happy with his work, and he constantly had to evolve to work harder and smarter so that he could stay in the shadows and keep Cape Madre safe. He wouldn't be able to do it forever, and when he died, someone would have to take over. Someone who had been touched by her. Someone who understood the importance. Bark had a hard time imagining that person to be Newt Goodreaux.

"How'd it happen?" Newt asked.

Bark hesitated, scratching the scruff of his chin. What if Newt didn't really understand? It might turn ugly, and Bark might have to make some hard decisions. And that would just be more work. So much work. But, what the hell. Maybe if he took a chance on Newt, it would engender loyalty.

"On the *Mayhem*. A few years ago now," Bark stated.

Newt stood up and used his free hand to move his folding chair closer to Bark, dragging it along the worn carpet and making a weird *whooshing* sound. Maybe a little too close, but at least now Bark could make out Newt's expressions, though he could have done without the overwhelming smell of fresh-cut grass.

Bark continued, "Caught a dolphin in the nets. Didn't notice until it was too late. Had it dead on the deck. If I brought it in, they'd fine me. Couldn't afford that."

Newt nodded as if he understood. No doubt, Newt had fished up a dolphin or two. It was an unavoidable hazard of the job.

"So, I took it out to the vortex. Tied some weights to it. Figgered it'd sink so deep that no one'd ever find it. Or at least not quickly enough to lead back to me, ya know?

"Went off without a hitch. I watched that poor thing sink down to the depths, only to be remembered by me. Ain't nobody more sad than me to see a creature like that die. Never feels good when it happens. But that's how it goes."

Bark stopped to see if Newt wanted to interject, but Newt chose to fill the silence by finishing off his water instead. Newt smacked his lips and made an *ahh* sound when he finished, which seemed intentionally dramatic.

"Fired up the motor to go back in and the boat didn't go nowhere. I mean, the motor was runnin'. Should've been moving. But wasn't. Not an inch. Felt like a truck stuck in mud."

Newt leaned forward, clearly intrigued by the story. Bark wondered if Newt had a similar story of his own. He must've. Or he wouldn't have asked the question.

"Go back to see what's holding me up, and there's just this mass of slimy, slick grayish purple stuff everywhere. I didn't know what it was at first. Didn't look like anything I'd ever seen."

Newt jumped in. "Like a shark, but not one solid mass."

"Right. More flexible and squishy than that. When it started moving and writhing, I became even more intrigued. Thought about getting something to try to dislodge it. Next thing I know, I'm in the water. Something pulled me in by the ankle. It hurt like the devil. Squeezed hard. No hope of getting away."

"You thought you were gonna drown, eh?" Newt offered.

Bark bent down to roll up his right pants leg, then flipped on his flashlight to shine it down at his ankle. The long-healed scars stretched all around, perfectly circular. They had started as bruises years ago, but eventually gave way to these strange, inconceivable scars. And the pain. The never-ending pain.

"Did this to me," Bark said as he moved the light up and down his lower leg. "Jerked me around and under. I said my last prayers. I thought it was all over. But then I was just out there. Floating. Alone. That thing was gone. My boat was still fairly close. Managed to swim to it. Climb up. There wasn't nothing broken, best I could tell. So, I just carried on. Went about my business. Didn't have no money for the doctor, anyway."

Newt nodded his head now, fast and furious as if he gained strength from hearing Bark tell the tale. He stood and lifted his shirt, motioning towards his mid-section to get Bark to point the flashlight there. Newt's scars stood out against his dark skin, and the circles along his waist were bigger than those around Bark's leg. It looked like someone had taken a large cup and traced the top of it onto Newt's skin in a kind of gruesome tattoo. Bark didn't say anything. He didn't know what he could say, but at least now he could be sure that Newt most certainly understood.

Once Newt seemed satisfied that Bark had taken in the whole of it, Newt dropped his shirt and sat back down in his chair. "Kinda the same for me. There's so much competition out there now, and me and *Mama Jean* were having a tough go of it. I knew y'all said that there weren't no fish to catch out there in the vortex, but I thought maybe if I trolled deeper or used some different bait. There had to be something down there."

Newt paused and looked down towards the floor, surely reliving his own encounter with her. Bark flipped off the flashlight and balanced it back on his thigh. Though lots of folks were scared of the dark, in Bark's experience, facing one's demons tended to be easier when no one could see the pain. Newt looked up again, and Bark could just barely make out the whites of Newt's haunted eyes.

"I sat there for hours and ain't nothin' happened. Didn't catch no fish even after trying every piece of bait in my box. I tried running the nets as deep as Mama Jean would let me, and I didn't come up with even a single thing. It's not just that there ain't no fish out there. It's that there's no life at all. What I wouldn't give to go down to the bottom out there and see what it's like. I betcha there ain't even seaweed down there."

Bark sat silently, taking in the story, wondering if Newt would be able to stop embellishing long enough to actually get to the point. Newt liked to talk. It was a miracle that he hadn't told this story to every person who would listen. Did she do that to him? Keep him quiet? Bark could believe it. She had a way of making sure things went by her plans. Ways that Bark never understood, but had been a slave to since he first encountered her that day.

"Anyway. It was hours, like I said. Two, three, maybe four? I don't know. I wasn't keeping too close a count on it. Not like I had anyone back on land waiting for me. Hell, even y'all probably wouldn't have noticed if Ol' Newt and *Mama Jean* never came back. For me, it started with the water. It was calm that day, without many waves and hardly any boats kicking up wakes. At least near the vortex. So, when the water out in front of me started..."

Newt motioned with his hands, wriggling his bony fingers like he was playing with a puppet. "Bubbling, I guess? Not like boiling water exactly, but sorta. Like something was coming up from the deepest parts of the ocean. And there she was, breaking through the surface and sending out a wake of her own that shook Mama Jean just a little. It was the first time I saw her, but I didn't even know what I was looking at. It just looked like a tiny island had appeared in the middle of the vortex, really. I thought it might be some trash or something, but then... then she opened one of her big black eyes and she looked at me. Into my soul, Bark."

Bark knew those eyes well. Not from his first encounter, but from the other ones. Those pools of black were unnatural and powerful, demolishing a lifetime of certainties. But there was love in those eyes, too. A creature who understood things about loyalty and friendship. She was like one of his cats in that way, begging for attention and care.

"I didn't know what to do, but running didn't feel right, so I sorta just stood there for a while and we watched each other. She blinked and rotated around and eventually I saw both of those big black eyes sticking out of her head. Well, I guess it's her head. I don't really know. But that's where eyes go, so that's what I've always assumed.

"I talked to her. Told her I didn't mean to hurt her none. Asked her what she was, where she came from.

All sorts of things. She didn't answer, of course, but I talked to her like I would my own dog — well the dog I used to have, rather, before she got run over out there by the mail truck. Jean was a good dog, God rest her soul."

Newt motioned with his hands in some semblance of the cross, but Newt wasn't Catholic. Bark suspected he'd just seen that on the television, then adopted it as some way of invoking help. Bark didn't believe in God. Not anymore. God wouldn't have made something like her.

"Then the tentacles came, over the side of *Mama Jean*. I wasn't scared then, though I ought to have been, I suppose. They just kinda moved toward me and I petted'em. I remember that part. I just stroked one of'em. It was smooth and wet and strangely comforting like one of them stress balls you see on the desks of people who have desks. You and me ain't the type to have desks, though, are we Bark?"

Bark shook his head. The *Mayhem* had a desk below deck, but that old thing wasn't the type of fancy desk that Newt meant.

"She started to coil one around my waist, and that's when I really started getting scared. I tried to dodge out of it, but those tentacles there were huge. There weren't no getting away at that point. Once she started squeezing, I worried that she'd kill me. I begged her to let me go, but she just jerked me forward, twisted me around.

"My head hit the side of *Mama Jean* on the way out. Must've lost consciousness because next thing I knew I was underwater, struggling to swim back to the surface, but she held me down. Not in and out, like what happened to you or that kid out there. She just held me. I knew I was gonna drown. I tried to pry it off me, ya know? But she held on too tight. It all seemed so weird at the time. I'm sure I was more scared than I remember now, but it just all felt like it was supposed to happen and there weren't nothin' I could be doing about it except to give in.

"Then she let go. My stomach hurt something fierce, but my legs worked well enough to kick me to the surface. I came up right next to *Mama Jean*, like she was there waiting to save me. I climbed up and laid on the deck for a long time, Bark. A long time. Just trying to process it all. To make sense of it."

Bark replied, "You'll never make sense of it, Newt. There's no sense to be made."

"Yeah. I suppose so. My stomach and my head hurt, but I just didn't feel right telling nobody about her. She was too special. I didn't want them going in there and hunting her down. The way I figger it, I went into her home and caused a ruckus. So, I left as soon as I was able. That's my whole story."

The end result of which was no more complicated than Bark's, but still took way longer to tell. Newt was so incredibly tiresome. But he and Bark shared the same path, of that there could be no doubt.

Silence cloaked the room again as the two men sat across from each other. It just didn't seem like any conversation could top that. Bark felt happy to have had the conversation, though. It felt strangely reassuring to know that he wasn't alone as he had once thought.

After a few minutes, Newt asked, "How come it works this way, Bark? You and me. We're ok, right? But Joe. It was harder for Joe."

Bark thought about it for a few seconds, but quickly realized that no amount of thought would ever provide the real answer. They were dealing with things that couldn't be understood. Of all the years on the sea, nothing prepared him for this. For her. But Bark did have thoughts on Joe. A lot of them. Too many of them. Too often.

"I shoulda helped him, Newt. I coulda maybe steered him the right direction. Helped him cope with it. It's a mighty tough thing to get through. I thought I was doing right by him keeping him away. But maybe I was wrong."

Newt motioned to the door next to Bark. "Why didn't she kill *him*?"

"Why didn't she kill you? Or me? Or Joe? I don't know why she does anything, but I reckon she needs some of us."

Newt nodded as if he agreed and understood. "What's gonna happen to the kid now, then?"

Bark took a deep breath, exhaling all the air in his lungs before answering, "I don't know, Newt. I just don't know."

CHAPTER 16

Popeye, the previously friendly black cat that guarded *Madre's Mayhem*, stared down at Miriam as if he meant to eat her, his alert eyes jerking with every move she made at the bottom of the ramp.

She hollered up the ramp for Bark but got no response.

"He lives on a boat?" Macy asked.

"I don't know if he lives here. But this where I met him."

After yelling his name again without any success, Miriam started up the ramp. Macy grabbed Miriam's wrist, stopping her progress.

"What are you doing? You can't just walk into someone's house!" Macy protested.

Miriam considered Macy's position. Technically, it would be trespassing, but it was a boat, sitting out in the water. It's not like she was going to steal anything. Bark was old, and it seemed likely that maybe he just couldn't hear her.

Miriam pried Macy's hand loose. "You stay here. Keep watch. I'm just going to poke my head in. See if he's below deck or something."

Macy's eyes burned with defiance, and the slightest bit of anger. "I am *not* comfortable with this."

Miriam didn't understand Macy's discomfort. Finding Tanner meant *investigating*, after all.

"Don't you want to find Tanner?" Miriam pleaded.

Macy looked up the ramp at the deceptively menacing cat, then back to Miriam. "I do. But trespassing? That's illegal."

It felt kind of nice for Macy to be the buzzkill for once.

Before Miriam could try to convince Macy to let her go up the ramp, her pocket buzzed. Once. Twice. A phone call, not a text. She didn't recognize the number.

"Hello?" Miriam asked, tentatively.

"Ms. Brooks. Detective Wallace. I'm here at your hotel. Needed to talk to you."

Miriam felt her heart jump in her chest. Had he found Tanner?

"I'm not at the hotel. Macy and I are down at the docks. Did you find him?"

Wallace paused and cleared his throat. "It's best that we talk in person. I'll come down and meet you in the Shady Shark parking lot. Does that work?"

The elation that Miriam first felt at hearing the detective's voice started to abate. This didn't sound like good news. Good news didn't have to be delivered in person.

"Um, yeah," Miriam stammered out. "W-We'll be there."

As she slid the phone back into her pocket, Macy looked at her with wet eyes. Though she hadn't heard the conversation, she seemed to sense what might be coming. Miriam turned away from *Madre's Mayhem* and headed toward the parking lot of the Shady Shark Motel.

"Is it Tanner?" Macy asked as she strode alongside.

Miriam only nodded.

***

Detective Wallace pulled up beside them as they leaned on Macy's old beat up Sentra. The two hadn't exchanged many words since the phone call, but Miriam could only assume that Macy felt the same trepidation bubbling in her stomach. They both stood to greet Wallace, but as he came around the front of his Crown Vic, he didn't offer any handshakes. He looked sad. Worried. Apprehensive.

That could only mean one thing.

Miriam didn't expect her voice to crack when she tried to ask the question. She had to stop and try again.

"Tanner? Is he..."

She couldn't complete the sentence. She couldn't bear to honor the possibility with words.

Wallace swallowed hard, speaking slowly. "We're not sure."

Miriam felt her chest loosen a little. "Not sure" meant that Tanner still had hope. It suddenly became easier to breathe.

"This morning," Wallace continued. "A jogger found a severed leg on the beach. It might be... could be... It's from a male. About Tanner's age."

A leg? Could Tanner survive losing a leg? The odds seemed low, but if anyone could do it, surely Tanner could find a way.

"So, that doesn't mean he's... gone," Miriam said. "Just maybe injured."

Wallace didn't seem to want to participate in the hope. He took a beat, reached into his pocket and pulled out an old-fashioned cloth handkerchief. He handed it to Macy, and only then did Miriam notice the tears streaming down Macy's face. Miriam refused to cry. Not yet. It wasn't over yet. She needed Macy to be strong right now. Like her.

Detective Wallace continued, "If you don't mind coming down to the ME's office with me, maybe you can identify whether it's his leg? There's some identifying marks that we think might be able to prove it for sure."

"Like what?" Miriam asked.

"A tattoo. On his calf."

Miriam took a deep, unrestricted breath.

***

"I can't do it." Macy's eyes were swollen and red as she stared out the windshield from the driver's seat. "I want to support you, Mir, I really do. But I just..."

Miriam understood. How could she not? It's not like she looked forward to seeing a severed leg, but it couldn't be Tanner's. Miriam felt sure of it. Detective Wallace had come to her sad and dejected, but the minute he mentioned the tattoo, Miriam knew that she had nothing to worry about.

Macy turned to Miriam and finished her thought. "I'm not a superhero like you. I can't just look at icky things and be ok."

Superhero? Is that what Macy thought of her? Miriam couldn't decide if Macy meant the label as a compliment or an insult, but she felt a swell of pride in her chest, nonetheless. Miriam spent so much time comparing herself to others — to Macy, specifically — that she found a deep level of comfort in knowing that she had enviable qualities. Though, being able to "look at icky things and be ok" could hardly be qualified as a superpower.

"Just stay here," Miriam offered. "I'll go in. Tell him it's not Tanner's — because it isn't — and then I'll come back out here, and we'll get some lunch."

For the briefest moment, Macy looked like she might be sick. "Ew. You're gonna go eat lunch after seeing a severed leg?"

Why not? She'd seen all manner of dead things. Not very many humans, admittedly.

"Maybe. We'll see." Miriam tried to couch her answer so as not to seem too freakish.

As she stepped out of the car, she turned and tried her best to give Macy a reassuring look. It didn't seem to work.

Miriam took off towards the glass doors of the medical examiner's office, spending the time thinking about whether her complete lack of fear made her weird. Probably. But it wasn't the only thing.

Detective Wallace waited inside the door, leaned up against the wall and staring at his cell phone. When Miriam stepped in beside him, he shoved it into a hidden pocket inside his suit jacket.

"You ready for this?" he asked.

Miriam nodded and followed as he led her to a room labeled "Examination Room A." He took a deep breath and pushed open the door. All the lab's chemical smells came rushing out, reminding Miriam of biology class and the hours she'd spent dissecting animals. She found a strange comfort in it, even though she knew that most would find the smells objectionable.

On a metal table in the middle of the room sat a leg, as promised. Long and strong, Miriam could see why someone might assume the leg belonged to Tanner. It certainly belonged to someone close to Tanner's build. Maybe a little shorter, by the looks of it, and maybe a little less toned. Though she had to admit that she'd spent very little time studying her cousin's legs.

As they approached the table, a man in a lab coat joined them. He offered an outstretched hand. "Dr. Gearhart. Nice to meet you."

"Miriam Brooks," she responded while shaking his hand.

Gearhart seemed more like her, indifferent to the smells, or the severed leg sitting on the table. Detective Wallace, on the other hand, looked as if he meant to run away.

"So, this is what we've got," Gearhart said. "White male. Probably 6'3" or so. Exercises a lot, I think. Oh. And this—"

Miriam eyed the circular wounds along the thigh, but Gearhart didn't draw attention to them. Did they honestly think she wouldn't notice? Tanner or not, the owner of this leg had encountered the kraken.

Gearhart took the time to pull on latex gloves before twisting the leg around on its side so Miriam could see the back of it.

He motioned to a picture on the leg's calf. "Tattoo. Pretty set. I think it's been there a while. Months, at least."

That ruled out the slim possibility that Tanner had surreptitiously gotten himself inked in the last few days. Miriam read the inscription and studied the ferocious image of a tiger. Same mascot as their old university, but Tanner didn't play any sports there. *State Champs* implied high school.

"A high school tattoo," Miriam said. "Probably football? Based on the size of the leg."

Gearhart smirked, seemingly suppressing a full smile. "Astute. Yeah. Good theory. But, uh... is it your cousin's?"

Miriam hadn't even considered it, really, because she was so certain that it couldn't be. But Gearhart and Wallace couldn't read her mind.

"No. Can't be," Miriam said. "Tanner doesn't have any tattoos. And our high school never won state in anything."

Gearhart shot a glance at Wallace. Back to square one for them, Miriam supposed. She found it intriguing, though, that someone else had encountered the kraken. Still, severed limb or not, she wouldn't believe that Tanner might be dead.

"The kraken did this?" Miriam asked. "Ripped his leg off?"

Gearhart looked surprised at the question, waiting for a nod from Wallace before answering. "Uh no. I think it was sawed off. Before the kraken, I think."

Sawed off? What the hell kind of place was Cape Madre where people were getting dismembered? At least this meant that she could hope to find Tanner intact, though maybe with some broken ankles.

Reminded of his injury, Miriam pointed towards the ankle on the leg. Not that they needed any more proof. "Ankle looks fine. The kraken grabbed Tanner by his ankles. There'd be injuries there."

Wallace looked surprised. "Damn. That makes sense. You told me that. Sorry. I should have noticed."

Miriam didn't take offense, shrugging at his unneeded apology.

She liked mysteries, but typical homicides were outside of her wheelhouse. She'd have to leave that to Detective Wallace, but the crossover with the kraken did stoke her interest. Was it merely a coincidence? Did someone kill a guy then toss his body parts overboard only for the kraken to happen upon it?

"Maybe whoever did this meant to *feed* it to the kraken," Miriam suggested. "Clearly the kraken got its tentacles on it after the victim's death, since there's no bruising."

Gearhart raised an eyebrow, sending a brief wave of embarrassment over Miriam as she remembered her atypical knowledge of these weird things. She could tell immediately that neither Gearhart nor Wallace cared for the implication. Wallace, in particular, looked distracted, seemingly lost in thought. She supposed he had a lot more to worry about now, the first of which would surely be identifying the actual owner of the leg.

In truth, Miriam didn't like the implication, either. If the kraken dined on people, then she would have to confront the possibility that Tanner hadn't turned up because he'd been eaten. She pushed the thought from her mind, forcing herself to remain impartial. To be a scientist. Especially here, with strangers.

When Wallace didn't engage, Gearhart answered, "But it hasn't been eaten."

"True," Miriam said. "But this is just a *part* of the body."

Wallace finally zoned back in. "Thanks for the help, Ms. Brooks. I need to get going. I have some things to take care of."

He ushered her to the door as Gearhart offered her a wave. She nodded in response.

Once they were out in the hallway, Miriam took off for the door, eager to tell Macy that she didn't need to worry. Wallace clomped along behind her.

She turned before she stepped outside. "My offer's still on the table, Detective. I can help you catch this thing."

Detective Wallace pursed his lips and nodded.

CHAPTER 17

Tommy rushed across the parking lot, mentally flipping through the facts. A kraken was bad enough, but now he had a probable homicide. Did the two relate to one another? No way to tell, really, but if murder was involved, he'd have more than the chamber of commerce to answer to.

As much as he didn't want Tanner Brooks to be dead, he had been sure that Tanner's leg sat in the ME's office. And if it wasn't his, then...

His heart thumped against his ribs, the bile rising in his throat. Maybe he was just hungry — he hadn't eaten all day — but he knew that the painful burning in his chest would be hanging around for a while yet. He needed to make sure that they shuffled resources to investigate the severed leg. Who could it possibly even belong to?

Tommy slammed the door back and stepped into the precinct, only to immediately be met by three teenagers standing from chairs along the wall. They appeared eager to see him, but he didn't recognize them. Not at first.

"Detective Wallace!" one of two boys exclaimed. "We need your help!"

There were uniforms at the desk, and a number of detectives ready to help out the local tourists. Tommy didn't have time for this.

"Talk to the desk officer. He'll help you out," Tommy suggested.

Grabowski, a pudgy young officer, pitched in from the desk. "Wouldn't talk to me, Detective. Said they'd wait for you."

Tommy sighed, resigning himself to surveying the three kids before him. Two boys. Fit. Looked like jocks maybe. And a girl. Pretty. Dark hair. Her hand was intertwined with one of the boys. Tommy's mind unexpectedly pictured them in less clothes, as a reminder of where he'd last seen them. A push-up bra accentuated the girl's form-hugging shirt, but during their last encounter those curves had been hidden under an oversized t-shirt.

The investigation into Hannah Huang seemed so distant and unimportant now that Tommy couldn't remember the last time he'd thought about it. He'd filed it away in his head as completed, really, sure that she had skipped town and headed back to Dallas. Emma Chu had woken up, though he still needed to get over to visit her. Hannah Huang just didn't matter to his investigation anymore.

The boy not attached to the girl spoke: "Justin hasn't come back. Since that night. With Hannah."

Tommy flipped through names in his head trying to put it all back together. Brady. This kid's name was Brady. And Justin had been out with Hannah the night before she checked out of the motel.

Still not convinced that he needed to deal with this, Tommy suggested, "Did you try calling him?"

Brady sighed. "Of course we did. Goes straight to voicemail. That would only happen if his phone died. Why wouldn't he charge his phone?"

"Fill out a missing persons report with Grabowski over there. We'll look into it first chance we get."

"Come on, Detective. Help us out. You were worried about Hannah before. And Justin was with her," Brady begged.

Tommy felt a twinge of obligation, but he refused to give into it. As much as he might like to take on every case, he knew that he didn't have the bandwidth. Not now, especially. He would just have to tell Brady more firmly that—

The logo on Brady's shirt caught Tommy's eye for the first time, sending his heart down into his stomach. His mind focused into gruesome clarity. From the front of the ratty old shirt, a tiger roared above a banner.

State Champs.

Dammit.

"All right. Come with me," Tommy said as he pushed past the trio towards his glass-lined office.

Once he ushered them into the tiny room, he excused himself to steal a chair from next door. He slid it in next to the two already in front of his desk and motioned for them to sit down, then closed the door and took his own seat.

"Tell me about your shirt," Tommy said.

Brady looked down in surprise. "What's that have to do with anything?"

Tommy folded his hands in front of him and just stared into Brady eyes, summoning as much intimidation as he could to force him to just answer. Brady's shoulders slumped as he silently retracted the question.

"We all got one last year. After we won state," Brady explained.

"Who's we?" Tommy asked.

"The whole team. Me. Justin. Frankie." Brady motioned to the kid beside him.

"What about tattoos? Did you commemorate the occasion with a tattoo?"

Brady seemed to push down the confusion before standing up and lifting his leg to prop his dirty shoe up on Tommy's desk. In the moment, Tommy didn't mind.

"Yeah, some of us," Brady said.

An exact match. It could have been Brady's leg on that cold metal table, and Tommy wouldn't have been able to tell the difference. How? Who? The questions swirled around in Tommy's head, each one trying to connect to an answer that he didn't have. To hell with the kraken. Now he had real work to do.

And his number one suspect had to be Brady.

He was the last person to have seen both Justin and Hannah alive. Tommy leaned back in his chair and tried to catch his breath, to clear his mind and reset. Could Justin be alive somewhere, without a leg? And where was Hannah? He shuddered to think of both dead and dismembered, their body parts floating in the warm waters of Cape Madre.

"I don't understand, Detective. What does my tattoo have to do with anything?" Brady asked.

Tommy stood and answered, "Stay right here. I'll be back in a coupla minutes, okay?"

The confusion evident on all three of the kids' faces told Tommy that none of them had anything to do with any of this, but he still had to stick to the rules. Play things by the book.

And that started with interrogations.

***

Nothing.
Brady and his band of misfits were innocent.

Tommy would've staked his career on it. The good news was that he finally got some help. Another detective had been assigned to the case and would start first thing in the morning. The coast guard would also start a search to look for the rest of Justin's body.

It didn't bring much solace. Tommy wanted to believe that Justin's murder and the mysterious kraken had nothing to do with one another, but he couldn't shake the feeling that they were more intimately connected than just the leg ending up in the kraken's tentacles.

Tommy's stomach rumbled. Still nothing to eat, and now dinnertime approached. He needed more than food, though. He needed refuge. A place to unwind and get his bearings.

He stood from his desk and cracked his back before slipping on his suit jacket. Nothing more to do today. As he rounded the corner out of his office, he stopped suddenly at a group of people headed his way. Grabowski, the desk officer, stood at the head of them.

Dammit. One more thing that he'd let slip through the cracks.

Tommy held in the overwhelming urge to sigh. "Mr. Chu. Mrs. Chu. Emma."

He offered his hand to Emma, since he hadn't formally met her before. She shook his hand limply, offering a shy smile. She wore a shirt that he recognized from the hospital gift shop, evidence that her luggage had been taken away when Hannah left town. Or worse.

"Thanks Grabowski. I got it from here," Tommy said.

Grabowski scurried away and Tommy ushered the family into his office, taking the time to get them situated before sitting down behind his desk. He studied each of their faces. Mr. and Mrs. Chu seemed considerably less stressed compared to the last time he'd seen them. Emma looked rested, alert, and a little bit embarrassed.

"I'm so sorry," Tommy started. "I meant to get down to the hospital this morning, but it's been a crazy day."

"Not a problem, Detective," Mr. Chu responded. "You just mentioned that you wanted to talk to Emma before we left town, and since she's been discharged, we'll be leaving in short order."

Tommy nodded. "I understand. Thanks for coming down."

Whatever had happened to Emma seemed of little consequence in light of recent developments, but Tommy knew he needed to at least try to hunt down all the leads. Maybe whatever happened to Justin and Hannah somehow related to Emma's attack. And, though he refused to believe it, a small voice at the corner of his mind insisted that Emma would go crazy when she woke up.

Like Joe.

"What happened out there, Emma?" he asked.

Emma shifted in her chair and tucked a strand of dark black hair behind her ear. "I was swimming with Hannah, but she saw somebody on the beach she wanted to talk to, so she went back in. I didn't mind. The water was nice."

Anticipating tears, Tommy pushed a box of tissues towards Emma's side of the desk. She took one preemptively.

"Next thing I know, I feel something around my waist. It happened fast. Then I was under water. I tried fighting it off, but it just squeezed tighter. It hurt. And then, I just woke up in a hospital bed."

No tears yet. Her account seemed anti-climactic, not really telling him anything he couldn't have already surmised.

"So, you don't know who rescued you?" Tommy asked.

Emma shook her head.

"What do you think did this to you?" Tommy motioned to her stomach as he said it.

She shrugged. "I don't know. An octopus? A squid?"

Without him asking, she slid the cheap t-shirt up to reveal the bruises on her stomach. Along with the incisions from her surgeries, Tommy could see the clear circular patterns of the kraken's tentacles. Certainly, there could be no question as to what happened to her.

Mrs. Chu swatted at her daughter's hand. "Emma. Cover yourself."

Emma rolled her dark brown eyes and gave Tommy a smirk. He lifted one corner of his mouth to return the sentiment, but quickly returned to the stoic cop-face expected of him.

Tommy leaned forward to indicate a switch in topics. "You came here with a friend? Hannah Huang?"

Emma nodded. "Yeah. That's right. Did you talk to her? We went to the hotel, but she already checked out."

"I didn't, no. Did you try getting in touch with her, by chance?"

"With what? I didn't have my cell phone in the water with me. I assume Hannah has it." Emma looked sheepishly to the ground. "We weren't supposed to be here. I guess she just freaked out? Took all our stuff back to school."

Tommy exhaled sharply. Certainly, that had been his theory as well, but current evidence suggested something much more sinister. He didn't want to alarm Emma and her family, but he also didn't know how to get the information he needed without doing so.

"Do you know someone named Justin? Stayed in the room next to you?"

Emma darted her eyes sideways before answering. "Um, yeah. He and Hannah were hanging out a lot."

Tommy didn't like this dynamic. "Mr. Chu, Mrs. Chu. I know this is going to sound weird, but could I talk to your daughter alone, please? You can wait outside. There are some chairs there."

Mrs. Chu shook her head. "Emma doesn't have any secrets from us."

She most certainly did, but Tommy didn't want to argue that. "I understand, Mrs. Chu. It's just procedure."

It wasn't really. Not at this stage. Emma Chu didn't have to even be here if she didn't want to. Tommy gambled that the Chu family wouldn't press the issue.

Mr. Chu patted his wife on the arm, staring into her eyes and giving a curt nod. Without any more words, they shuffled out of Tommy's office. Once the door closed behind them, Emma practically melted in the chair, taking on an entirely new and relaxed persona.

"Thank you," she said, her dark eyes now glittering in the fluorescent light.

Tommy repeated his question. "Tell me about Justin. For real."

"Yeah. He'd been hanging out with us. Him and his friend, Brady. Hannah was really into them."

"Both?" Tommy asked.

"Yeah," Emma replied. "Why do you ask? What do Justin and Brady have to do with anything?"

Tommy took a deep breath, weighing his possible replies. He preferred to keep her in the dark until he knew for certain that Hannah Huang was dead. Emma had spent the last few days in a hospital bed and most certainly couldn't be considered a suspect in Justin's murder.

"Brady and his friends reported Justin missing," Tommy said.

Emma didn't look particularly concerned. "Maybe Hannah chose him over Brady? She was totally boy crazy."

Maybe. But none of that mattered. None of this seemed to matter. Tommy's stomach protested again, as he felt irritation tug at his mind. He couldn't do it anymore. Not today.

"Emma," he said. "Thanks for talking to me. I can't give you all the details right now, and I can't make you do it, but I would really appreciate it if you'd stay in town for a few days. I might need to ask you some more questions."

Emma sighed. "But I'm so tired, Detective. I just wanna get home and get back to normal. As far away from the ocean as I can get."

Tommy puzzled over her reply and realized that he had steeled himself against the possibility that she might have an overwhelming urge to hunt down the kraken. But of course she didn't want to do that. No sane person would. Which, of course, left him only with the conclusion that Joe hadn't been sane.

Tommy nodded. "Of course. But this is important. I need to make sure Justin and Hannah are safe, and you might be the key to figuring that out."

Though she looked put out and annoyed, she nodded. "I get it. Just tell my parents that you're making me, yeah?"

"No problem. Thanks for the help."

Emma popped out of her chair and left Tommy to the silence of his office. Though he was no closer to solving Justin's mysterious disappearance, he at least felt relief at the fact that Emma seemed fine, and appropriately horrified of the water and the monster that had almost killed her.

He forced himself up, talked briefly with Emma's parents, then locked up his office. His mind swam with everything he'd learned over the course of the day. So much information. So little of it useful. Not for the first time, Tommy questioned his fitness as a detective.

As he slid into his car, food became his only goal. Hot, greasy, artery-clogging food.

CHAPTER 18

The docks looked ominous in the waning sun, each boat a misshapen skeleton against the skyline. Once again, Miriam and Macy stood on the wooden planks beside *Madre's Mayhem*. Popeye, the black cat that had judged them from the top of the ramp, lazily cleaned himself on the bow. Other cats meowed at their feet, one of them snaking around Miriam's legs. They seemed hungry.

"Mr. Bark!" Miriam yelled up the ramp.

Nothing.

"Guess he's not here," Macy suggested. "We should come back tomorrow. In the daylight. When it's not so creepy out here."

Miriam would not be deterred this time. Whether or not Bark was here, she meant to get on his boat and have a look around. Though the most useful information surely existed in Bark's head, Miriam imagined that some scrap of useful, material evidence might be found somewhere in this hull.

"I'm going up. You can stay here if you want," Miriam said.

Macy exhaled sharply, placing her hands on her hips. But she didn't say anything. Not this time.

Miriam stepped up the ramp, causing Popeye to stop his bath and consider her, his tongue frozen in place as he sized her up. She didn't resume her climb until the cat continued licking his paws, as if his approval mattered more than propriety. The ramp creaked with each step, but the docks were nearly empty. No one seemed to care that she was there.

Once on the deck, she took in the view of the old, dilapidated planks stretching across the floor. Everything seemed dirty. Ancient. On the verge of disappearing into dust. A *thump* startled her— a cat had landed from a perch somewhere above. It ran down the ramp with its tail tucked between its legs.

The topside seemed starkly appointed, with very little that Miriam could even consider evidence, so she made her way up to the small, enclosed cockpit just above her entry point. Unlike Newt's *Mama Jean*, the cockpit had no door. She ran her fingers along the instrument panel as she crossed through it, looking for anything suspicious, but she came up empty again.

Though it felt more invasive and harder to justify, Miriam decided that her only course was the hold. She made her way back to the deck and found the wooden square frame with a knotted rope sticking out one edge. She pulled it up and gingerly flipped it back to ensure that the bang of the hatch against the deck didn't make too much noise. She considered that a need to be quiet meant she'd crossed a line, but then she forced herself to think of Tanner, causing her to push on.

The stairs down into the dark room below were steep, but Miriam navigated them deftly, quickly descending until she found even footing. The light from above only lit a few feet in front of her, causing the hold to seem dangerous and unsafe. Her heartrate spiked. She should have brought a weapon.

Without the help of her eyes, she listened intently for anything that might represent a threat. Only when she could ensure that she wouldn't need her hands for defense did she fish her phone from her pocket.

The light illuminated the room's corners. While the deck was clean, the hold was filled to the brim with stuff: boxes, nets, tools. An empty table sat in the middle of the room, its legs bolted to the floor with steel brackets. The smell of fish down here hung heavier than in the salty air above.

Miriam spun around in a slow circle to get a sense of the size, unveiling another door slightly ajar. Where to start? She decided on the room, pushing gently on the door until there was resistance. With ease, she slid her thin body through the narrow opening.

Smaller, this room was as an office, with a metal desk bolted against the wall and a folding chair in front of it. Pictures hung along the walls. Rubbermaid file boxes sat behind the door. A map unrolled across the desk, each corner duct-taped down.

Miriam pulled the chair out of the way to stand over the desk, shining her light on the worn map. Somewhere along the way, Bark must have laminated it, but water stains wrinkled the paper inside the plastic, implying that it hadn't always been that way. Miriam studied it, taking in the coastline and the waters of Cape Madre, fixating on the inky scrawls drawn over the plastic covering.

As she tried to make sense of it all, she became aware of steps above her. Someone had come aboard *Madre's Mayhem*. She quickly turned off her phone light and folded herself into the small space under the desk. As gently as she could, she dragged the chair back so that it sat in front of her.

As her heart pumped wildly, she became aware of the sound of her own breathing. Miriam tried to calm herself by closing her eyes and focusing on her extremities, her chest, and, finally, her lungs, just as her father had made her practice hundreds of times. With no weapon, her only option would be to hide and wait.

The steps moved around on the deck but zeroed in quickly on the hole leading down to where Miriam hid. The more she studied each step, the more she began to relax. Bark's feet would surely make louder sounds than she now heard.

"Mir?" a fevered whisper rushed into the room, confirming Miriam's suspicions.

Relieved, she squeezed out from under the desk and made her way to the bottom of the steep wooden staircase. Macy's wide eyes peered down into the hold.

"Everything ok?" Miriam asked, mirroring Macy's whisper.

Without an answer, Macy turned around backwards and started down the stairs, using the framing to steady herself on the descent. Miriam stood aside to make room for her.

On flat ground again, Macy hissed, "What are you doing? I thought you were just gonna see if he was here!"

Miriam could feel the nervous energy pouring off her best friend, but she refused to let it stop her investigation. She turned the light back on and motioned for Macy to follow her into the tiny room. Neither girl had any trouble slipping through the narrow crevice, but Miriam imagined that Bark would have to wriggle and squeeze to have any hope of making it through. Why make it so hard on himself?

"Look at this," Miriam said, abandoning the whisper.

Macy stood beside her and looked at the map. Miriam could tell that Macy wasn't really studying it, but Miriam's mind went to quick work correlating the marks, trying to make sense of what they all meant.

Miriam pointed at a circle drawn in black ink. "This here. I think it's the vortex. And here." She pointed at an X drawn in green nearer the shore. "I think this is where Emma got attacked."

Macy touched the X and whispered, "Why would he be tracking that?"

Miriam shrugged, but on some primal level, it made sense. Bark knew something about the kraken. Something that no one else had figured out. Miriam didn't know what yet, but she intended to discover the truth. Because the truth would lead her to Tanner.

Macy pointed at another green X, far off the coast but nowhere near the black circle. "What's that, then?"

Miriam didn't have the answer. Joe Hampton, maybe? Miriam had assumed that his attack had taken place in the vortex just like Tanner's, but maybe not. If it had come to shore for Emma, maybe it also lurked in other parts of the water.

Or maybe there was more than one.

Of course there had to be if the species had survived all this time, but Miriam pushed that frightening thought out of her mind. She had no evidence for that yet, and until she did, she preferred to focus on only what she could account for.

"Maybe that's where Joe got attacked?" Miriam offered.

Macy nodded, her red curls causing strange shadows to bounce around the room. "And the red Xs? What are those?"

The hastily-drawn red Xs covered the blue ocean region. The sheer volume of them sent a chill up

Miriam's spine. If each X corresponded to some encounter with the kraken, then that meant its appearances were more prevalent than she would have guessed. But did they mark attacks? Sightings? Or maybe something else that she hadn't considered.

Miriam eyed the markers in the plastic case affixed to the wall, fighting the urge to mark a new X for Tanner. Though all of this felt wrong, she did admire Bark's careful attention to detail, and once she figured out the meaning of it all, she felt confident that this map held secrets that she would need to kill the kraken and save Tanner.

"You should take a picture," Macy suggested.

Already on it, Miriam used panoramic mode to scan over the entirety of the map. Though dark, she'd be able to edit the photo to bring out the most important bits once she got to a computer.

That done, Miriam scanned the rest of the room. She didn't want to press her luck by going through each box.

"Let's check out the other room," Miriam said as she led the way back through the doorway.

Once through, Macy turned on the light of her cell phone as well, bathing the hold in a more reasonable amount of cold, white light. Though Miriam would have dutifully fanned out to cover more ground had she been with Tanner, she could tell that Macy had no interest in leaving her side. They inched along, their backs to the center of the room so they could study the stuff lined against the walls.

"It smells like ass down here."

Not the description Miriam would have used, but it did smell bad. Worse than she would have imagined, even for a fishing boat. It didn't surprise her, though.

Based on the outer image of the *Madre's Mayhem*, Bark clearly didn't spend a lot of time cleaning.

They moved along past wooden crates full of ropes, rusted tools, and five-gallon buckets. As they swept their lights past a handheld scale, they both stopped their lights on the unexpected sight of a plastic yellow backpack. It sat atop a black roller bag with a red ribbon around one of the handles. Both seemed misplaced among the hold's other accoutrements.

Miriam crept forward until she could see the tiny red-and-white Pokeball emblazoned on the outside pocket of the backpack. Bark did not seem like a Pokemon fan. Miriam's mind started to form a theory, but it still eluded her conscious thought, manifesting only in her quickened heartrate and clammy hands.

Kneeling next to the roller bag, her eyes followed the red ribbon and found a luggage tag attached at the other end. Miriam looked up to Macy and then turned it around so that she could read the name.

Emma Chu.

"What does it say?" Macy asked, her voice shaky and unsure.

Miriam shot to her feet. "It says we need to get out of here."

She didn't know exactly why, but every impulse shooting through Miriam's veins told her that something was horribly wrong. Maybe he had found it, she reasoned, and taken it aboard for safekeeping. With Emma in the hospital, Bark might not know how to return it to her. But that didn't feel right.

Eager to leave, but still curious, Miriam swept her light around the room, past the table and to the other side of the hull. She saw more luggage, hidden under a large net. Surely, Emma Chu hadn't brought this much luggage for one week in Cape Madre. Bikinis didn't take up much room.

She tried to keep a tally in her head as she counted off the bags. She guessed there were enough for at least two people. And if Emma was one of them, who was the other?

Macy stood nervously at the bottom of the steps. "Come on. We should go. You said so."

It's true. Miriam had said that, but she needed more information. She needed something more concrete. Something that could bring the confusion into sharp focus.

She spun, trying to catch a glimpse of anything that could help. As her light drifted past the floor, she noticed the wood beneath the table was dark and stained. She stopped and lifted the light, her eyes following the legs of the table until she could make out the unmistakable color of blood splattered across the table.

Bark was a fisherman. It could just be from fish, right? Miriam tried to tell herself that she was blowing it all out of proportion. Bark was a nice man. A man of the people, by all accounts. Most likely, the darkness and adrenaline of trespassing had just spooked her. All of this could be explained. Somehow.

"Come on!" Macy insisted.

The light glinted back at Miriam, reflecting off something new. Something shiny. Something metal.

A saw. Specifically, a bone saw. A big one that would be capable of sawing apart large fish, of sawing easily through bone and tissue. The teeth of the blade were stained blackish red.

Yes, maybe Bark had used it for sawing apart fish. Or maybe...

J.P. BARNETT

"Go!" Miriam shouted as she ran towards Macy.

Macy climbed up the stairs awkwardly and slowly, causing Miriam to push against her butt to hasten their exit. When they both emerged on deck, Miriam took a deep breath and searched the docks. She didn't see anything other than the outlines of the boats and the furry shadows of the cats.

Macy helped her lower the door into place, then they sprinted down the ramp and across the docks and into the parking lot of the Shady Shark Motel. Macy leaned against the car, gasping for breath, as Miriam replayed all they'd seen.

"Let's go," she said, nudging Macy to get into the car.

Only when they were safely on the road did Miriam finally take an unencumbered breath.

This was bad.

Her mind reeled with possibilities. Bark had sawed off some guys leg. Almost certainly. Maybe her passing thought at the medical examiner's office hadn't been as fanciful as it'd seemed.

As she put it together, her hope that Bark might have fished Tanner up and saved his life evaporated. No, if Bark had found Tanner, then it would surely be too late.

Miriam yelled at Macy, "We need to go see Detective Wallace. Now!"

CHAPTER 19

Crack!

The sound woke Bark from a deep sleep. It took him a few seconds to get his bearings and realize that the sickening pop came from his nightmares. During waking hours, he did a good job of keeping the memories at bay, but the bloody mess of meat and bones couldn't be completely compartmentalized. It's not that he didn't regret what he did, but the opportunity had just fallen into his lap, allowing him to a test a theory that might have saved more people than it hurt.

He still didn't know if his theory would hold.

Newt had been gone for hours, long enough that Bark wondered whether he meant to come back at all. Maybe he had decided to abandon the call. Or worse, he had been caught in a lie and confessed to everything. At any rate, Bark needed to get down to the docks. Every minute Newt delayed brought more frustration.

Bark stood and stretched his back. Sleeping in a chair invited a lot of pain for a man so long in the tooth.

The kid still hadn't woken up. Maybe for the better. Bark could already tell that he needed to refine his kidnapping technique. The teenagers had been drunk and too eager to get a tour of a fishing boat, but if he'd be making a life of detaining people, he'd need

J.P. BARNETT

to figure out how to keep people unconscious in a more elegant way. He vaguely remembered TV shows mentioning chloroform, but he had no idea where he'd even buy something like that.

Bark hobbled to the kitchen and pilfered a bottle of beer from the unplugged fridge. It wouldn't be cold, maybe not even cool at this point, but at least it would still serve to dull his senses, and the pain.

Once he drained the entire thing, he sat the bottle on the counter and made his way back to the chair. He didn't want to commit to anything too rashly. He needed to wait. To see where she might pop up next. The iceboxes on the Mayhem still held remnants he hoped to use in order to keep her at bay a while longer.

Before sitting down, Bark quietly twisted the handle of the bedroom door, parting it just slightly so that he could peer inside. He had sat in the darkness long enough that his eyes could easily make out the shapes in the room. The kid laid on the bed, his arms stretched above him and handcuffed to the headboard. Still there. Still safe.

The room smelled of piss. An inevitable consequence of keeping someone chained up without the use of a bathroom. But Bark wasn't about to inject a catheter into this kid. What he smelled like didn't matter.

Bark nearly crapped his own pants when he heard a voice in the darkness. "Who are you? Where am I? What happened?"

Dammit. Surprisingly, the kids voice wasn't nearly as frantic as Bark might have expected.

"You were in an accident," Bark replied from the doorway.

The handcuffs rattled as the kid twisted his wrists, trying to make sense of the situation. It would all start clicking into place soon, and the gentle questions would surely give in to desperate screams. Bark didn't want that.

"Stay calm. I know this seems weird, but it's for your own good," Bark offered, trying to keep the inevitable panic at bay.

"Where's Miriam?" the voice asked.

A good question, which Bark couldn't answer. Alive, as far as he knew. But she wouldn't be coming to this kid's rescue.

Bark sighed and picked up the baseball bat leaning against the back of his chair. He really didn't want to do this.

The kid startled. "What's going on?"

Just one whack. If Bark could make it a good one, then hopefully the kid would just go back to sleep for a while. He stepped into the room and lifted the bat before crossing over to the bed.

"Listen, kid. I don't want to do this, but you gotta keep quiet. Y'hear me?" Bark said as menacingly as possible.

Bark inched forward. From here he might be able to get in a hit, but he'd need to move closer to be sure. He tried to think of another way, but he felt cornered. The house was old. The walls were thin. If the kid made a racket, someone might hear, and then everything would get much, much worse.

Surprisingly, the kid didn't yell as Bark moved closer, the bat slowly rising above his head. Maybe the confusion of it all had left the kid paralyzed, but Bark could see the whites of the kid's eyes watching intently.

Another step, and Bark moved to slam the bat into his prisoner's head when the kid's sneaker-clad foot slammed into Bark's belly, shooting pain through his abdomen. The kid screamed, as if the kick hurt him as much as it had hurt Bark. Bark swung the bat down with less force than intended, missing his target and landing on the mattress.

"Help!" the kid yelled.

Bark doubled his grip on the bat and reared back for another shot, but the kid twisted this time, screaming in pain as he wrenched his own wrists to avoid the bat. Bark felt anger rising in his chest, no longer regretful about having to silence this kid. He'd strangle him if he had to.

Another wild kick caught Bark in the thigh. He backed up, dragging the bat along the covers, then letting it *thunk* to the floor.

"Help!" the kid yelled again.

Bark lifted the bat, intent on rushing in and striking before the kid could react. Bark lunged forward. The bat flew down. The kid screamed and pulled on the cuffs, and Bark only barely registered one of the cheap chains snapping before the bat stopped.

Almost impossibly, the kid positioned his free hand alongside the chained one to catch the bat flying at his head. Though the kid grunted at the force against his fingers, he still managed to dig in with an unrelenting grip. Before he knew it, Bark lost his balance and fell onto the bed.

They wrestled each other for the bat, but the fact that Bark's hands weren't confined gave him the upper hand. In a few short seconds, Bark straddled the kid, pressing the bat across his neck and pushing down hard. The kid kicked his feet, but he couldn't buck off Bark's weight. The kid sputtered and gurgled as the bat crushed into his windpipe.

Bark wondered if this might kill the kid. He didn't want that. Not if he could help it. He loosened his grip on the bat, and the kid gasped for air. Maybe this experience would be enough to keep him quiet.

Suddenly, the kid shoved the bat forward, catching Bark right in the nose. Blood gushed out, dripping onto the bat, the sheets, the kid's face.

"Goddammit!" Bark exclaimed, scuttling off the bed and holding his nose.

No more Mr. Nice Guy. Bark slammed the bat into the kid's knees, gaining strength from the howls of pain. Then into his stomach. And, while the kid crumpled in pain, Bark took the shot he needed the most and cracked the bat into the kid's skull. His body went instantly limp.

Bark breathed hard and dropped the bat on the floor before crossing over to check for a pulse. Not dead. Good.

He dragged the bat back into the living room, dropped it on the floor next to the chair, and then slammed the door shut.

"Dammit! Dammit! Dammit!" Bark yelled to beat away the pain, both hands squeezing at the bridge of his nose. He didn't know if it was broken, but it hurt like hell.

At least they had running water.

He made it to the kitchen, turned on the tap and splashed some water onto his face. He couldn't see well enough to know how much blood there was, but the stinging and the volume of blood on his hands told him it was probably a lot.

As he started to get a handle on the pain, he heard the screen door squeal, then the front door swing open.

"Perfect timing, Newt. Perfect timing," he said, as he held a dish towel up to his nose.

"Bark?" a female voice echoed into the room. "What are you doing here?"

Goddammit.

He rounded the corner back into the living room and stared at the silhouette of Stacy Hampton. He stopped, trying to fight through the pain to find an answer that would make sense. Something that would make her leave.

He watched her head spin down to the bat, then back up to him, the waning light shining through the door enough for her to surely see the carnage on his face. And the blood on the bat.

"I heard screaming. Are you ok?" she said, clearly more cautious than she'd been when arriving.

"I'm fine. I just... fell."

He knew immediately how stupid it sounded.

"What are you even doing here?" she asked again.

"Just helping Newt out with something."

She hadn't moved from the doorway yet, and Bark wondered whether she believed him. Maybe it didn't even matter, as long as she left without knowing what really happened.

"No electricity?" she asked.

"Uh, no. Newt hasn't used the place in a while. Um. Thinking of fixing it up. Seeing if maybe he can rent it out."

She seemed to be relaxing. "Well, I appreciate him mowing the yard. It was getting to be a real eyesore."

"I'll tell him you said so."

She started towards him. "Do you need some help? Are you okay?"

Instinctively, Bark held up a hand and spoke more sternly than intended. "I'm fine. Fine. It's fine. Just a nosebleed. Don't worry about it."

She persisted, reaching up to his face and tugging on the towel. Bark held fast, despite the pain it caused. He jerked away and turned his back to her.

"I told you I'm fine. Just go back home."

She responded sharply, "Stupid men and your stupid pride. I'm just trying to help."

He could feel her eyes rolling behind him, and then he heard her move away.

He turned back and let out a mirthless laugh. "Yeah. What can I say? I'm a man of the sea. We're tough."

"Oh, don't I know it."

She stood by the door now. It was nearly over. Bark held his breath, waiting for her to leave, when Stacy turned at a noise behind her.

"Help!" the kid's voice pierced through the walls of the living room.

Stacy jumped and turned towards the door to the bedroom. It was closer to her than Bark. He'd never make it before she would be able to get there.

"Who's that?" she asked, stepping towards the door before she got an answer.

"Stacy!" he yelled, causing her to pause briefly as her hand hovered above the knob. "Don't go in there."

She looked back at him, but he couldn't make out the expression on her face. For a moment, he thought that maybe she would heed his direction, but then she twisted the knob and pushed the door wide open.

"Thank god! Help me. Please!" the kid pleaded.

Bark dropped the towel on the floor as Stacy stepped inside the room. The panic flooded his veins as he realized what he would have to do. He heard the bed creak as she sat on it, promising the kid that he would be okay. Asking him what happened. Maybe it hadn't registered yet, or maybe her nurturing instincts had overridden her good sense. Either way Bark needed to act fast before she could turn on him.

He scooped the bat up on his way to the room, never missing a step. Lord help him. He didn't want to do this, but he was too far in now.

"Watch out!" the kid yelled to Stacy.

Stacy spun and jerked her hands to her face. "Bark! What the—"

She never finished her sentence. The force of the bat slammed into her arms, smashing them against her face until the bat cracked into the crown of her head. She slumped over on the kid as he stammered in the dark, offering words of apology to a woman who couldn't hear him. The kid jerked at the handcuffs, trying to get both hands to her head. Trying to comfort her. To hold her.

The kid didn't even know her.

Bark did. Bark loved her. Just like he had loved Joe. He tapped his forehead, trying to beat away the throbbing behind his eyes. This wasn't how it was supposed to go.

The boy screamed and yelled. No words. Just unbridled anger and hatred.

Bark needed quiet. He needed to regroup.

He raised the bat above his head again, rushed over, and clocked the kid on the head as hard as he could. He didn't even check to see if he had killed the kid this time. He just dropped the bat in the middle of the floor and stumbled back into the kitchen for another beer.

CHAPTER 20

Tommy understood the irony of it: a cop, two hands anxiously gripping the wheel, trying through a haze of alcohol to focus on the road. He meant to only eat a burger and some cheese fries, but then he ordered a beer. And another. And another. He wasn't proud of it. Or rather, he didn't think he would be in the morning.

He might not be over the legal limit, he reasoned with himself, and he wouldn't be going far. All excuses he'd heard a million times from a million different tourists. Somehow, they seemed truer when he told them to himself. He'd never had a drinking problem, but the day had stolen his resolve. It happened sometimes. He was only human.

He didn't know why he drove there, but as he pulled his Crown Vic along the curb and stared at Stacy's house, he regretted the decision. What did he expect from her? He couldn't hang his worries in this place. She couldn't handle the weight. But she told him to keep an eye on Emma, and now he had new information.

Across the street, someone rummaged in the back of a truck.

"Well if it isn't Newt Goodreaux!" Tommy exclaimed as he stumbled out of the car, internally assessing whether he'd come across as a little too excited. Tommy Wallace was a jolly drunk.

Newt stood up quickly, banging his head against the steel cross bar of his fishing pole rack. The clang echoed through the neighborhood.

"T-T-Tommy."

Did Newt have a stutter? Tommy couldn't remember him ever having a stutter before.

"Finally cleanin' up this old piece of crap?" Tommy asked.

Newt rubbed the back of his head, a sour expression on his face. He glanced down at a bottle of bleach in his hand and forced a smile. "Yessir. Need some extra money. Gonna rent it out."

Tommy nodded his approval. "Good plan."

He crossed in front of his car and started down the walkway to the familiar blue door, barely noticing that Newt practically ran inside. Tommy's knocks fell muted on the door, dispersing into silence almost as quickly as he made them.

While waiting for Stacy to answer, he tried to compose himself. She'd seen Joe come home drunk and wild-eyed far too many times. Tommy couldn't be that way with her. He imagined himself a rock, steadfast and unmoving. A place where Stacy could lean until she caught her breath.

No answer. He cupped his hand above his eyes and peered into the elongated window next to the door. Everything looked normal, in its place. Neat and clean, as always. Lights shone throughout the house.

A glance towards the driveway revealed Stacy's car, so signs pointed away from her being out on errands. Not that she left on errands very often anymore.

He knocked again.

Tommy looked at his watch this time, willing himself to focus. After a full minute with no answer, he tried the handle, twisting it open and parting the door. He peered through the foyer and into the living room, trying to make sure every little thing stood in place. He shook his head and told himself the alcohol was just making him paranoid. She might just be in the shower. Still, it seemed atypical for her to keep the door unlocked.

Creeping inside, he turned down the hallway, taking note of the half-empty glass of tea on the end table in the living room. Stacy kept things tidy; he'd never known her to leave glasses lying around.

By the time he made it to the first bedroom, the unnerving silence goaded him into drawing his gun, but he tucked it back into the holster almost immediately. With it out, he'd only scare Stacy when he found her.

Each step made Tommy feel more uneasy. Everything seemed so normal. Like she'd vanished in the middle of a typical evening at home.

"Stacy?" he hollered for the first time, realizing that he should have led with that.

No answer.

Tommy picked up his pace, moving past the spare bathroom into the master bedroom. He flipped on the light. Nothing out of the ordinary. The quilt lay stretched across the queen-sized bed with military-like precision. The master bathroom was empty, too, though water droplets clung to the sides of the garden tub. Tommy squeezed the towel on the rack. Still wet.

Tommy considered that she might be outside, tending to the yard, but that job had largely fallen to him in recent months, so he doubted it. With no reason to suspect anything strange, Tommy felt foolish, but then wondered if maybe he'd finally developed the "gut" so many other cops talked about. He felt it in his bones. Stacy needed help.

With the haze of the alcohol starting to evaporate, Tommy moved faster through the house, the backyard, the front, his dreadful suspicions hardening. Outside, he peered down the street in both directions just in case she'd gone for a walk.

He stopped in the driveway and considered his options. Reporting her missing felt premature, and even if he did, he'd catch the case anyway. All matters related to the Hamptons fell to Tommy — an unspoken understanding between him and the chief.

A flash of light caught his eye, bouncing through narrow slits of the boarded-up windows across the street. Tommy stalked across the narrow stretch of pavement. Maybe Newt knew where Stacy had gone.

He didn't bother knocking before pulling back the screen and stepping into the house through the already-open door. Cloaked in shadow, the room was mostly empty. The late afternoon light silhouetted a few chairs, some beer bottles on the kitchen-adjacent counter, and a baseball bat leaning against the hearth of the fireplace. The caustic smell of bleach assaulted his nostrils.

A flashlight shone into the room from a door on his right. Tommy moved his hand to the butt of his gun.

"Tommy," Newt said, his eyes wide and alert in the dim light. "Careful there. I'm cleanin' the carpets."

Tommy took a step back, glancing down to see his footprint outlined in the white carpet. It seemed a strange color choice, but as he widened his field of view, he realized the white was localized to the area directly in front of the door.

"With bleach?" Tommy asked.

Newt didn't answer, but his eyes stayed carefully trained on Tommy. Newt Goodreaux could often be described as energetic, but he seemed nervous and defensive now.

"You ok, Newt?"

Newt finally dropped his eyes and nodded, the light bouncing up and down across the living room. "Yessir. Just, uh, the bleach gettin' to me, I guess. Been working on it a while."

Tommy wished for his own flashlight, feeling suddenly uncomfortable with Newt being the only source of clarity.

"Why you using bleach to clean carpets, Newt?"

"So much work to do." Newt changed the subject. "I underestimated how much work there was. Why you here again, Tommy?"

The question stung, reminding Tommy that he had come to find Stacy. Newt being too damn stupid to know how to properly clean carpets hardly seemed important. "Looking for Stacy. Thought maybe she'd come over here to visit. Or maybe you saw her leave?"

Newt inflated, almost imperceptibly, to take up more of the doorway into the bedroom. "Uh. N-no. I ain't seen her. Maybe she went down to the store."

Tommy cocked his head towards the door. "Her car's in the drive."

"Oh," Newt said before trailing off. "Well, she ain't here. I need to get back to my cleanin', if you don't mind."

Tommy felt the distinct impression that Newt wanted him gone. Newt was a slimy asshole, sure, taking advantage of tourists when he could, but he wouldn't hurt a fly. Yet, Tommy still felt like he'd latched on to the very end of a thread that led somewhere significant.

"Newt. Listen. What's got you all riled up, man? What are you not telling me?"

Tommy could see Newt's Adams apple bob up and down as he swallowed hard. Time slowed as the two men eyed each other in the wan light.

"Sorry, Tommy," Newt said finally. "I just... I still feel bad about that kid, ya know. I know it wasn't my fault, and these things just happen, but I feel so bad about it. I didn't mean for nobody to get hurt."

Tommy didn't expect that answer. He'd talked to Newt after Tanner's disappearance and come up with no reason to hold Newt responsible. Even then, Newt hadn't expressed the regret that he did now.

Newt continued before Tommy could reply. "Just trying to keep busy. I know it don't make no sense." He ran the flashlight across the living room. "This gives me something to do, ya know?"

As the light washed across the room, Tommy's peripheral vision caught stains along the wood-grain of the baseball bat leaning against the hearth. Streaks of red. Paint? Maybe, but the drops and splatters looked much more like a crime scene.

Like blood.

Tommy jerked the gun from its holster and pointed it straight at Newt, knowing that his actions might be premature. Newt jumped and threw his hands in the air, losing his grip on the flashlight and dropping it on the wet carpet.

"Jesus, Tommy! What're ya doin'?"

Tommy nodded down to the flashlight. "Kick that over here."

Newt hesitated at first, then nudged the flashlight toward him. Tommy kept his gun pointed at Newt as he knelt to pick up the flashlight with his left hand and shone it directly on Newt's frightened, worried face.

"What's going on, Newt?"

Newt protested, "I told you. Just cleanin' the house up."

"What's with the bat?"

Newt turned his head to look towards the fireplace, causing Tommy to tighten his grip on the handle of the gun. The rattle of the gun seemed threatening and loud, even to Tommy. Newt didn't answer the question. He hung his head, closed his eyes and pivoted one of his feet back, taking up less of the doorway. Tommy braced for sudden movements but forced himself to give Newt the benefit of the doubt. His hands still up, Newt cocked his head into the bedroom.

"Back up. Against the wall over there," Tommy said as he motioned to the back of the room.

Newt complied and Tommy followed into the room.

"I swear to God, Tommy," Newt blubbered. "I didn't do it. I wasn't even here, I tell ya. I promise. It wasn't me."

Tommy swept the flashlight across the room, taking in the white splotches where Newt had already bleached the carpet ... as well as other dark stains he hadn't gotten to yet.

Then, he saw the bed, where a blue-and-white comforter lay stained with what Tommy immediately assumed to be blood.

"Please, Tommy—"

Noticing his gun had drifted, Tommy centered it back on Newt's chest. "Shut up, Newt."

Handcuffs dangled from the headboard. Tommy tried to piece the scene back together in his head. Someone tied up to the bed. Beaten. Bloodied. Worse?

Tommy spun towards Newt, bringing his flashlight-hand up to help support the gun. Newt crossed his hands in front of his face. "What did you do to Stacy, Newt?" Tommy yelled.

He could see one of Newt's big brown eyes through a slit in his fingers. "I told ya, Tommy. I didn't do nothin'. I wasn't even here."

Tommy took a step forward and rattled his gun, going against all his training to remain at a safe distance from a potential threat. Newt jumped again and Tommy very nearly pulled the trigger. As his finger tensed, he realized that he'd been compromised; that he couldn't trust himself to make rational choices.

"I swear it. It's true," Newt whimpered.

"Is she even alive?" Tommy asked.

Newt lowered his hands and nodded into the blinding light. "Yessir. I think so. I think she is."

"Where is she?"

"I-I dunno."

"Turn around," Tommy demanded.

Newt turned around and put his hands behind his back, resigned to his fate. Feeling along his belt, Tommy remembered that he'd thrown his cuffs into the backseat of the Crown Vic when he went off duty. With no restraints, he grabbed hard onto one of Newt's wrists and twisted his hand back, ignoring Newt's yelp of pain.

Tommy leaned over to Newt's ear to make sure that the bastard could hear him clearly.

"Newt Goodreaux. You're under arrest."

CHAPTER 21

Newt didn't resist as Tommy jerked him out of the back seat of the Crown Vic. The whole drive over, Newt had blubbered about how he didn't do it. Tommy had arrested the wrong man, Newt insisted. Tommy wanted to believe it, too. He'd known Newt far too long to believe that he would do something this horrendous.

Quiet now, Newt marched dutifully ahead of Tommy into a thankfully-empty waiting area, then through the glass doors into the bullpen. Tommy could feel confused eyes burning into him as he made his way back to an interrogation room. Most of these cops had known Newt their whole lives, and, though he could hardly be considered perfect, he'd never been paraded around in handcuffs before.

The small interrogation room was a converted supply closet, boasting none of the trappings of the fancier ones on TV. The door contained the only window. A camera peered down from the corner, recording everything that transpired. Tommy had always viewed that camera as a boon, but the urge to beat the truth out of Newt made it feel more like a liability today.

Tommy pushed Newt down into a wooden chair, slung his jacket on the back of the other, and paced back and forth across the tiny room.

"You understand your rights?" Tommy asked. "You don't have to talk to me if you don't want to."

He'd gone through the formal list before shoving Newt in the car, but getting it on record seemed prudent. If Newt had done something to Stacy, Tommy couldn't afford to let him get away with it on a stupid technicality.

"Yeah, of course," Newt said. "Don't need no lawyer, Tommy."

Tommy felt somewhat certain that Newt absolutely needed a lawyer, but he didn't really care whether Newt made wise choices so long as they were clearly *his* choices.

Tommy stopped his pacing, unbuttoned the cuffs on his sleeves, and rolled them up to his elbows, trying to sort through his approach. He could call in some help, but it wasn't uncommon for initial interrogations to be done by solo detectives. Cape Madre didn't have the resources to do everything in pairs.

"What'd you do to Stacy?" Tommy asked, a little more bluntly than he would have liked. He resumed his pacing.

"I didn't do nothin' to her, Tommy. Bark did."

Tommy stopped. In the entire car ride over, Newt had insisted his innocence, but this was the first time he'd mentioned Bark. Tommy couldn't believe it. Wouldn't believe it. If Cape Madre bothered to recognize a Citizen of the Year, Fred "Bark" Barker would be an automatic nominee, and eventual winner.

"Seriously, Newt?" Tommy asked, sliding into the chair across the table. "You expect me to believe that? Why would Bark be at your house?"

"He was looking after that boy," Newt said, leaning forward in his chair and clasping his cuffed hands in front of him. "Tanner."

Tommy felt his face blanch. A headache started creeping across his temples.

"You're gonna have to give me more than that, Newt. None of this makes sense."

Newt licked his lips, glanced up at the camera and then back at Tommy. "Bark found the boy. After... you know. The incident. Floatin' in the water out there. Brought him back in. Needed somewhere to keep him, so asked to use my old place out there. I agreed. We had to keep him safe. Had to make sure he didn't go do what Joe did, ya know?"

"No," Tommy replied. "I don't know, Newt. Explain it to me."

"Well, I mean, we coulda brought him in or let him go, or something. Been heroes, I suppose, but that wouldna done him no good. He would've just found a way back out there. To see her."

"See who?"

Newt kept rambling without answering the question. "It was Bark who figgered it out. After Joe. Once you spend some time with her, you just kinda wanna go see her again. She's beautiful. In all my years on the water, I ain't seen nothing so beautiful. So, I get it. I understand why people wanna see her again, but with Joe it just kinda took him over, ya know? And Bark was worried this Tanner kid would do the same thing."

Rolling over so easily had become Newt's MO. Every time Newt ran into the law, he became a fountain of platitudes and promises. Still, Tommy felt uneasy at how quickly Newt wanted to spill the beans on this particular issue.

"Are you talking about the kraken, Newt?" Tommy asked.

"Um. I suppose so? Is that what you call it? She don't have a name, I don't guess, so that's as good as any. She lives out there, Tommy. That water belongs to her. We're just borrowin' it."

Krakens. Boys thought dead. Stacy. Joe. It all swam around in Tommy's head, the facts crashing into each other like angry waves. Could any of this even be remotely true? Or was Newt telling stories to save his own ass? The latter seemed more likely, but Tommy had seen a lot of weird stuff in Cape Madre in recent days.

"So, you're saying Bark has Tanner and Stacy?" Tommy asked.

"Yessir. The both of'em. Took'em out on the *Mayhem* I reckon, but he didn't tell me where he was headed. He just had to get out of there, ya know."

No more time for talking. Not until Tommy made sure that the coast guard dispatched their only Cape Madre-based ship to find Stacy. They were already looking for Tanner, so it wouldn't be out of their way.

Tommy stood from his chair, leaving his coat behind as he opened the door. Before he could step foot into the hallway, he heard shouting across the bullpen.

"Just let me talk to Detective Wallace!"

He'd only seen Miriam Brooks calm and collected, but he still recognized her voice through the panic. The desk officer, Grabowski, held his hands out in front of him to keep Miriam from moving farther into the bullpen. She stopped trying when her eyes locked onto Tommy's. She cocked her head towards Grabowski, silently begging Tommy to call off the enforcer.

Tommy let the interrogation room door shut behind him with a bang, as he rushed over to the commotion. "I got this, Grabowski."

"You sure, detective?"

"I'm sure," Tommy replied as he cast a sideways glance towards Miriam. "Ms. Brooks won't cause any trouble."

Through the glass door, Tommy saw a pale-faced Macy Donner rocking back and forth in a chair.

"I think I know where Tanner is," Tommy said before Miriam could launch into whatever news she brought with her.

Whatever her mission, Tanner neutralized her urgency. "He's alive?"

"I think so. I need to get the coast guard after him. Can you just hold on here? One second? I'll be right back. I promise."

Though she looked unsure of the agreement, Miriam nodded, and stayed put.

A quick glance told Tommy that his chief sat behind her desk, happily typing away on her keyboard and ignoring the drama unfolding in her bullpen. She never liked the drama. And she certainly wasn't going to like this.

***

The adrenaline of a good argument coursed through Tommy as he stepped out of the chief's office. He'd won, though. The coast guard would be immediately dispatched to search for *Madre's Mayhem*. And the bigger coup — Tommy got permission to bring on a monster hunter.

Miriam hadn't moved from her spot, blocking the door out of the bullpen with her arms wrapped defiantly around her chest.

When he got to her, Tommy tried to sound upbeat. "You've just been deemed a subject matter expert, Ms. Brooks. Ever participated in an interrogation before?"

Her mouth curled up into a faint smile. "Um. Not really."

"That's okay. You'll catch on."

He motioned with his head for her to follow. She did so, after briefly sharing a perplexed look with Macy. Tommy escorted her to the interrogation room, let her in, then slid a chair from the corner so that the two of them could sit side-by-side across from Newt.

Newt sat with his head hung low, his foot tapping against the shiny linoleum.

Tommy started. "Okay, Newt. This is Miriam Brooks. She's an... expert on sea life. I'm going to need you to tell her what you know."

Newt didn't look up before mumbling, "I 'member her."

"Tanner's alive?" Miriam asked.

"Yes'm. Bark has him."

"And why didn't he bring him in. To the hospital?" Tommy asked.

Newt looked up at Tommy before dropping his head again, which Tommy took as a protest of the repeated question. But Tommy wanted Miriam to hear this for herself. He wanted to know whether it meant something. Whether it fit with whatever crazy theory she had about the kraken.

Newt regarded Miriam, his eyes dark and wet. His sharp, narrow face seemed older now, resigned and exhausted. He steepled his fingers in front of him, the handcuffs rattling against the cheap, wooden table.

"To make sure," Newt answered.

Tommy egged him on. "To make sure of what?"

"That she hadn't changed him like she did us."

"And who is 'she', Newt?"

Newt swallowed hard. His lip quivered as he tried to speak, but then he stopped and folded his fingers in from the steeple, as if to say a prayer before he answered.

"She don't have no name. But you call her the kraken, I guess?"

Miriam leaned forward, enthralled. Tommy studied the faces of both Newt and Miriam in turn, confident that Newt wouldn't let the silence hang.

"She attacked us. Bark. Joe. Ol' Newt here. And then she let us go. It took a while at first, ya know, before either of us realized what was going on and even still, I don't really understand it. Bark thinks he does. He made the connection and finally understood after what happened to Joe. See, he tried to keep Joe from her. Thought it'd be better that way. But it was worse. Way worse. Joe wouldn't quit."

"Wouldn't quit what?" Miriam asked, strangely confident for someone who'd never participated in an interrogation before. Whatever panic she'd brought into the room had already begun to give way to curiosity.

"Trying to get to her," Newt answered. "To... help her, I guess? Hell, I dunno how it all works. She needs us. We gotta take of her. Make sure she eats. Stays healthy."

"Help her? She tried to kill you. Why would you help her?" Miriam asked, clearly exasperated.

"Well, I... because..." Newt stopped suddenly, his eyes searching the room, looking for the solution to a question he couldn't answer.

"Where's Tanner?" Miriam demanded, changing the subject.

Newt refocused, the confusion of the previous question evaporating from his face. "Bark has him, like I said. On the *Mayhem*, I suppose. Though I don't for sure."

Miriam slid back in her chair and stood up, looking at Tommy. "We have to go get him. Now!"

Tommy held up a hand. "I've already dispatched the coast guard. They're redirecting to go find him right now."

"I need to be there with them!" she yelled into the tiny room.

"Ms. Brooks," Tommy said calmly. "They're trained to apprehend vessels out on the ocean. They'll find him. They will save him. But I need you here now. To figure this out."

Her eyes narrowed as she processed his plea. Tommy could tell it took a lot of willpower for her to slink back into her chair. Before she could change her mind, Tommy urged Newt on. "Why do you take care of her, Newt?"

He shook his head, as if answering would be painful. "I dunno, Tommy. I dunno. I dunno. I told you. We just have to. She's alone. She needs us."

"Did Bark feed him Emma's friend?" Miriam asked out of the blue.

Tommy assumed she meant Hannah Huang, but his mind instead went to Justin's cold, sawed-off leg sitting on the table at the ME's office. Miriam had posited that maybe it'd been detached as fodder for the kraken, but Bark? Surely Bark hadn't done that.

"Maybe," Newt said. "I dunno, really, but I know that he doesn't wanna do that. He just wants to keep the city safe, ya know. We both do. That's all we want and to do that we need to keep her out in the deeper water. Away from the beach. She came too close. Bark had to do something to keep her out there. To protect her. To protect us. To protect Cape Madre."

Tommy cleared his throat. Was this what Miriam had come to tell him? That Bark had murdered two co-eds and fed them to a giant sea creature? He wondered how she could possibly know that. He hadn't known her long, but he suspected that perhaps Miriam Brooks had done a bit of sleuthing of her own.

So maybe it was all related, after all. It seemed unbelievable, but the facts were starting to align. The kraken attacked Emma, and for some reason Bark thought he could keep it from happening again by feeding it Justin? And probably Hannah? Though Tommy struggled to believe that Bark could murder anyone, if it meant saving Cape Madre, then perhaps Tommy could see it. That might be enough to push Bark over the edge.

"Help us out, Newt," Tommy said. "You help us catch Bark and sort all this out, and I'll make sure it all falls on him."

"I have been helping, Tommy," Newt stammered. "I don't wanna see this end bad."

Frustrated and tired, Tommy slammed his fist into the wooden table, causing both Miriam and Newt to jump. "Then tell me the truth, Newt! What the hell is going on here?"

Newt bumbled and mumbled and shook his head, tears welling up and spilling across his dark cheeks. Like Tommy, Newt was frustrated. Confused.

"I dunno, Tommy," Newt blubbered. "I really don't know. I don't know why he took Stacy. He was just trying to keep the boy safe, ya know. Stacy must've come over? He didn't tell me, honest! But Bark don't want no trouble. I don't want no trouble."

Tommy leaned forward, feeling the rage getting the better of him. Newt had to know more. Tommy couldn't believe the facts as they'd been laid out in front of him. Newt was being irrational. He seemed confused, yes, but maybe that was all an act. Newt acted almost like a victim.

A hand lightly touched his bare forearm and Tommy felt himself almost instantly cool off. He looked towards the young girl beside him, her eyes begging him to calm down. It seemed out of place and surreal that Miriam could so quickly regain her cool, but she sat there collected and serene, despite the fact that Tanner was in real danger. Just like Stacy.

"Hey, Detective," Miriam said. "He's clearly upset. Maybe we take a break?"

For someone with no experience with interrogations, Miriam read the situation surprisingly well. Tommy nodded and stood up, promising Newt that they'd be back.

***

Tommy poured the scalding coffee down his throat and hardly noticed the burn. He needed caffeine fast, but he also needed something to do while he worked through Newt's interrogation and everything that Miriam had just revealed. He believed her, even though he didn't want to. Somehow, for some reason, Bark had gotten mixed up with this kraken, and it had led him to murder.

It seemed consistent at least, even if it didn't make sense. Memories of Joe turned Tommy's stomach, forcing him to make the connections. Joe acted weird, too. No murders, but he'd become a different person. A person that neither he nor Stacy recognized. The same thing must've happened to Bark. Maybe to Newt.

And Emma?

Tommy made a mental note to send some uniforms to her hotel to keep an eye on her. Though, she hadn't seemed particularly interested in the kraken when he'd last spoken to her.

"I helped you, Detective," Miriam said from across the small round break-room table. "Now you help me. Get me out there to find Tanner. To hunt this kraken."

Tommy wasn't sure she'd helped him much at all. Not yet. But some part of him still believed Miriam would be useful in stopping the madness descending on Cape Madre.

"Call me Tommy," he said. "And I already told you. The coast guard's on it."

"They might be able to find Bark, but they won't stand a chance against the kraken."

Miriam's single-minded focus made Tommy uncomfortable. Was she any better than Bark or Newt or Joe? Maybe she'd never been influenced directly by the kraken, but it just didn't make sense to him that someone would be so foolhardy. The coast guard had guns and training. Miriam Brooks seemed to have nothing but tenacity.

"It's late," Tommy said with a sigh. "I'm tired. You're tired. You and Macy go back to the hotel. Get some sleep. I promise, I will let you know the minute I hear something."

Miriam stood and glided out of the office without a reply. Though he'd only been a detective for a little while, Tommy could tell when someone meant to break the law. Miriam would go for Tanner at whatever the cost. He figured someone should probably stop her.

As he filled up a second cup of black coffee, Tommy decided that it wouldn't be him.

CHAPTER 22

"We need a boat," Miriam said, snapping her seatbelt in place.

Macy looked at her incredulously, with no clear intention to start the car until Miriam explained. Miriam's head raced with possibilities and plans. Tanner was alive. And that meant she could get him back.

"Tanner's alive," Miriam said. "Bark has him."

"The guy who's boat we infiltrated?" Macy asked.

"Infiltrated?" Miriam laughed. "Yeah, I suppose that's what we did. We must have just missed him, because Newt thinks he took the boat out with Tanner on it."

Macy unbuckled her seatbelt and threw herself across the seat, swallowing Miriam in an unexpected hug. The smell of makeup and hair product filled Miriam's nostrils, forcing her to turn her head away from the red mess of hair to catch a breath. Miriam tentatively wrapped her arms around Macy, slightly uncomfortable, but happy to share the excitement with someone.

Macy then popped back into her seat, strapped back in, and started the car. "Okay. So, we need a boat."

Her hands on the wheel, Macy waited for instruction, but Miriam didn't have any to give yet. Yes, the boat. Weapons would be nice, but she'd have to improvise without them. Dangerous, perhaps. But what choice did she have? If the coast guard could manage to find Bark without running into the kraken, then maybe she could take the time to plan a proper hunt, but the situation as it stood required action.

"How do we get a boat?" Macy asked.

"Newt's. Go to Newt's," Miriam said, before she'd even really thought about it.

"Um. Okay," Macy stammered. "And where is that?"

Right. Miriam had so much information from Tommy that she hadn't relayed to Macy yet. But they couldn't afford the time now. Macy would just have to trust her.

"Stacy's. Go to Stacy's."

Macy nodded, threw the car in drive, and drove to the highway that hugged Cape Madre's coastline. The hour was late, so the beach was empty, but with the blockades up it seemed especially eerie. Miriam wondered when the beach had been shut down. Did Tommy do that?

"He took Stacy, too," Miriam added.

Macy didn't say anything, but Miriam watched her mouth turn down, and only then noticed that Macy's left leg bounced up and down. What did that mean? Was Macy nervous? Scared?

Miriam laid a hand on her friend's outstretched forearm. "You don't have to come with me."

Macy nodded, glanced at Miriam, then wrestled her arm away to wipe her nose. "No. You can't do this alone. I don't know what I can do to help, but what's the worst that could happen?"

Death. Violent, terrible death.

But that certainly wasn't an answer that either of them needed to hear out loud, so Miriam chose to remain quiet.

"Catch me up," Macy requested. "If we're going to do this, I need to know what you know. Not just bits and pieces."

Macy flipped the turn signal and veered the car away from the coastline, up into the suburban hills. They didn't have much more time, but maybe Miriam could relay it all. Or enough of it.

It came out fast, Miriam's words tumbling over one another as she described the interrogation of Newt, but Macy kept up, nodding and "mmhmming" with each new nugget of information.

They were parked in front of Stacy's house before Miriam finished, but she kept going anyway, the car idling quietly in the dark. Once the facts were out, she focused in on the part that really bothered her. The part that she couldn't explain. The part that felt like it had an explanation she just couldn't grasp yet.

"That's really weird," Macy said once she had time to speak. "It's like they're in love with the kraken or something."

"Yeah," Miriam responded. "It felt almost like Newt didn't even know what he was doing. I mean, he knew he was doing it, but even his own actions seemed to confuse him."

"Maybe Bark brainwashed him?" Macy offered.

Miriam considered and quickly dismissed the notion. "I don't think so. It sounds like Bark's just as far in as Newt. And Joe was too."

"What about Tanner?" Macy asked. "Is he gonna be that way?"

"I hope not," Miriam replied, herself wondering what it would mean if Tanner also became enamored. Surely, he wouldn't, though. He'd seen enough to have perspective.

Macy turned off the car. "Maybe they can't help it. Maybe something's wrong with them."

Diplostomum pseudopathaceum.

Macy's statement jostled something loose in Miriam's brain, and it forcefully surfaced. The fish that ate the snails. The birds that ate the fish. The snails that ate the bird droppings. A circle of life. A complex parasite intent on keeping itself and its hosts alive. Could this be it? Not that particular parasite, of course, but something else. Something new.

Miriam had been intent on hunting down a kraken, a giant sea creature straight out of pirate myths. Maybe her cryptid was smaller than she expected. Maybe it lived inside the kraken. Inside Bark. Inside Newt. Inside Emma.

Inside Tanner.

"A parasite!" she exclaimed.

Macy looked confused. "Huh?"

"What if the kraken infects people with a parasite? Through its tentacles. Or its suction cups. Doesn't matter. Somehow. And what if the purpose of that parasite is to protect its host?"

"You're talking about the poop thing again, aren't you?" Macy asked.

Miriam felt the electricity firing through her; something she took as a sign that she was at least on the right track. "Well, I don't know if that's a part of this particular one. But it would explain everything. If Bark and Newt were infected, then maybe it's driving them to protect the kraken. To feed it. To..."

"Love it?" Macy finished the sentence.

Could a parasite do that? Probably not exactly, but close enough that other humans might interpret it that way. But maybe it was just a survival mechanism. The details were surely complicated and impossible for the two of them to fully understand, but if Miriam could get Tanner back, then they'd have a willing test subject. They could isolate it. Study it. It would be a huge breakthrough. Maybe even more exciting than the kraken itself. To nerds like her, anyway. The media would surely prefer the kraken.

"We need to find Tanner," Miriam said. "Then we can test him and find out."

Macy shrugged. "Why not just test Newt? They have him already, right?"

Of course. Miriam reached for the phone in her pocket, then paused. If she called Tommy now, he might catch on and stop her from what she intended to do. No, she'd call him after.

"Maybe. But we gotta get out on the water first," Miriam said.

"Uh, we're in the suburbs. There's no water here."

"No, there's no water. But I'm hoping that we'll find the key to a boat."

"Stacy has a boat?"

Pointing to the dilapidated house across the street, Miriam replied, "No. But Newt does."

***

She knew it was a long shot. Surely, circumstances favored the key to the *Mama Jean* being safely tucked away in Newt's pocket. But Tommy had told her that he'd caught Newt trying to cover up the scene, and if that meant getting dirty, then maybe he'd emptied his pockets. Miriam could only hope.

"You know this is like grand theft boat or something, right?" Macy said as she trailed Miriam into the house.

Shadows stretched across the entry room, barely visible in the tiny amount of moonlight creeping through the wooden planks boarding up the windows. Miriam extracted her phone from her pocket and clicked on the flashlight. Macy followed suit.

"Fan out," Miriam commanded. "Look for keys."

"So, we're ignoring the felony part of it. All righty, then." Macy stepped away into the bedroom.

Before Miriam could properly investigate the living room, Macy screamed and stumbled back onto the linoleum that pretended to be a foyer, tears shining in her eyes.

"So... much... blood," Macy eeked out.

Miriam didn't feel the panic that Macy did, partially because she knew about what Tommy had seen, but also because she knew that Tanner was alive when he'd left the house. Whatever injuries he might have sustained, they could be mended. Healed. If they could find him in time.

"It's okay, Macy. He's fine. He's alive. It looks worse than it is."

Macy nodded, "Um, I hope so. Yeah. I know. I just... it freaked me out. I'm gonna stand right here if that's okay."

Miriam patted Macy's shoulder, then swept the room with her flashlight. A bloody baseball bat against the hearth. A rickety chair pushed against the wall next to the bedroom. Miriam tried to put herself in Newt's shoes.

"You can stay there, but follow me with your light," she told Macy as she turned off her own light and slipped the phone into her pocket.

Miriam walked into the room and reached into her pocket, as if to pull out imaginary keys. She reached her arm out and searched the room for somewhere she might hypothetically put them. The furniture was sparse, the mantle serving as the only surface. But it sat empty, and coated with dust.

If he didn't take them out of his pocket right when he came in, then when? Probably when he realized he'd be cleaning. She glanced through the tiny hole above the kitchen sink and saw a blue cap to a large plastic jug. A cleaning supply of some sort. One that might have been stored under the sink — it's where her dad had always stored such things.

Engaging the light on her phone once more, Miriam said, "I'll be right back."

She went around the corner into the small galley kitchen. She skimmed the light over the counters, frustrated with no promising gleams of metal that might be keys. She rounded back to the living room, where Macy stood expectantly.

"Did you find them?" Macy hissed in a frantic whisper.

Miriam shook her head, still surveying the house. They needed the boat. She couldn't see a path forward without it. As she played out mentally the kind of man Newt was, her mind latched on to one last possibility.

"Come on!" she shouted, not bothering to whisper as she bounded out of the house.

Newt's beat-up truck sat along the curb, fishing poles leaning into racks, as if they served as fortification against attack. But Cape Madre was small, Newt's truck was worthless, and he seemed like just the kind of guy who might...

Miriam opened the driver's side door. Hoisting herself up into the driver's seat, she reached for the visor, flipped it down, and smiled when the tangle of keys literally fell into her lap. No guarantee that this ring held the key she needed, but it was her best hope.

She held them up for Macy to see through the windshield. "Bingo!"

***

The parking lot of the Shady Shark Motel almost felt like home. As soon as Macy put the car in park, Miriam pounced out of the car and jogged towards the *Mama Jean*. She carried with her the baseball bat found at Newt's. Macy thought it crude to be carrying a bat bathed in Tanner's blood, but it was the only weapon Miriam had quick access to, and she found gleeful irony in using it to rescue him.

Macy followed across the parking lot. The docks seemed deserted, which gave Miriam some comfort. Everyone knew who owned the *Mama Jean*, and she didn't want anyone trying to stop her.

The dock that previously served as the home for *Madre's Mayhem* sat empty now, confirming Newt's theory that Bark had taken Tanner out to sea. They were on the right track. Miriam felt sure of it.

Miriam scrambled onto the boat just as Macy caught up, breathing hard. "What if none of those keys work?"

Stretching out a hand to pull Macy on the boat, Miriam replied, "You sure 'what if' a lot."

Both on board, Miriam made her way to the cockpit and tried the keys in the ignition. It only took two tries before she found the right one, cranked it, and heard *Mama Jean's* motor sputter to life. It had been a while since Miriam piloted a boat, and never one quite this big.

Macy joined her inside. "Don't forget to call Detective Wallace. Tell him about the *Diplo*... parasite thingy."

Right. Miriam pulled her phone out, navigated to her recent calls, and tapped the number that would connect her to Tommy. Hopefully he wouldn't protest too much when she asked him to take the ridiculous action of testing Newt for brain parasites.

The phone rang once.

Then a ring tone echoed into the night air. Weird. Miriam glanced to Macy to see if maybe she was receiving a call, but Macy's wide eyes looked as confused as Macy.

A second ring.

The ring tone again.

Miriam hung up, put it all together, and whirled to her right just as a shadowed figure came around the corner through the door.

"Couldn't let me do it on my own?" Miriam said to the shadow.

Still without his jacket, sleeves rolled up, tie discarded, Tommy Wallace stepped into the cockpit. Miriam worried that he'd come to stop her, but when she scanned his tired, scruffy face and saw the desperation in his eyes, she knew that he wouldn't. He needed to find Stacy, just like she needed to find Tanner.

"I should be arresting you for grand larceny," he said.

"Grand larceny," Miriam mused, feeling a little like a comic-book villain. "So, it's *not* called Grand Theft Boat. I'm impressed, Detective Tommy. That you managed to find us."

He shrugged. "I knew you'd go for a boat. Asked Newt if he had his keys. When he told me where he'd left them, I knew it was the only play you had."

Macy fidgeted, sheepishly. "Are we in trouble?"

Tommy sighed. "Probably. But we'll figure it out after we find Stacy."

"And Tanner," Miriam added.

He nodded. "And Tanner."

CHAPTER 23

Sunset urged him to turn back, but Bark refused, pushing the *Mayhem* onward towards the vortex. With Newt cleaning up the house, Bark bore the slightest hope that maybe he'd still be able to sort all this out. There'd be questions about Stacy, but Bark felt up to the task of misdirecting the law as necessary. As long as Newt could keep his mouth shut.

The door to the hold sat open, so Bark could hear when his passengers awoke. There'd be no need to keep them quiet out here, and he hoped he'd be able to talk to them before...

"What the hell am I doing?" he said out loud.

He struggled to make sense of it, but he felt like he'd been put on autopilot and couldn't take control of the situation. He felt cornered. Claustrophobic. Stuck in a horror movie that he couldn't escape. He played through alternate scenarios in his head, imagining the fallout from turning himself in. Prison, for sure. Maybe the death penalty if they found out about the other two kids.

Bark thought of himself as a selfless man. He lived in poverty and gave away as much fish as he sold. He spent what little money he scraped up to feed damn near every stray cat in Cape Madre. And none of it mattered now. None of it added up to anything. He wondered if his good deeds would even make a dent on the ledger when he passed to the other side.

Through the swish of the wind and the swash of the water hitting the hull, Bark heard the slightest hint of a voice. He cut the engine on the *Mayhem* and let her coast to a stop, bobbing up and down with the waves. He didn't bother to drop anchor.

He slipped below down the steep ladder, tough on his old knees, but easy in the way of all practiced things. When his feet planted on the floor, he looked to see Stacy and the boy — Tanner, he thought Newt had said — whispering to one another. When they saw him, they popped to attention, their eyes wide with fear.

Both still sat with their backs against separate legs of his table, tied with a precision of knots that Bark had perfected through years of sailing. They looked so helpless and defeated.

The silence stretched on. Bark stared at his captives, trying to figure out what to say. How to tell them that he couldn't help what was happening. Neither of them struggled or yelled this time. Not yet, anyway.

Bark broke the silence. "I'm sorry."

"Sorry?" Stacy spat sharp words. "You're sorry?"

Bark always liked Stacy. The only good thing that had ever happened to Joe. To see her in pain, both physically and emotionally, tore Bark up inside. Even with the blood dried on her face, Stacy was still pretty in her own unique way.

Bark tried to speak with sincerity, but his croaking voice sounded menacing. "This isn't what I wanted to happen, Stacy."

"What? You mean you didn't want to hurt me? Just him? What the hell is wrong with you, Bark?"

So many burning, leading questions, but he deserved the vitriol, he supposed. For a brief moment,

Bark considered that maybe he could convince Stacy to keep quiet. To let him kill the boy and walk away from it all. That'd be the last of it, he decided. After that, this damn monster could take care of itself.

Guilt surged in him from that last thought, stronger even than any associated with betraying Stacy. He'd never be able to walk away from such a beautiful creature. And Stacy would never be able to keep quiet. The goodness in her would prevail, and she'd turn him over to the authorities. He'd rot in prison, and then what would happen? To Cape Madre? To the magnificent natural wonder below?

"I can't explain it. I want to. I just. I have to keep everyone safe."

Stacy stomped a foot against the wooden planks of the floor. "How is this keeping anyone safe?"

"It might get worse if I don't."

Without an answer, Stacy struggled against the ropes and screamed into the belly of the hold, the shrill echo muted into silence almost immediately by the small space. When she stopped, her chest heaved up and down, full of rage she couldn't release. For the first time, Bark considered that Stacy might want to kill him.

"You won't get away with it." Tanner's voice broke into the conversation with confidence and conviction. "Miriam won't stop until she finds you."

That little girl? Bark certainly had no fear of her. Tanner presented a threat — or at least he had before Bark beat him with a baseball bat — but Miriam? What could she possibly do to him?

Before Bark could formulate an answer, a foreign voice wafted down from the top of the stairs, far away but loud. "Fred Barker. This is the US Coast Guard.

Show yourself. We *will* board your vessel and employ deadly force if necessary."

"Dammit!" Bark muttered, taking a few long steps to the half-open door leading into his office. He slipped through the tiny opening, barely able to shove himself through, and opened the top left drawer of the desk. He preferred using a fishing pole to a gun, but he'd been to the range. He knew how to use it.

Once he squeezed back through the door, he slipped the pistol inside the waistband along the small of his back and, with no further glance to his captives, started up the stairs. When he stepped up on the deck, he blinked against the Coast Guard cutter's blinding light.

The voice from the bullhorn: "Put your hands up. Don't make any sudden movements."

Instantly, Bark dropped to the deck and rolled behind the boat's four-foot wall. His bones creaked and ached but he managed the maneuver, shielding himself just as bullets flew over his head. One bullet popped into the fiberglass hull below. One splintered wood from the deck.

He jerked the pistol from his waistband, reached up, and blindly fired towards the cutter. Someone yelled, "Take cover!"

"What the hell am I doing?" Bark repeated to himself.

He couldn't hold off the Coast Guard with an old rickety fishing boat and a pistol. This would be the end. All the hard work would fail here. Either by arrest or by death. In the moment, death seemed preferable, so Bark lifted the gun again, firing more rounds across the void between the *Mayhem* and the cutter.

They didn't return fire, leaving Bark to wonder what happened, but his questions were answered when he heard the *thump* of the cutter's launching ramp against his hull. They were boarding, and unlike all the other times when they just wanted to perform a friendly inspection, Bark suspected this time would come with far more violence.

When he heard the first set of boots hit the deck, Bark slid the pistol away from him and put his hands above his head. He tried to get up, but without the use of his hands for support, he couldn't manage it. The sound of officers flooded the deck now, causing Bark to lose count of his assailants.

"Keep your hands up!" the first officer yelled at him. "Face down!"

Bark kept his hands above his head and wriggled until he felt the hard wood of the deck pressing against his chest. In an instant, he felt a knee fall hard into his back, knocking the wind out of him. Bark yelped from the pain, but the officer above him didn't seem to care.

Three officers stood within Bark's field of view, no doubt itching for any excuse to shoot him. That made four, leaving probably at least six unaccounted for if the cutter was at capacity. It was the only vessel the coast guard had at Cape Madre. If he could escape this, it would be a long time before anyone else would come for him.

The officer on his back reached up and jerked Bark's left hand down, twisting Bark's arm and wrenching his elbow, causing even more pain. A cold, metal handcuff slipped around Bark's wrist as he moved to offer his other hand.

Just as the handcuff touched his right wrist, the weight on his back vanished. A scream pierced the air. Hesitant to make any sudden moves, Bark lifted his head just in time to see tentacles wrapping around the legs of the officers in front of him, each one striking the deck in unison before being dragged away. Some of them held their guns, others dropped them.

None, however, stood a chance.

Bark shuffled himself back up, handcuffs dangling from his left wrist as he tried to get a better sense of what might be left of the threat. Strangled screams issued from the water, disappearing beneath the waves as quickly as they rose. Bark kept himself low, gathering up two of the sidearms the officers had dropped. More would be coming. He needed to be ready.

The deck shook with the weight of another officer boarding the deck, followed by a gunshot that nearly grazed Bark. He grabbed one of the guns and fired a round towards the young, fresh-faced man—a rookie, probably. The bullet hit him somewhere, but Bark couldn't be sure exactly where. The kid fell to the deck almost instantly but rolled to his side and squeezed off another round.

Bark spun, not really knowing if he could dodge a bullet, and understanding that he couldn't when pain shot up his leg. It didn't bring him down, though. Not yet. He fired again at the prone officer and watched as the officer's body went still. Not the first-person Bark had killed, but it still shocked him.

Five left.

He peeked up over the side of the hull, where the searchlight had been swiveled toward the water; where dark tentacles snaked out in every direction, on both sides of the cutter. Bark heard gunshots, but they weren't for him.

On the port side of the cutter, Bark saw an officer behind a giant harpoon gun affixed to the deck. He'd never seen that before. If they were kitted out to fight her, then that meant they knew what to expect. For the first time, Bark had enough breathing room to realize that Newt had betrayed him.

A loud *clunk* sounded across the waves as Bark watched a huge harpoon fly towards one of the arching tentacles. The splash in the water told him that the harpoon missed its mark. The cutter lurched as the kraken grabbed hold of the starboard side and tilted it low into the water. The officer manning the gun lost his balance, but quickly righted himself with the harness he had strapped around his waist. They were too prepared. Ready to kill her.

Bark took a step, fighting back the blinding pain in his leg. The muscles all worked. He suspected that the bullet had only grazed his shin. Good. He needed to get to the other boat. There'd be more than just the guy with the harpoon gun, but he didn't care. She needed his help.

He grabbed his pants leg and forced his leg over the wall, dropping down onto the cutter's ramp and almost losing his balance to the pain.

"Freeze!" someone shouted at him from the other end of the ramp. A woman this time, short and stout, with good sea legs under her, pointing a sidearm at Bark from only a few feet away. She wouldn't miss, and the effort of getting off the *Mayhem* had lowered his guard. He put both hands up but didn't let go of the guns.

She took a slow, measured step toward him, impressively restrained considering the madness going on around her. From his new vantage point, Bark could see other officers firing pistols into the water. Bark doubted very much that pistols were going to stop her.

Bark didn't move. He didn't have a way out, and he felt certain the officer on the other end of the ramp would pull the trigger if she felt threatened. He let the guns fall out of his hands, where they rattled along the metal ramp before bouncing off into the ocean below. She took another step, this time quicker, surer of her success. Within seconds she stood in front of him, close enough that he could get the full measure of her almond-shaped brown eyes and stern features. He dropped his hands in front of him and she expertly used one hand to latch the other handcuff to his right wrist. Though he couldn't give himself up easily, he felt relieved to know that he wouldn't be able to do anymore harm.

The fight raged around him, tentacles slapping the cutter's deck and twisting the boat. The ramp skidded across the hull of *Madre's Mayhem* until it lost contact entirely. The officer in front of him spread her feet apart, bracing against the sudden movement, but Bark reacted too slowly and lost his balance. He tumbled through the air and crashed into the water below.

Each kick through the salty brine sent shivers of pain from the gunshot wound, but Bark still managed to work his way back up to the surface. He gulped for breath between each wave that battered his face. Without the use of his hands, he wouldn't be able to stay above the water long. The *Mayhem* was too far away. He'd have to make for the cutter and deal with whatever that meant. He laid out on the water and kicked, using his hands in front of him in small motions, hoping that it would help propel him along.

Miraculously, he managed to hold his breath long enough to make it to the hull of the cutter. He eyed the side of the ship until he found the small handholds of a built-in ladder along the side. Would he even be able to make it up in his state? He didn't know, and some mental nudge urged him to just give up.

But he couldn't. He wouldn't.

As he made his way up the small indentations, another officer flew over his head in the grasp of a tentacle.

Four left.

To his right, he saw the kraken's head pop above water, the bulbous mass of flesh surrounding her big inky eyes. The boat lurched again as Bark realized that she'd grabbed hold of both sides now, pulling the cutter towards her. She was big, but not big enough to eat a boat.

Bark scrambled, fighting through the pain until he finally managed to sling himself onto the deck of the cutter. No one seemed to notice. Two officers now stood at the rear of the boat, firing rounds towards the kraken's head. She didn't flinch, either because the bullets didn't hit or because they didn't faze her. That left a guy at the harpoon gun out of Bark's view, and the woman. Who would be—

A boot struck him hard on the left side of his ribs, causing Bark to cough and wheeze. For the life of him, Bark couldn't understand why she hadn't shot him yet. He rolled onto his back, gasping for air and resigned to whatever fate came.

Bark felt the deck shift under him, gravity pulling him towards the aft section of the cutter. The woman lost her balance, tumbled into his chest, and scrambled to get her footing. Bark rolled and twisted, managing to grab hold of the railing along the side. How the hell was the kraken tilting the boat up? Even Bark didn't realize she was that strong.

As he got himself situated, hot pain shot up his leg again, this time from the force of the agent holding onto his ankle. Bark looked down at her wild eyes and realized that this woman no longer meant to subdue him. Now she needed him to survive.

With his good leg, Bark kicked hard at her knuckles, over and over, struggling to keep his hands gripping the wet railing. Partially because he knew he couldn't support the weight of them both, but also because he knew he'd have to sacrifice her if he wanted to escape.

The woman was strong, latching on to his good leg with her other hand so he couldn't kick anymore. His hands slipped, but he barely managed to regain control. They'd both fall soon enough.

Then a tentacle shot over the railing, towards the agent, the purplish tip wrapping around her throat. The woman clawed with one hand at the suction cups tightening around her but found no purchase against the kraken's oily skin. The force pulling on Bark slackened as the tentacle supported the weight of the officer.

Crack!

At first, Bark thought it might have been the boat, caving to the pressure of being upended, but his stomach churned as he realized that the sickening pop came from the now lifeless agent. Her hands released as she fell away from Bark into the water. A glance down confirmed that the two agents had also fallen in.

One left.

The kraken lifted her head farther out of the water, revealing a huge beak serrated with terrifying white teeth. Bark had never seen this part of her before, but the stress of keeping himself aboard the vessel left no time for wonder. The water around her swirled and shifted as she seemed to inhale everything around her. One of the agents screamed as his leg lodged into the crooks of her teeth.

Bark didn't see the rest. He refocused, managing to pull himself up enough to steady his good foot onto the railing. When secure enough, he glanced down, only to see half of one of the agents floating out to sea. He could only assume the other half now slid down the kraken's gullet. Why had he bothered to dismember those teens at all?

The boat started to correct itself, tilting back to its normal horizontal position. The kraken's head lowered into the water, leaving only her eyes staring back at Bark. A harpoon collided into the water next to her, causing her to disappear beneath the waves and reminding Bark that he wasn't safe yet.

When the boat crashed back down, Bark fell to the deck and scrambled up to his knees, searching for any sign of a gun. When he couldn't find that, he hobbled over to a fire suppression cabinet, punched the glass, and pulled out a crowbar. Blood trickled from his knuckles, but the pain easily faded into the background as he moved to find the last of the Coast Guard officers.

Bark made his way around the cockpit and peeked around the corner at the harpoon gun. The officer unshackled from the harness and sprinted to the aft section of the boat to check on his compatriots, never suspecting that Bark might have been aboard. Once the officer crossed in front of him, Bark slammed the crowbar down into the crown of the agent's head and watched as the young man crumpled to the deck.

Bark dropped the crowbar, doubled over with his hands on his knees and took a big long breath, coughing and tasting the salty water burning in his throat. He fought the urge to sink to the deck and instead made sure that none of the officers in the water still lived. A few rounds surveying the deck made it obvious that they'd all drowned — or worse.

He found a set of universal keys in the officer's pockets, managed to get the handcuffs off, then, welling his strength, heaved the harpoon officer over the railing. He didn't know if the crowbar had killed the harpooner, but if not, the water would.

The cutter now sat unmanned, silently floating alone in the water. *Madre's Mayhem* had drifted away, so Bark worked his way to the cockpit of the Coast Guard vessel.

Bark knew they'd be coming for him now. In greater numbers and with more weapons. Though no one would know the entire situation, he harbored no doubt that one of them had radioed back to shore.

As he slid across the water to the *Mayhem*, he tried to work out the next step, but came up empty. Did it even matter if he got rid of Stacy and Tanner?

By the time he climbed back aboard his own ship, the agony and pain overtook him. He collapsed onto the deck of the *Mayhem* and tried to catch his breath, forcing his brain to stay awake and fight for an answer, but he could only come to one conclusion.

There was no way out of this one.

CHAPTER 24

With Miriam driving, Tommy slipped into the seat across from Macy at the front of the boat, wiggling this way and that to avoid the sharp edges of the worn leather poking out. He tried to remember the last time he'd gone out on a boat. His stomach sloshed with every wave, but he couldn't be sure whether it came from impending sea sickness or worry.

"You ok, detective?" Macy asked across the way, her voice elevated to cut through the wind.

"Yeah. I'm ok." Tommy nodded, then changed the subject, motioning up to Miriam through the plexiglass windshield. "How does she know where we're going?"

Macy smiled. "Saw a map on Bark's boat. Mir has a thing for maps. Memorizes them like instantly. It's spooky."

"She seems to have a lot of weird skills," Tommy mused.

"Yeah." Macy giggled. "You haven't even seen the really weird stuff yet."

Tommy tried to imagine what the really weird stuff might be. He had a hard time squaring the young, mousy-haired girl with the stories he'd read about her killing the beast of Rose Valley. She looked innocent, unassuming, and shy. Yet, somehow, he believed that she possessed the skills it would take to rescue Stacy — currently, his only goal.

It didn't seem too far-fetched for Tommy to go off the book to get a job done; he was the cop who always looked the other way, after all. But this seemed crazy even for him, and he couldn't help but appreciate the irony of his actions being so uncharacteristic as to bring into question whether they were his at all.

"You think she's right?" he hollered to Macy. "That they're being controlled?"

Macy shifted in her seat, taking a beat to look up at Miriam and then back to Tommy. She shot him a half smile, and he thought he caught a wink but couldn't be sure in the dim light.

"First thing to learn about Mir is that everything goes a lot smoother if you just assume, she's right. She's always right about these sorts of things."

A parasite controlling Bark. And Newt. Causing Joe to do something so stupid that it got him killed. Tommy couldn't decide if that made Joe's death easier or harder to accept. Maybe if he'd listened to Stacy. Tried to get Joe medical help. Maybe a doctor could have found the parasite and cured him. And then maybe Stacy wouldn't be held captive by someone in the thrall of a kraken. It sounded outlandish even in his private thoughts, but Tommy tended towards believing Macy about Miriam's accuracy in such matters.

The motor on the *Mama Jean* slowed down, growing quiet enough for Tommy to hear the water again. Was this the vortex? It looked just like regular ocean to him. As he scanned the horizon, though, he saw a boat in the distance, a shadowed, angular monstrosity that could only be a coast guard vessel. It had to be the USCGC *Orvar*; the only coast guard boat assigned to Cape Madre. No sign of the *Mayhem*, though.

Tommy hopped up and made his way to the cockpit, holding on to the railing to keep his balance, lamenting that he never spent the time to earn his sea legs. Miriam fiddled with the radio.

"I didn't want to turn this on," she said. "But something seems off. I'm gonna try to raise them."

Tommy leaned against the doorframe and peered back out towards the cutter. Its searchlight bobbed up and down with the waves, haphazardly pointing into the ocean. He hadn't seen the ship enough to know what the silhouette should look like, but the front seemed sharper and longer than he would have imagined.

"Coast guard vessel, please come in, over," Miriam said into the handheld microphone, as if it all came second nature to her. Tommy wondered if she had a handheld radio license. Seemed consistent with her weird set of skills.

While she waited, Miriam moved towards Tommy and stared out across the horizon. "Looks like its launching ramp is deployed. They wouldn't sail like that."

She stepped back to the radio, turned some dials, then tried again. Tommy felt like he should be helping, but he didn't know what he could do, so he pulled his sidearm from his side holster and double-checked that it was loaded. It was the only weapon they had save for the bloody baseball bat, but Tommy couldn't bear the thought of having to shoot Bark.

Miriam hung up the mic, then cranked the motor back up.

"Gonna go check it out," she said.

Tommy only nodded, holding on to the frame of the door as *Mama Jean* surged forward. In a matter of minutes, they pulled up alongside the *Orvar*. A chill shot up Tommy's spine when he could see the deck in disarray, covered in water. As Miriam suggested, the launching ramp extended out over the waves. Something was certainly wrong.

"Um guys," Macy yelled from the front of the boat.

Miriam and Tommy both rushed to the front and peered over the edge, following Macy's gaze to the water where something floated. A pair of pants, maybe? The blue fabric billowed, until a wave caught it and *thunked* it against the side of the *Mama Jean*. Tommy swallowed hard.

Miriam put an arm across Macy's chest and pushed her back away from the edge, confirming to Tommy what he suspected. A pair of pants, yes, but the legs were still in them and the torso was gone.

"Ew. Ew. Ew!" Macy exclaimed, collapsing back onto her bench. "Is that…?"

Miriam frowned. "I'm going over there. Stay here."

"I'm coming with you," said Tommy.

Miriam stopped and studied him, leaving Tommy to wonder whether she would deny his request. Though she couldn't, of course.

"Will you be okay over here by yourself?" she said to Macy.

The girl looked shaken. Unlike Miriam, Macy didn't seem to have a handle on things at all. She nodded slowly, then stood up. "I'll wait in the cockpit."

The three of them made their way to midship, where Macy peeled off, leaving Miriam and Tommy to cross over to the *Orvar*. Miriam grabbed a nearby rope and started tying it into a noose.

"Did the kraken do all this?" Tommy asked while she worked.

"Not sure, but probably. How many people would you say were on this boat?"

"I don't really know. At least a handful. Maybe five? Ten?" Tommy responded, considering the insanity of ten trained coast guard officers now dead to some legendary monster.

Miriam tossed her noose over the gap between the *Mama Jean* and the *Orvar*, barely missing one of the mooring anchors on the side of the ship. Tommy half-expected her to nail it on the first try.

As she tried again, Tommy hollered across the water, "Hello?"

No answer.

On the second try, the loop hit its mark. Miriam pulled, tightening the rope.

"Wanna help here?" she asked with a hint of exasperation.

Tommy scrambled behind her and picked up the rope. Together they heaved, the two boats drifting towards each other across the waves. Before long, the two hulls clinked together, and Miriam began tying one end of the rope to the railing of the *Mama Jean* so that they could cross over.

Tommy joked, "Nice work. Were you a boy scout?"

Miriam hopped over the railing and into the *Orvar* before answering. "Dad thought boy scouts were amateurs."

Of course. Of course he did. Tommy worked his way over next, pulling his sidearm from the holster the second he reached even footing. Miriam lit the way with the white light of her cell phone.

The *Orvar* seemed quiet. Eerie. They boarded on the port side of the ship. Other than the water on the deck, things seemed normal. As if all the officers had decided to go for a swim.

"Watch out," Miriam said, putting an arm up before Tommy could take another step.

He looked down and saw broken glass all over the deck. Probably not sharp enough to cut through his shoes, but certainly better safe than sorry. He followed the shards to a fire suppression container on the side of the cockpit, its glass broken, but most of the contents still intact.

"A fire?" Miriam asked rhetorically. "Surely not a fire."

Tommy surveyed the equipment inside the case and tried to account for what might be missing, but he came up empty. Maybe the glass had been broken accidentally. For a kraken attack, he expected more gore, but somehow the surreal silence unnerved him more than a hypothetical deck full of blood.

They rounded in front of the cockpit and made their way to the starboard side, where Miriam rushed towards a large metal gun bolted to the deck plating. It looked old and rusted, with a leather strap hanging from the butt of the gun.

Miriam ran her hand along the shaft, as if to appraise its worth. At her feet, in a metal case also bolted to the deck, were a stack of metal harpoons. They were huge. The kind Tommy could imagine one might use to take out a great white shark, or whale. With nothing except the kraken nearly that large in the waters of Cape Madre, Tommy wondered why the coast guard even had such a relic.

"Man," Miriam said. "I wish we could take this with us. This is what we need."

"Ship's too big for us to pilot," Tommy said. "And I don't think we've got the manpower to move that thing."

"Yeah," Miriam responded. "Probably they use a crane to mount it. No matter, though. I'm sure they've got weapons onboard somewhere. I think that should be our priority."

Clearly, there existed little hope of finding any officers alive on the *Orvar*. Trying to picture what might have happened to them made Tommy want to throw up, so he pushed the images away and followed as Miriam worked her way around the ship. Past the harpoon gun, they found a crowbar on the deck, along with a hint of blood. The first they'd seen. Neither of them touched the crowbar.

"Fighting a kraken with a crowbar?" Tommy asked. "Seems like poor odds."

Miriam knelt and studied it, and only then did Tommy notice the faintest drops of blood trailing off towards the side of the ship as Miriam traced the path with her light.

"I don't think the kraken did this," she said.

Tommy shuddered at the thought of the crew turning on one another, trying to escape a creature that they couldn't understand. It seemed impossibly unlikely that it would have come to that.

Miriam stood up and shined her light back towards the bow of the ship. "Launching ramp." She pointed the light back to the crowbar. "This."

"Bark?" Tommy asked.

Miriam shrugged. "Maybe. I think they definitely docked with another ship, and surely our kraken's not clubbing people with crowbars."

Tommy considered the possibility. Clearly, the creature was smart, so maybe it could pick up weapons and use them. But why do that when it could just strangle people to death, or drown them, or, as his roiling stomach reminded him, eat them?

"How many more coast guard ships are stationed here?" Miriam asked.

"Just this one," Tommy responded.

Miriam sighed. "So, we're alone, then."

"Corpus Christi isn't far. They'll send back up."

"This will all be over by then," Miriam said, shaking her head.

Tommy didn't respond. The two of them found the metal stairs leading downward and descended into the dark hold. Miriam found a light switch in short order, though, and for the first time since they'd boarded the *Orvar*, Tommy felt a little bit comfortable, glad for at least the illusory safety of the light.

Miriam slipped her cell phone into her pocket. "We need to find weapons. Traditional guns are fine, but handheld harpoon guns are better."

"You don't think they hit it with those big harpoons upstairs?" Tommy asked.

"Hopefully, but I doubt it. If they took out the kraken, there'd still be someone here."

Fair point, though Tommy preferred to believe that some brave officer spent his dying breath firing a harpoon straight into the kraken's brain.

As they searched, Tommy asked, "I seem to remember something about octopuses having multiple brains."

Miriam nodded, snaking her way through a bunkroom, Tommy in tow. "Yeah. Nine of'em. Kinda. It's complicated. And the plural is Octopi. Still, though. Hit the central brain, and it'll die."

At the end of the bunkroom, they found a smaller chamber full of weapons. Miriam immediately started sifting through them. Tommy searched the walls and found a rack of perfectly-spaced harpoon guns.

"This what we're looking for?" he asked.

"Perfect! We should take'em all. And all the harpoons too."

She motioned down to a large case filled with harpoons. Dozens of them. More than they'd be able to carry in one trip. Tommy reached down and cradled as many as he could carry in the crooks of his elbows, while Miriam pulled two of the guns from the wall. Together, they made their way back to the port side to the *Mama Jean*.

"Macy!" Miriam hollered. "Come help us here. Take these and put them inside."

Macy appeared in a heartbeat. Over the course of multiple trips, she emptied their arms into the cockpit. After two more trips, they had six harpoon guns and what seemed like an inexhaustible supply of harpoons.

Both happy with the haul, Miriam and Tommy stepped back onto the *Mama Jean*, and Miriam leaned over to unlatch the *Orvar*. It immediately drifted away in the waves. Tommy hated to watch it go, feeling as if they'd lost some level of protection.

In the cockpit, Miriam checked a handgun she'd pilfered for ammo. Tommy hadn't seen her take it.

"What's that for?" he asked.

She sat the gun on the dashboard and started up the *Mama Jean's* motor.

"That's for Bark."

CHAPTER 25

The chain dragged against the chamber as the anchor *splooshed* into the water and began its two-hundred-foot descent to the seafloor, just on the precipice of the vortex. Bark surveyed the calm, moonlit water for any sign that she might have followed, but nothing bubbled to the surface. Though she'd shown no signs of injury, he worried that the coast guard had landed a few hits.

With *Madre's Mayhem* anchored, Bark made his way to the deck, dropped a first aid kit, and slid down beneath the wall, collapsing under his own weight and trying to fight off the emotions threatening to overwhelm him. He had always been so good at moving on, doing the next thing, and putting the past behind him, but now it promised to all catch up with him. All his decisions. All his mistakes. The dark side of all his goodwill.

He rolled up his pants leg and studied the bullet wound to his shin. With all the blood, it was hard to judge the severity, but he could still walk and maneuver. He hissed when he poured alcohol over the wound, which looked only like a decent-sized scrape. With medical tape and gauze, he dressed it as best he could, then leaned back against the wall to let the pain dissipate.

Since leaving ten dead officers in the water, Bark had considered his options, concluding that he could never return to Cape Madre. Or to America. His only option was to run. To push the *Mayhem* past waters that it had never seen to find a port somewhere in Mexico, or maybe the Caribbean. Though he often thought he might live forever, he knew the years were catching up with him, and with any luck he could live out the rest of his life before the authorities found him.

He pulled a rough hand across his cheek, at the nagging feeling of something there. It came away wet. A tear.

Bark tried to conjure up the last time he'd cried, but his brain only wanted him to think of her. Waiting for him below the waves. Waiting for the next offering. But when he ran, who would take up his mantle? In trying to survive, Bark would doom Cape Madre to pain, death, and surely the complete destruction of its livelihood.

But, none of that mattered anymore. She couldn't save him. He pushed himself back up on his feet and stared at the dark passage down to the hold. Before he could run, before he could shirk his responsibilities in the name of survival, he had one last task. One more horrific thing to hang on his conscience.

He climbed down the steep stairwell into the hold, where he turned on an LED lantern. Shadows danced eerily along the inner hull.

"What did you do, Bark?" Stacy said calmly.

Bark wondered what it had all sounded like from down here. The gunshots. The shouting. The screaming. He wondered whether his captives felt hopeful during the chaos, before realizing with dread that no rescue would be coming.

Bark finally replied, "Only what I had to."

The bonesaw sat on the table, still bloody from the two drunk teenagers. The memories haunted him. The girl, especially, was tiny. Smaller than some fish. Stacy and Tanner were both bigger, the latter closer to the jock with the tiger tattoo. The thought of having to carve them up sickened him.

Bark sighed and slipped into his office for bullets to refill his gun. Flipping the light on, he paused to consider the map taped to his desk. He'd diligently marked every time he saw her. Every time she attacked someone. Every time she surfaced near him. Every time the two of them sat in silence together, with nothing but the sounds of the waves between them.

He didn't know why he mapped it all, but he gave in to the compulsion once again and marked a green X to signify the loss of the Coast Guard officers. Bark managed to keep her on a tight leash. Other than Joe, and the two college kids, no one had died until today. When judging life on an absolute scale, Bark gave himself accolades for saving at least a few lives.

The bullets rolled around the drawer when he opened it, floating freely along the bottom. He fished two out and loaded the pistol that he pulled from the waistband at the small of his back. He'd only need two.

Bark slipped the gun back into his waistband before squeezing back into the hold, not quite ready to pull the trigger. He desperately wanted absolution. He wanted Stacy, at least, to understand that he couldn't just turn himself in. He didn't want to take other lives, but now it had come down to his own life or theirs, and he tried to convince himself that, when it really came down to it, anyone would make the same decision to save their own life.

Intent on having a reasoned conversation, Bark walked across from Stacy and slid down to the floor, sitting eye level with her but far enough way that she wouldn't be able to lash out at him. The boy, handcuffed to the other end of the table, turned his head to the left so that he could see.

When Bark finally spoke, his voice strained under the tears trickling down his leathery cheeks. "I wish I could explain it, Stacy."

She didn't say anything, but her eyes stared intently at him, judging him. Bark continued, "I'm so sorry about Joe. I wanted to save him. Honestly, I did. I knew how it felt to be attacked by her. I knew that drive to go back. To find her again. To spend time with her. I didn't want Joe to give in to it like I did, so I did the only thing I could think of."

Stacy shifted, her own eyes starting to bubble with tears. If he thought she'd stay calm, Bark would have released her. Comforted her.

Instead, he kept talking. "I blacklisted him, Stacy. I made sure nobody in Cape Madre would take him on. The fisherman. The marinas. No one. I figured if he couldn't get out on the water, the urge would just pass. And he'd go back to normal. Go back to you. He stole a boat once. Did you know that?"

Stacy shook her head and whispered, "No."

"He did. But I caught him before he got out here and forced him right back to the docks. I didn't know it'd be that strong. I didn't know he'd try to swim to her. How could I know that?"

He paused again, searching for any sign of forgiveness from her. Or, at the very least, the acknowledgment that Joe's death affected him as much as her. But she remained steely-eyed and distant. He supposed he didn't really deserve any more than that.

He stood and reached around for the pistol, then thought better of it. He couldn't do it. He couldn't watch Stacy die. He knew that letting her drown out in the ocean was the coward's way out, but his heart just couldn't take the pain of shooting her, much less dismembering her.

Somberly, Bark worked on dislodging the knots that kept her tied to the table. She let him work in silence, exchanging looks with Tanner that Bark couldn't understand. He considered that they'd worked on some plan to overpower him, but he couldn't believe either of them stood a chance in their current states, so he soldiered on until the ropes came loose, and Stacy went free.

He stood along with her, thankful that she remained calm.

"Let's go," he said, motioning towards the steps.

He followed behind her, on guard to any attempt at turning on him, but her spirit seemed broken. Behind him, Bark heard Tanner wrestling with the ropes, pulling against the table and grunting in protest. Confident that Stacy would remain compliant, Bark turned his back to her.

"Stop it!" he yelled at the boy. "I'll let you go next."

Their eyes met, and then Tanner did the most unexpected thing: he smiled, and as Bark tried to process the meaning of it, he felt the nauseating impact of Stacy's shoe between his legs. He doubled over in pain. Remembering the gun in his waistband, he grasped for it just as Stacy did the same. The gun fired downward, missing them both and splintering the wood.

Bark twisted, trying to maintain his grip. Stacy won in the end, and he turned to see her pointing the muzzle of the gun at him. He put his hands up, wondering if this might be the end. Maybe he owed his life for Joe's. He didn't think she could do it, though.

"Shoot him!" Tanner yelled.

Stacy's arms tightened, her elbows locking and rattling the gun in place, but her finger didn't budge.

Bark bet his life on her inability to pull the trigger. It was a good bet— he lashed out and knocked the gun from her hand before moving in and striking her face. The gun clattered to the ground and Stacy crumpled at his feet. Leaving the gun on the floor, Bark jerked Stacy up by her collar.

Blood trickled from her mouth, her eyes open but dazed. The anger burned brightly enough that Bark wanted to hit her again, but he thought better of it and pushed her up the stairs, her feet slowly plodding along. She lost her balance halfway up, but Bark caught her and slammed her onto the deck.

Once beside her, he pulled her up again and held her face inches from his own, staring into her bloodshot eyes. She focused in on him, and he thought she might say something, but instead she spit blood all over his face, the warm goo oozing down his cheeks.

Enraged, Bark dragged her to the edge of the *Mayhem*, looked at her one last time, and heaved Stacy's frail body into the still waters of the vortex.

CHAPTER 26

Miriam's carefully-considered gambit worked, as the *Mama Jean* cut across the water in near silence. She studied the deck of the ship in front of her and saw no evidence that Bark knew of their presence. She wouldn't be able to stop *Mama Jean* from crashing into the side of *Madre's Mayhem*, but she hoped that the element of surprise would be in their favor. Miriam didn't fret about the old man who waited for them, though. She worried about the unstoppable kraken waiting beneath the waves.

As their boat inched closer and closer, Miriam made out the silhouettes of Stacy and Bark emerging from the hold. She was still alive, and if Bark hadn't killed Stacy, then that meant Tanner might be alive, as well. The hope buoyed her spirits, but when Tommy pulled his gun from the holster, it brought her back to reality, causing her to grab the gun she'd taken from the Coast Guard cutter. She'd shot a man before — or at least a government experiment that had once been a man — so she felt confident that she could pull the trigger if she had to.

But she knew that couldn't be the plan. Though they could probably justify killing Bark in cold blood as the two boats sidled up beside one another, Tommy had made it clear that he wanted Bark alive.

Closer. Just a dozen yards away now. Macy stood at the bow of the ship, resolutely holding on to a rope that Miriam had given her. Once they touched, Miriam would toss the rope up, hopefully onto something sturdy, and then she and Tommy would scramble up as quickly as they could.

A good plan that broke down the moment they watched Bark throw Stacy over the side of the boat.

Tommy gasped and ran from the cockpit to the bow of the ship. Miriam was surprised when he didn't jump in the water, his body seemingly frozen in fear. She knew what she had to do. From the cockpit, she took off in a dead run and dove into the water without saying a single word to Tommy or Macy, her head barely missing the hull of *Madre's Mayhem* before descending into the water.

By sheer intuition, Miriam managed to skirt along the bottom of the *Mayhem*, hoping her breath would hold long enough to make it to the other side. The strange muffled noise of the two boats knocking together told her that Bark would now be alerted to their presence. When she could spare a hand, Miriam felt for the gun tucked in her shorts. Still there.

The pressure in her lungs built, but she ignored the pain, knowing that she had minutes. She needed to stay alert and focused, and hope that Tommy could keep Bark at bay long enough for her to get Stacy to safety. When the hull started to creep back towards the water, she knew she didn't have far to go.

She broke the surface, gasped for air and looked around for any sign of Stacy.

Though bloody and confused, Stacy sat treading water, understandably surprised to see Miriam. With Miriam's hair darkened by the water and matted against her face, Miriam doubted that Stacy would even recognize her.

Miriam swam to Stacy and looked into her eyes. "Are you okay?"

Stacy only nodded, her eyes vacant. She was clearly in shock, which limited Miriam's options. Getting back on the *Mayhem* would be a daunting task, but *Mama Jean's* lower profile gave them a fighting chance. It was longer than Miriam wanted to stay in the water with a potential kraken lurking nearby, but swimming around *Madre's Mayhem* was their only option. With Stacy hooked under one arm, Miriam set out towards the bow.

A gunshot rang across the water. Miriam swam faster.

***

Tommy clumsily worked his way up to the deck of *Madre's Mayhem*, leaping over the wall to see Bark there and charging him. He tried to avoid him but proved too slow, falling to the ground as Bark's leathery hands grasped for his throat. Tommy worried that Bark would go for his gun, but Bark's huge body prevented him from reaching across to get it himself.

The old man was strong. Stronger than he had any right to be. Tommy bucked and shifted and tried to throw Bark off him but instead just felt the vice-grip of Bark's hands. Tommy tried to plead but could barely even breathe, left only to stare into Bark's hateful eyes. Tommy had never seen such eyes on Bark before.

Tommy clawed at Bark's meaty hands, to no avail. At least Miriam would save Stacy. At least Tommy's sacrifice would serve a purpose.

Clunk!

Just when Tommy considered giving in to the larger, stronger man above him, Bark's hands went slack, and he rolled off to the right, clutching his head and rattling off a string of expletives. Tommy was left looking up at the flushed, anxious face of Macy Donner, now staring with disbelief at the baseball bat in her hand.

The time to worry about Macy would have to come later. Hearing Bark scuttle across the deck, Tommy jumped up, pulled his gun from the holster and fired a round towards where he guessed Bark to be. The shot missed wide, and Bark took the opportunity to crawl across the deck and slip head-first into the hold. Tommy heard him hit the bottom hard.

"Stay here!" Tommy warned Macy.

Tommy inched towards the hold carefully, unsure of what might happen next. He felt certain that Bark would have a gun. Above the hole leading downward, Tommy peeked over into the darkness. He could barely make out Bark's silhouette at the bottom of the stairs, a gun pointed up toward Tommy's head. Tommy dodged out of the way, but Bark never pulled the trigger.

Bark's gruff voice echoed up, "I don't want to kill you, Tommy!"

"Yeah?" Tommy asked. "Could've fooled me."

Tommy tried to find an angle that would give him the advantage, circling around, but unless he learned to ricochet bullets, Bark had him in a standoff. Tommy looked at the hold's heavy wooden door and started concocting a plan. If he couldn't take Bark out, maybe he could lock him up, sail the *Mayhem* back to port and then deal with it.

"Leave. Get back on your boat and go home!" Bark yelled.

"Not gonna happen, Bark."

Bark's gun cocked. "If you don't, I'll kill the kid."

***

Miriam wrapped a blanket around Stacy's shivering shoulders, frantically looking around the boat for Macy. If she wasn't on the boat, that meant she went over to the *Mayhem* with Tommy. It didn't make sense that Macy would have left the safety of the *Mama Jean*. The adrenaline shot through Miriam like a bullet train, now driven by a need to protect the two most important people in her life.

"Stay here, ok?" Miriam said, trying to get Stacy to focus. "I'll be right back."

Stacy rocked back and forth on the bench curved around the aft section of the boat. She needed help, comfort, and probably a doctor, but Miriam either didn't have or couldn't spare any of those things. She patted Stacy's shoulder one more time and bound towards the bow, scrambling up the side of the *Mayhem* just in time to hear Bark threaten Tanner's life.

Tommy eyed Miriam quietly, his face sullen and hard. Macy sat against the wall of the deck, clutching tightly to the bloody baseball bat.

Miriam assessed the situation and quickly realized what Tommy surely already knew — a head-on attack against Bark would only mean Tanner's death. But if they left, Bark would likely kill Tanner anyway. There had to be another way. A way to turn the tables. She searched the deck, her eyes judging the usefulness of everything she saw.

She looked again, this time searching the wooden deck, her eyes landing on bullet holes.

Miriam motioned with her left hand for Tommy to keep Bark talking, while she quietly got to her hands and knees and crawled slowly towards the holes. If they went all the way through, then maybe she could get a good angle on Bark. Guess where he was by his voice. Though it was a long shot.

"If you do that," Tommy shouted. "Then you'll be a murderer, Bark."

"Ain't nothin' new, Tommy."

"Prison. Forever. Maybe the death penalty. Do you want that?"

Miriam made it to the holes and inserted one of her fingers all the way through. She wondered why there were bullet holes in the deck of *Madre's Mayhem* and decided that she could thank the Coast Guard for that. Her angle would be limited, but she could at least get a shot down. If it didn't hit Bark, it might at least startle him enough. Or it might get Tanner killed.

"I'm sorry, Tommy," Bark hollered up, the slightest hint of strain in his voice. "I didn't want it to go this way."

"You're sick, Bark," Tommy said. "We can help you. If you just give yourself up now."

Miriam judged Bark's location and knew there'd be no hope of a direct hit, but she placed the muzzle of the salt-water drenched gun against the hole, hoping that it would still fire. She conjured up the image of the hold in her mind, trying to imagine where he might have Tanner. She needed verbal confirmation. She needed to know she wouldn't hit him.

"Tanner?" she yelled suddenly. "Are you alive?"

Almost immediately, his voice reverberated up. "Miriam? I'm here!"

Perfect. She could tell that Tanner sat somewhere closer to the bow of the ship, far away from the hole that she meant to use as a distraction. She exchanged a look with Tommy, hoping that he understood the stakes. Once she fired, Tommy would have to act fast before Bark could get his bearings and kill Tanner.

Bark yelled up, "You brought that stupid girl?"

"Yeah," Tommy replied while shooting her a smirk. "She's persistent."

Bark let out a short, sharp laugh. "Well, now you know the kid's alive. So, I mean it. I'll shoot him."

Tommy widened his eyes and gave Miriam a sharp nod. She took a deep breath, tightened her muscles, and squeezed the trigger. Tommy leaped into the hold, skipping the stairs entirely. She heard the thuds and echoes of a scuffle, but no gunfire yet. She scrambled over and dropped down into the dim light of the hold, where Tommy sat on the floor, blood trickling from his hairline.

Bark held a gun at Tommy's head, an evil smile on his face. Miriam didn't spend time to formulate her plan. Bark hadn't registered her arrival into the hold yet, and she had to take advantage of it. She pulled up her pistol, aimed, and fired.

***

To Tommy, it seemed like the bullet had torn through Bark's shoulder in slow motion, blood and tissue spraying out like snowflakes drifting to earth. A shoulder wound wouldn't kill Bark, but it at least caused him to drop the gun. Tommy scanned for his own gun, found it, and scooped it up. He shoved it into his holster, certain that Bark wouldn't need to be threatened now.

Bark clutched his right shoulder, blood seeping through the cracks in his fingers. He started to turn towards Miriam but fell to his knees before he could make a full turn. Then onto his back. Bark coughed and sputtered.

Tommy moved to Bark, kneeling above him. The man's eyes no longer held the hateful vitriol from before. Tommy brushed Bark's hands away from the wound, took the handkerchief from his back pocket, and pressed down hard. It wouldn't be enough, Tommy knew, but it would help. Maybe give Bark a fighting chance to make it to a hospital.

He didn't expect the sadness to weigh on him as it did. He didn't just need to save Bark to be a good person. He *wanted* to save him.

"You ok, Tanner?" Miriam asked, breaking Tommy from the moment.

"Yeah," Tanner replied. "I'll be fine. Help him first."

Tommy didn't pay attention to what Miriam did, only barely registering her slipping through a door to another room.

Holding his handkerchief firm, Tommy said, "We'll get you back to a hospital, Bark."

Bark faintly nodded, his eyes hazier by the second.

Tommy kept talking. "Why Bark? Why'd you do all this?"

He could see the corners of Bark's mouth trying to form a smile, but before he could get there, he coughed and moaned. "I... I wish I knew, Tommy."

Miriam appeared again, this time holding a sizable first aid kit. She went to work immediately, brushing

Tommy aside as she dressed the wound with expert grace.

As she worked, Tommy muttered, "Thank you."

"I'm not a monster, Detective," Miriam said without missing a beat. "I don't want anyone to die. Help me here."

Tommy took her cue and helped lift Bark up slightly so that Miriam could get to the entrance wound on his back. Bark groaned in pain. Tommy marveled at Miriam's skills. The resilience. The maturity. A kid. The same basic age as all those kids that ruined his life every spring break, but this time someone he could look up to. He never expected to find a role model in someone so much younger than himself.

"Is Stacy...?" Tommy asked.

"She's fine," Miriam responded. "On the *Mama Jean*. In shock, I think, but fine."

Miriam studied her work, and then nodded.

"Okay," she said, ushering Tommy to gently lower Bark back down. "We still need to get him to a hospital, but I think we can move him over to the *Mama Jean*."

With that, Miriam stood and crossed over to Tanner, hugging him before going to work on the knots holding him to the table. Tommy sat next to Bark, surprised when he felt a rough hand close around his own. He looked down at Bark.

"Thanks, Tommy," Bark whispered.

Tommy squeezed the old man's hand, trying to offer comfort whether or not Bark deserved it. The emotions coursing through him were complicated and difficult to understand, but he would figure those out with time. He took a deep breath, finally allowing himself to detach from the situation. They got Stacy and Tanner back. Apprehended Bark. But it wasn't over.

Almost on cue, *Madre's Mayhem* sank deeper in the water, rocking harder than it would from any wave one could expect this far out.

A scream echoed from outside.

***

Tanner's face was swollen and bruised. He looked hungry and tired. He smelled bad. But most of all, he was alive. Miriam felt whole again, ecstatic to have him back. It wasn't their way to heap praises and love on one another, but she knew he felt the same.

By the time the boat rocked, Miriam was working on the last of the knots. When Macy's scream rang out, Miriam desperately wished she could be in two places at once. She couldn't protect Macy and Tanner at the same time, though. The best she could do was to get everyone in one place.

"Can you walk?" Miriam asked Tanner.

He pushed up to his feet gingerly, holding the table for support. He'd be able to hobble along, but he was in no shape to fight a kraken. Neither was Stacy. Nor Macy, for that matter. As much as Miriam wanted to complete the task, she recognized that circumstances didn't allow for it now. She slid herself under one of Tanner's arms and took the brunt of his weight from the table.

"We gotta go," Tommy said from across the hold, trying to pull Bark to his feet. Bark cussed and moaned, but Tommy managed it just as the boat rocked again, almost sending both men back down.

Miriam shuffled forward, Tanner in tow. She ignored the protests of pain that escaped his throat with every step and forced him to push on. The stairs were difficult, but Miriam went behind him, pushing up with all her strength. If he slipped and dropped his full weight on her, she'd stand no chance of keeping him up, but Tanner's strong biceps proved up to the task of heaving himself up, even with limited use of his ankles.

Miriam took in the situation and saw the tentacles curling around the boat. She wondered whether the *Mama Jean* was similarly afflicted. Macy was no longer onboard. The baseball bat rolled around on the deck. Miriam counted off the tentacles. Four. All wrapped around the boat she stood on. That left four more unaccounted for. She could only hope that the kraken used them for support instead of going after the *Mama Jean*.

Tommy's labored grunts pulled Miriam's attention back down to the stairwell, Bark's pained face looking up at her. Below, Tommy supported Bark on his back, but the old man was far too heavy and large for Tommy to walk up the stairs that way.

Miriam nodded to Tanner and they both dropped to their knees, reaching down and instructing Bark to grab hold with his good arm. Together, Miriam and Tanner heaved Bark up onto the deck, Tommy pushing from underneath. Bark screamed in pain. Miriam didn't know if he'd make it, but she wasn't going to leave him to die. She'd done the revenge thing with Cornelius. She wasn't going to do it here.

Besides, was any of this really Bark's fault?

Once all four were on deck, Miriam dragged Tanner along towards the *Mama Jean*. Halfway there, he resisted, hanging back and surveying the deck, his eyes wide with wonder.

"She's... amazing," he said. "Just give me a few minutes."

Miriam's heart broke. Not him. Not Tanner.

"No!" she forcefully spat out. "We're going."

When he continued to resist, she shouted to Tommy, "Detective! Help me!"

Right behind her, Tommy lowered Bark to the ground, spent a half second surveying the insane tentacles whipping around them, and took up Tanner's other side. His added strength provided enough leverage to pull Tanner along to the edge of the boat, until they looked down at the bow of the *Mama Jean*. Macy stood at the bottom, gesturing frantically. No sign of the kraken on this side of the boat.

The drop wasn't far, but Miriam knew it'd be painful for Tanner. She couldn't make herself care. Getting him away from the kraken took priority. With Tommy's help, they heaved him over the side and lowered him as far as they could before dropping him down and letting him fall the last few feet. Macy immediately scooped him into her arms and cupped his face, muttering words Miriam couldn't hear.

A tentacle lashed out and grabbed at Tommy, but he evaded just in time. The two rushed together to get Bark, going through the same routine with him after Macy helped Tanner hobble away. Tommy jumped down next, leaving Miriam alone on *Madre's Mayhem*. The boat shook and shuddered. What did the kraken mean to do?

A tentacle snaked towards her methodically. She managed to grab the bat rolling on the deck and slam it down against the tip, grazing the smallest of the suction cups. It retreated briefly, long enough that Miriam was able to turn and hop down onto the *Mama Jean*.

She counted six tentacles now, all wrapped around the now-abandoned *Mayhem*. It creaked under the pressure. As Miriam started the engine on her own boat, the hull of the *Mayhem* cracked, a string of broken metal snaking up the side. Like legends of lore, this kraken was about to sink a sizable ship. And that meant they had time.

As Tommy and Macy tended to Stacy and Tanner, Miriam, for all she could, pushed the *Mama Jean* away from the creature she'd come to kill, away from any chance to learn more about a monster that defied existence. With Tanner safe, now she could mount a real hunt. A real expedition.

With the distance between them growing, Miriam looked back to see the kraken slide off the broken pieces of the *Mayhem*. Though she couldn't be sure, it seemed to lurch in their direction as it slipped below the waves.

CHAPTER 27

Tommy set the handset down on the thin metal casing of the CB radio and breathed a sigh of relief. They weren't back to shore yet, but at least now he could count on a couple of squad cars and ambulances when they got there.

He looked at Macy, sitting with Tanner's head on her lap. At Bark, stretched out on the bench across from them, unconscious and fading fast. Stacy sat in silence at Bark's feet, staring into the distance.

"You think Bark'll make it?" Tommy asked Miriam.

"I don't know," she replied, hesitating. "I-I'm sorry that I shot him."

Tommy didn't answer right away, trying to process the complex emotions surging through his veins. Probably Miriam had done the right thing, but Tommy still felt guilty, as if letting Bark shoot him might have brought Bark to his senses and put an end to all this madness.

"You did what you had to," he finally said.

He bent over and picked up one of the harpoon guns they'd stacked on the floor, then a bolt of ammo. Loading it proved easy enough, and soon Tommy felt a little bit safer.

"Those bolts are heavy," Miriam said while he worked. "And slower. You'll have to aim higher than you would with a gun. It's a different kind of skill."

Tommy nodded, understanding the truth of what she said without really processing the reality of it. He hoped he wouldn't need it.

They stood next to each other in silence while Tommy recapped the entire bizarre situation in his head. They'd left the *Mayhem* severely damaged, on the precipice of the deepest waters in the gulf. The ship had taken its secrets with it, and that meant Tommy would never get the luggage that Miriam had seen. He wondered how Bark had done it. Overpowered two co-eds before dismembering them and, he could only assume, feeding them to that creature.

And then what? He'd taken Hannah's hotel key, gathered up the luggage, and left the key in the room so it looked as if she'd just checked out? He might have been old and ragged, but Bark was clever. So clever that Tommy never suspected him, which made Tommy feel foolish and naive.

He turned to Miriam. "Here's the thing I don't understand about your parasite theory."

Miriam nodded with a look on her face that told him she welcomed the intellectual challenge.

"Yeah? What's that?"

"So, the kraken attacks and then they get infected. Makes'em want to get back to the kraken. Take care of it, I guess. But what about Emma?"

"What about her?"

There had been no time for Tommy to tell Miriam about Emma, but she was the missing piece that he couldn't fit into the parasite theory. "I talked to Emma before I came out here. She seemed fine. Scared. Worried. Never wanted to set foot in an ocean again. That doesn't square with all of this."

Miriam shrugged. "Maybe it has some sort of incubation period? That would make sense, right? Maybe she'll change her mind still."

"Maybe," Tommy admitted. "We'll keep an eye on her just in case, but she was attacked before Tanner. And he already seems to be smitten with that thing."

Miriam stared out at Tanner for a few beats before responding, "There's something we don't understand."

Something? There were a million things they didn't understand. Tommy couldn't keep up with the number of things that currently perplexed him. The fact that Miriam just kept moving forward, as if the world hadn't been turned upside down, amazed him. He was tired, hungry, and running out of the will to continue. Someone would have to hunt down this kraken, but if he could just get them all safely back to shore, he'd make sure it wasn't him.

"How much further?" he asked.

"Not long. Ten minutes maybe."

Tommy took his harpoon gun and stalked out to the back of the *Mama Jean*, staring out across the endless, abyssal ocean. The moon bounced brightly off the water, rendering every crest a tentacle, every shadow a fleshy mass protruding from the water. Tommy had never particularly liked the ocean, and now he felt the stirrings of a proper phobia.

Soon, though, he could get back to normal police matters. Like arresting the murderer bleeding out on the other end of the boat.

It would be a hard road from here. For Bark. For Tommy. For the entire city of Cape Madre. Everyone loved Fred Barker. And even after what Bark had done, Tommy couldn't quite convince himself that Bark deserved the derision.

As he surveyed the waves, he thought he saw a loop arch out of the water. Then another. He squinted and focused, hoping that the shadows played tricks on him, but he couldn't ignore the rounded tip of a tentacle that popped out of the water mere feet from the boat, the suction cup glinting in the moonlight. He thought his body didn't have anything else to give, but he felt his heartrate rise, the blood pounding in his ears.

"She's here!" he hollered as loudly as he could.

Miriam's head stretched out of the cockpit, trying to see what Tommy saw, but she couldn't get the right angle without leaving the wheel. Miriam had only one job right now: to steer. The kraken had to be his problem.

He sprinted to the opening beside her. "Just drive. I'll hold it off."

She looked dubious, but didn't protest. Tommy moved back to the aft section of the *Mama Jean* and raised the harpoon gun to eye level, trying to remember what Miriam had told him about the weight and the speed.

He focused on the water, trying to ignore the growl of the motor, hoping he'd be able to hear the splash of the kraken. Anything to zero in on his target. When he found nothing off the aft section of the boat, he moved to the bow, where Macy sat clutching Tanner's hand, fear reflecting from her eyes.

That girl had saved him from Bark back on the *Mama Jean*, and that meant something to Tommy. He'd lay down his life to keep her safe. To keep all of them safe. He told himself this more than he felt it, because he needed courage. He needed something to push him forward into the insanity of trying to fight a giant octopus, armed only with a harpoon gun meant for taking down sharks and rays. Fearsome creatures that somehow seemed laughable now.

Something slick and slimy arched out of the water, too close to the bow for Tommy to react. The boat moved too fast for him to get a shot off.

"Watch out!" he yelled.

The boat swerved at his command. Miriam's eyes focused on the horizon before them. Despite Miriam's best efforts, the *Mama Jean* skipped across the tentacle lying in the water and bounced into the air. Tommy squatted and held on to the edge of the boat as Macy and Tanner likewise braced themselves. The boat landed back into the water hard, sending Bark toppling to the deck. Stacy didn't even react.

Without thinking, Tommy set his harpoon gun down on the bench Bark had vacated and knelt beside the old man. He felt for a pulse and found one, faint but thumping away. He considered hefting Bark back onto the bench but decided the deck might be more stable.

"Tanner!" Macy yelled behind him.

Tommy spun to see Tanner propping himself up so that he could stretch his muscled arm across the gap. He fell back into his seat, with Tommy's harpoon gun in tow. At first, Tommy reasoned that Tanner being armed could only be a good thing, but when the barbed end of it trained directly on him, he knew nothing good would come.

Tommy didn't know Tanner, but a universal understanding of humanity told him all he needed to know. Tanner was panicked, worried. Angry.

"She won't hurt us," Tanner said. "Leave her alone."

Macy looked helpless next to Tanner's hulking form, confused and terrified. Tommy calculated the situation. The harpoon gun, slow and heavy. Tanner without the use of his legs. How quickly could he react? How much experience did he have with such weapons? If Miriam was any indication, the answer was plenty.

Tommy held up his hands, trying to simultaneously meet Tanner's gaze and scan the horizon for another breach from the kraken. "I'm just trying to keep everyone safe."

"Stop it!" Macy yelled at Tanner, slapping at his bicep but causing no shift in his aim. "What are you doing?"

"I'm not going to hurt anyone," Tanner said calmly. "And neither is she."

Tommy had his doubts, but for the first time the claim did make him wonder whether the parasite worked both ways. He assumed the kraken had followed in a mad frenzy before, but now he considered the possibility that she had come to save Bark and Tanner. He thought back to the attack on the *Mayhem*, trying desperately to remember any detail that would prove the theory. Then again, maybe it didn't matter.

While having been zoned out for much of his hostage negotiation training, Tommy tried to summon up anything he could remember. "Mr. Brooks. I don't want to hurt anyone or anything. I just want to get everyone to safety."

"We're already safe," Tanner replied.

Tentacles danced alongside the boat, arching out of the surf on both sides as the *Mama Jean* skimmed across the water. How did such a creature move so incredibly fast? It seemed even more surreal than the kraken itself.

Tommy turned towards Miriam, her eyes wide. She cocked her head gently to the right and Tommy took the meaning. As soon as his eyes turned back to Tanner, the boat swerved suddenly, causing Tanner to lose his balance.

Tommy lunged forward, grabbed the muzzle of the gun and forced the pointy end of the harpoon toward the sky. With Tanner seated, Tommy had leverage which he used to his advantage, twisting the gun out of Tanner's hands just as the boat came to a sudden halt. The motor still ran, sputtering and whining, louder now, as if the entire mechanism had been pulled from the water. Then the boat began to tilt forward, just slightly, the way a bus might as it slammed on its brakes.

Miriam yelled from the cockpit, "Get the motor back in the water!"

Tommy shot Tanner a stern look and bounded off to the aft section of the boat, unable to make out the scolding that Macy spewed Tanner's way. To his left, he saw the faint lights of Cape Madre. The fishing ships lining the docks. The flashing blue lights of the reinforcements. The fading dim bulbs of the Shady Shark "No Vacancies" sign. They were almost there. Tommy just had to free the boat from a kraken.

The writhing mass of flesh at the back of the boat seemed omnipresent and indistinguishable as any one piece of the animal. He supposed he stared at tentacles, but they'd wrapped around one another, engulfing the top of the motor while impressively avoiding the dangerous part at the bottom. Knowing very little about boats, Tommy worried that a harpoon might go through the flesh and into the motor, leaving them dead in the water.

"Here," Miriam said from behind him. She held out a machete that Tommy didn't even know they had. "I found it in the cockpit. Give me the gun."

Tommy obeyed, handing over the harpoon gun and taking the machete. Could he hack his way through this? He didn't have time to worry about it, slamming the machete's dull blade into the mass of flesh and slicing the slimy skin. It was too large and thick to cut through, but blood oozed encouragingly from the cut.

Miriam stood beside him, the harpoon gun pointing out to the water, moving jerkily from tentacle to tentacle as they swarmed around them. Yet she never took a shot, as if she was waiting for something.

As he brought the machete back for another whack, something grabbed his wrist. Without looking, he knew what it was. A hot poker of pain shot down from his wrist into his chest.

Miriam fired the gun. A loud, squishy *thunk* as the harpoon plunged through the tentacle holding Tommy at bay. Almost immediately, the grip loosened then snaked back into the water, the lodged harpoon clanging against the side of the *Mama Jean* as it disappeared.

"Dammit," Miriam exclaimed. "Needed that one for the head. I'll be right back."

She sprinted to the cockpit for more ammo. Tommy took another whack at the slimy mass engulfing the motor. His wrist yelled with pain. As he pulled back up, he saw the tentacles rising toward him from both sides of the boat this time. She wouldn't let him hit her again.

He ducked and dodged and hit the deck to avoid the tentacles coming for him. From a sitting position, he swung the machete wildly, hoping to force them away.

Miriam came around the corner in a flurry, holding a loaded harpoon gun in each hand. At first, he thought she'd somehow wield both at the same time, but she leaned one against the back of the cockpit, trusting the gravity of the boat's tilt to keep it in place. Though he expected her to shoot at the tentacles slowly writhing towards him, she instead ducked under them, looked towards the motor and fired.

K'thunk!

The tentacles swarming Tommy retreated in an instant and he scrambled up beside Miriam. The boat dropped suddenly as the twisted-up tentacles around the motor slid back into the water. Miriam dropped the gun and raced back to the cockpit. Tommy followed.

"How'd you do that?" he asked, quickly realizing that she couldn't be bothered to answer.

The lights of the shore drew closer, streaking towards them as quickly as the *Mama Jean* could push. Behind them, the waves rumbled and boiled, evidence of the kraken skimming beneath the surface of the water. They raced her now, and Tommy feared that they wouldn't come out the victors.

"Get the rope," Miriam yelled. "Get ready!"

Tommy made his way to the mooring rope coiled up on the deck and grabbed the end of it. The docks approached quickly, and Miriam showed no signs of slowing down. After a few more feet, Tommy could make out the uniformed officers on the dock, then paramedics hanging back near their ambulances. Surely, they could see the speed of the approach. They needed to move.

Tommy yelled above the whine of the motor, "Move!"

Closer.

Confusion danced across their faces.

"Move! Now!"

One of them seemed to catch on this time, scurrying away and motioning to the cop beside him.

The boat swerved hard, knocking Tommy to his knees, rolling Bark across the deck, causing Macy to hop from one bench to the other. Tanner and Stacy managed to brace themselves effectively. The side of the boat skimmed towards the dock at an ungodly speed. Miriam cut the motor just as the *Mama Jean* slammed into the side of the dock. The force of it almost knocked Tommy down again but he held his ground, vaulted over the edge, and planted his feet on the wooden planks of the dock.

The boat tried to careen away, bouncing off the docks and back into the deeper waters, but Tommy put all of his muscle into keeping it alongside him. After he managed to contain the momentum of the boat, he looped the rope around the mooring anchor, surely in a completely inappropriate way, but good enough to keep the boat close.

The cops and paramedics rushed in, following Tommy's direction to go for Bark and Tanner first. Stacy and Macy stumbled off the boat and retreated far into the parking lot, still visible but out of harm's way. Miriam jumped down soon after with a loaded harpoon gun, a handful of harpoon bolts, and the machete that Tommy had carelessly left on the deck. The *Mama Jean's* hull caved and cracked where it had collided with the dock. Tommy briefly wondered whether Newt had insurance.

Then, the cracks and dents didn't seem to matter so much, as tentacles slammed down over the *Mama*

Jean. On the other side of the boat, Tommy saw it for the first time. The bulbous mass of its head. The dark, knowing eyes. And a huge beak, open wide and revealing rows of terrifying, serrated teeth.

It seemed impossible. Surreal. A legend come to life. Fear coursed through him, but also the slightest hint of something else that he didn't like and couldn't suppress...

She was beautiful.

CHAPTER 28

The uniformed officers rightly retreated behind the doors of their squad cars, both vehicles carefully positioned so that the open doors could be used as barricades. They stretched their sidearms out in front of them, but both Tommy and a boat stood between them and their target. Though Miriam harbored no hope that the bullets from a standard issue pistol would do any significant damage to the kraken, she appreciated the show of support.

The paramedics strapped Bark into one ambulance and forced Tanner and Stacy to share another. They needed to go before things got ugly.

"Go with them!" Miriam yelled to Macy, motioning to the ambulance that contained Tanner.

Macy took a step towards the ambulance, then stopped, shaking her head and clearly screwing up her courage. "No. You might need me. He'll be fine."

Miriam studied Macy's mascara-streaked face, her hair long past the point of presentable. In front of Miriam stood a battle-hardened Macy, running solely on willpower and defiance. That didn't change the fact that Macy didn't know the first thing about survival or fighting. Or how to fire a gun properly. But Miriam longed for the emotional support that Tanner would usually provide, so she nodded.

"Ok," Miriam said. "But stay back unless I need you."

One of the paramedics hollered from the back of Tanner's ambulance. "You comin' or not?"

Miriam answered, "No. Go on. Get them out of here!"

The paramedic seemed more than happy to comply, slamming the door on the ambulance just as it started to bounce through the torn-up parking lot of the Shady Shark Motel. The second ambulance followed.

Tommy stood on the dock, still next to the *Mama Jean*, but in increasingly more danger as the kraken appeared and slammed her tentacles over the scuffed-up boat. The only weapon he had left was his own pistol. But he hadn't drawn it. He just stared at those huge black eyes, seemingly mesmerized. The fear that he had carried all night for the kraken seemed to evaporate before Miriam's eyes.

When she'd freed Tommy's wrist from that tentacle, she'd hoped that he would be able to stay with her until it was all over, but now she knew that she'd lost him. It was bad enough that Miriam needed to take down a kraken, but now she'd lost her staunchest ally. And might have to fight him first.

She sighed, wishing for a better way to carry her arsenal which she awkwardly held against her body, using her elbows and two hands. She'd need to be more agile if she had any hope of survival.

She dropped the spare bolts, used the strap on the harpoon gun to loop it around her shoulder, and carried the machete in her non-dominant left hand. If ever she would be the superhero that Macy claimed her to be, now was the time.

Miriam surveyed the scene carefully, turning doubt into surety, fear into strength, and worry into resolve. It all happened naturally, her mind moving so quickly that time inched forward in slow motion. The grueling training of her childhood. The pointless expeditions into the wilds. The relentless whip of her father. Now it all paid off. Now it would save a town.

Four uniformed officers. One compromised detective in love with a kraken. A well-meaning, but terrified best friend. And a kraken. An honest-to-God, living legend of the deep. If her survival wasn't at stake, Miriam might have taken the moment to revel in the grandiosity of it all. To appreciate that this was exactly the sort of thing her father had always wanted to find.

She marched forward, crossing the distance between her and Tommy in a matter of moments. She worried that the uniforms would take her as a threat, but she could tell by their wide eyes and shaking guns that they were too enthralled by the sight of an enormous octopus to pay her any mind.

With Tommy focused on the kraken in front of him, Miriam slowed her walk as she approached, trying to be as quiet as possible. When she got close enough without alerting him, she reached under his arm and pulled the gun from the holster. He spun on her, reaching for the gun himself only to find it missing. He looked hurt. Betrayed.

She used her free right hand to tuck the gun into the back of her shorts. She didn't want to shoot him. She just wanted to make sure he couldn't shoot her.

Several tears trickled down Tommy's cheeks. She could see him fighting the confusion, but the kraken interrupted any hope of a conversation. It lurched, using its huge tentacles draped over the *Mama Jean* to propel itself forward, up and up until the mass of its body crept over the cockpit. The hull creaked under the weight, all eight tentacles flailing wildly.

Miriam felt electricity in her veins as she waited for Tommy to make a move. She couldn't afford to turn her back to him.

A tentacle slapped into a light post along the dock, splintering the wood of the post. It rocked back and forth, causing Miriam to run her gaze down the shaft until she saw where the wood barely held together. Just as she found the weak point, it toppled down towards them. Tommy turned and Miriam jumped, pushing him out of the way as it came crashing down to the dock.

Back on her feet in an instant, Miriam watched Tommy crawl away towards the squad cars. Could he turn the four officers against her? She didn't have time to worry about it.

Another tentacle landed hard beside her, punching a hole straight through the dock and into the water, splitting the light pole in half. Miriam sprinted away from the middle of the *Mama Jean*, scanning the dock for cover. The echo of gunfire pierced into the air, but if any of the bullets struck the kraken, she couldn't tell. Its meaty gelatinous form seemed to absorb them.

As she ran, a tentacle shot out in front of her, causing her to turn the other direction, where another tentacle took the flanking position. She tossed the machete from her left to her right hand, reared back and slammed the blade towards the dock, focusing on her follow-through, expecting to hit the hard wood below. She didn't feel the thunk of the wood, but when the tentacle retreated, its bloody tip hung limply from the end.

For the first time, the kraken bellowed. An ungodly deep sound, like a tuba from hell. The tentacle behind Miriam wrapped around her ankles and pulled, her chest banging into the dock and knocking the wind out of her. The harpoon gun threatened to slip from her shoulder, but she used her left hand and caught it by the strap just as the kraken lifted her in the air.

The warm, slimy suction cups of the tentacle seared into the skin of her bare ankles. How long did she have now before the parasite would stop her from fighting?

Though she expected to be pulled towards the terrifying teeth of the creature, instead she found herself high in the air, dangling from her ankles, trying desperately to hold on to the weapons that seemed useless. Using her core strength, she did a sit-up in mid-air and hacked at the tentacle with the machete, but without any leverage it bounced off her target, barely slicing into the skin at all.

Then she came hurtling down, still grappled by her ankles and incapable of escaping a date with the hard pavement below. Worried that the machete would impale her, she tossed it blindly away. She couldn't give up the harpoon gun, though, so she held it above her head, the bolt pointing away from her.

It hurt. Bad. Every bone in her body jostled and shook, clanging together in unnatural ways. The brunt of the trauma pounded into her chest, as she felt something inside give way. A rib, maybe? She coughed blood onto the ground as the tentacles dragged her back along the pavement, over the splintered wood of the dock, then back up into the air.

From her vantage point, she saw one of the officers with a rifle now, firing across the water and hitting at the base of one of the kraken's tentacles. Another bellow issued forth.

This thing meant to clobber her against the pavement until there was nothing left of her body. She had few options. As her arc reached its peak, she fumbled with the harpoon gun, pulling it up and desperately trying to aim it upside down. The weight. The speed. She calculated it all in a matter of seconds, pulled the trigger, and bounced back as the harpoon flew from the shaft towards its target.

Bullseye! The harpoon plunged into one of the kraken's huge black eyes, which burst open in a spray of thick, translucent goop. Miriam hit the pavement with less force this time. The tentacle didn't let go, though, and as she flew back up into the air, she dropped the harpoon gun. It was of no use without another harpoon to load it with.

The useless pistol, miraculously still cradling the small of her back, was all that remained of her arsenal.

Below, another of the tentacles crashed down into the door being used as a barricade by the rifle-bearing officer, scattering the two men hiding there. The kraken snatched the door and threw it towards the retreating men, striking one of them. Miriam searched the ground for Tommy, unable to find him, worrying that he waited to thwart her attack.

Miriam's eyes found Macy next, kneeling on the pavement. Macy haphazardly held the harpoon gun up, trying to cram one of the bolts that Miriam left behind into the muzzle. Macy moved frantically, fumbling through the process, but Miriam saw the bolt snap into place just as the upward arc of the tentacle ended.

This time, it twisted, and instead of slamming Miriam back down on the pavement, she found herself face to face with the dark water. Moving downward, with only seconds to spare, Miriam pulled the pistol from her waistband, spun and fired as many rounds as she could into the back of the kraken's head. She didn't know how many rounds were left in the cartridge, but she hit the water before she could empty it.

Plunging into the salty brine, Miriam used the resistance of the water to try to free herself from the kraken's grip, but she only felt the pain in her ankles as she wriggled. Perhaps the kraken meant to drown her. As the water rushed past her on her way back up, she did her best to aim the gun towards the tentacle, as close to her own feet as she dared.

She fired, the gun kicking back lazily, the boom of the muzzle muffled and distant. The tentacle loosened its grip, and Miriam took the opportunity to kick away, wincing at each painful stroke of her leg. Her head broke above the water's surface, hidden from the kraken's watchful gaze. Miriam knew that it could sense the vibrations in the water, though, even with the bulk of its mass resting on the sinking hull of the *Mama Jean*.

She quickly sorted through facts in her head. About Octopi. About Krakens. Legends. Stories. With her weapons largely inadequate, Miriam needed some way to conquer this thing. Her mind provided her with one option. An unreasonable option. Likely even impossible.

She swam towards the *Mama Jean*, slower than she would have liked. The script played in her head: the brave pirate allowing himself to be eaten so that he could damage the creature from the inside, heroically saving his ship and his crew. This kraken was too small for that, but Miriam reasoned that a nugget of truth hid in those stories.

Once she made it to the boat, she scrambled up the side onto the sinking deck. It hurt to stand, and her ankles threatened to turn and collapse but she wouldn't allow it. Every labored step got her closer to the cockpit and the giant fleshy creature on top of it. She had only the pistol, unsure of how many bullets were left in the cartridge, and doubtful that it mattered at all.

She couldn't see what went on in in the parking lot, but the tentacles whipped and slashed through the air above her, slamming down and creating pops, cracks, and crashes with every hit. She imagined crushed cars and dead police officers, and Macy standing resolutely among the carnage, trying to help.

The bellowing roars increased, electrifying the air. Miriam now stood behind the creature, where she could see the tiny bullet holes in the back of its bulbous head, and the larger hole where the harpoon had exited after traveling through the eye. Individually, perhaps they meant very little, but the sum of the bullets surely amounted to something.

She released the cartridge from the pistol to check her bullet count. Two shots left. It would have to be enough.

K'thunk!

A harpoon flew past Miriam on the right, hitting nothing but the water behind her.

Next— a shrill scream.

Miriam looked up to see a huge tentacle clutching Macy by the waist, wrapped tight around her bare midriff. The tentacle picked her up, yet Macy managed to hold onto the harpoon gun with her right hand, and, in her left, an unloaded bolt.

Miriam checked her stomach. Her head. Her heart. So far, she felt no weird attraction to or admiration for the kraken in front of her. Only the overwhelming need to make sure it died a painful, horrible death.

"Macy!" she yelled.

Macy looked down and saw her, tears streaming from her big green eyes as she kicked her legs at air. "I tried, Mir. I tried."

Miriam scrambled up the side of the cockpit just as a tentacle found her. She fought through the pain, stomped a foot down to push the tentacle away, and moved up further. On the other side of the kraken's head loomed its mouth and remaining eye. Her target. Her only hope.

Another tentacle came for her. Against all odds, she dodged it, but it quickly came back. For support, she reached her arms around the kraken's massive head, pressing her body as flat as she could, inhaling the rotten fishy smell of its skin. It seemed to work, the tentacles trying and failing to find purchase. Mostly out of the water, its ability to move its head was limited, and Miriam used that to her advantage.

She scooted around, trying to ignore that her ankles wanted no part of supporting her weight. The head turned toward her, slowly, and then they were face to face. The serrated teeth gnawed and chomped towards her, rows and rows of them leading down a dark, ominous gullet. Though huge, it couldn't eat her in one bite, but she feared she wouldn't be able to keep it at bay forever.

Miriam looked up at Macy dangling in the tentacle above, still clutching the weapon Miriam wanted most. Their last chance hinged on an impossible throw — something that would only work in an 80s action movie. But desperate times...

"Throw it!" Miriam yelled up to Macy.

Macy didn't question it. If she doubted her abilities, she didn't show it. She tossed the bolt first, sending it through the air end over end. Miriam predicted its path, confident that she could catch it until a tentacle rammed into the back of her knee, causing her to lose her already precarious balance.

The harpoon got closer.

Miriam stretched and twisted, then felt cold metal strike the palm of her hand. Down on one knee, in front of a horrifying gaping maw, Miriam had a proper weapon. But she wanted the gun, needed its force to lodge the harpoon deep in the primary brain of this monstrosity.

Macy then threw the harpoon launcher. Her aim was off this time. Miriam wouldn't be able to catch it from her perch in front of the kraken, so she slipped off the cockpit and dove forward, her possibly-broken ribs crashing into the water and careening against the deck.

The harpoon gun landed in the water in front of her, so she scrambled along to get it, barely noticing that the deck underneath her began to shudder and sink. The *Mama Jean* groaned as it finally started to give up its valiant attempt to support the weight of something so remarkably huge. Before she got to the harpoon gun, she watched it sinking into the murky waters of the gulf and found herself with nothing to stand on as the deck melted away from her.

Miriam dove. Aiming for where she could only guess the harpoon gun would be, she struggled to move forward with one hand wrapped around the bolt. She blindly waved her hand in the water, praying for a bit of luck.

Her free hand hit something. The harpoon gun. She was sure of it. She wrapped her fingers around the muzzle of the gun just as she felt a wrenching pain in her thigh, pulling her back in an instant. Her fingers slipped from the gun, then got tangled up in the wet leather strap. She flew through the water at blinding speeds, into the air, where another tentacle wrapped around her waist.

She felt her broken ribs impaling her organs. Probably bleeding internally but she couldn't care about that, not now. She had a harpoon gun. And a harpoon. And the tentacles were pulling her closer to the exact place she wanted to go.

In the water now, the kraken's head seemed more alive, able to move and bend in ways that it couldn't before. Salt water ran down the beak, dripping off the teeth like blood.

It pulled Miriam closer.

The tentacle tightened, crushing her. Briefly wondering whether it was trying to turn her into an easier-to-swallow mash, she hastily loaded the bolt into the harpoon gun and stared into the kraken's one black eye. It bellowed, just as she got within feet of it. She could feel the hot exhalation run past her skin, could smell the rank breath diffusing in the salty air.

Miriam Brooks had spent a lifetime hoping to find something as mystical as this creature. Hoping to prove that the legends of man held an ancient truth. She'd seen a lot of messed up shit, but this thing was truly magnificent.

And ugly.

And she hated it with every fiber of her being.

"Miriam!" Macy screamed.

As the tentacles tried to cram Miriam head first into its waiting teeth, she pointed the harpoon gun up to the roof of the kraken's mouth, angling it toward what she thought might be the brain.

This thing could go straight to hell.

She fired.

A thunderous, aching groan.

The tentacles loosened.

As she fell, her arm grazed the thing's teeth, shredding skin. The mouth didn't chomp shut as she feared, and Miriam toppled into the warm salty water below.

CHAPTER 29

Her body refused to cooperate. Miriam tried to kick her feet to propel herself back to the surface, but she barely made any headway before the pain forced her to stop. Her right arm stung against the salty water, so she used the only good limb remaining, trying to leverage enough water to push herself up.

She didn't know if her shot had killed it, but she could hear muffled splashing all around her.

And then arms — not tentacles — wrapped around her tender rib cage. A soft presence pushed against her back. And then, in an instant, Miriam could breathe again, greedily sucking in all the fresh air she could.

Macy kicked along, no doubt in pain herself as she managed to get them both safely to the dock. She fished Miriam out, requiring a little of Miriam's upper body strength to get the job done. Miriam collapsed onto her back, grateful to be out of the water. By Macy's lack of urgency, she assumed the kraken was no longer a threat.

Miriam pushed herself up onto her elbows and stared out across the water. The *Mama Jean* had almost completely disappeared beneath the water line. The kraken floated on the surface, its tentacles stretched out haphazardly, seemingly dead, though Miriam didn't think she could fully accept it yet.

"I didn't know you could swim like that," Miriam said.

Macy pushed a lock of wet red hair behind one of her ears. "Yeah. I was totally a lifeguard in high school. I never mentioned that?"

Miriam almost laughed, but the pain in her ribs prevented it.

"Mostly for the boys, though," Macy said. "Didn't think I'd actually ever need to save someone."

Miriam turned her head towards the squad cars, one of them overturned and the other missing a door. Someone was beating on the back window of the upright car. Miriam squinted and saw it was Detective Tommy Wallace, watching the dead kraken with a pained expression.

One of the uniformed officers ran up to them. His nametag said Grabowski. "Ambulances are on the way. That was amazing!"

His red cherubic face regarded Miriam with more awe than she felt like she deserved. She asked, "What happened to Tommy?"

"Oh," Grabowski answered. "Detective Wallace, you mean? He told us to lock him back there and to not let him out no matter what he said. He said some pretty awful stuff."

Grabowski shuffled off to tend to one of the fallen officers. Miriam smiled and collapsed back to the dock. Was it over? Had she really just killed a kraken?

She reveled in the frustration that she could imagine creeping across her father's face as he read the news.

Take that, dad.

Macy stretched out beside her and they both stared up at Cape Madre's clear coastal skies. Stars speckled the horizon in every direction. Soon, she would be whisked away in an ambulance, and the pain shooting through every part of her body longed for the relief, but she found something meaningful and relaxing about lying there with her best friend, next to the carcass of an impossible monster.

She was exhausted. But also proud. Of herself. Of Macy. Tanner would still need to be cured, but Miriam felt confident there'd be a way. She thought of Cornelius and actually smiled, thinking of how excited he would be to study the carcass. So much to learn. So much to prove. And now it all fell to her.

"Are we gonna go crazy now, too?" Macy asked.

Miriam considered the question without an answer. Whatever the parasite did, it hadn't affected her yet. She felt nothing but derision for the creature floating in the water. Certainly, she wasn't wracked with the pain that she saw in Tommy's eyes. There was something about it they still didn't understand.

"Tommy said Emma didn't turn either," Miriam said.

"So, like, it doesn't affect girls?" Macy posited.

"Hmmm," Miriam hummed. "Maybe you're on to something."

She wanted to roll to her side so that she could look Macy in the eye, but when she tried, her ribs protested, so she stayed on her back and settled for turning her head. Macy did the same.

"In Greek times," Miriam suggested. "Sailors told tales of the sirens. Beautiful creatures of the sea that sang a song so beautiful that the men couldn't resist it, but women easily ignored the call. It led the men into treacherous waters and ultimately to their deaths... Maybe it wasn't a song. Maybe it was a parasite."

Ambulance sirens echoed in the distance. Miriam let out a dry chuckle, which hurt even though she couldn't help it.

"What's so funny?" Macy asked.

"The sirens are coming for us."

Macy laughed.

CHAPTER 30

Aside from the top-notch medical care, quarantine felt an awful like jail. Alone in his plastic prison, Tommy was starting to get stir crazy. He huddled on the bed, his hands between his thighs. The opaque plastic walls hardly kept out the heat. He couldn't be certain, but Tommy guessed they had him in a hangar. He didn't know why they had to keep it so cold, though. Surely, the natural temperature should be somewhere closer to the balmy air of Cape Madre.

Occasionally, he'd receive a visit from a nurse or a doctor or a pathologist, all transplants from Atlanta. He didn't understand all the lingo, but the word "parasite" was thrown around a time or two. The CDC took the threat of his affliction very seriously, but Tommy knew that they'd cured it. He could feel it. The longing. The frustration. It had all started to abate after the latest rounds of experimental drugs they'd pumped through his veins. The only things left were the overwhelming feelings of shame. At failing in his duty. At betraying Miriam when she needed him the most.

The nurses generally didn't like to talk, but Tommy managed to learn that Miriam, Macy, and Stacy had all been released within twenty-four hours of their captivity. Tests showed no signs of the parasite in their brains or elsewhere. He could only assume that Tanner, Bark, and Newt sat freezing in their own plastic hovels somewhere nearby, but not close enough that they ever answered the random questions he'd flung into the open space of his cell.

Rustling plastic alerted him to an impending nurse. The first doctor that attended to him had been a man, but after that, he'd only seen women.

"Good news, Detective Wallace," the stern looking nurse said as she appeared through makeshift flaps that acted as a door. "Looks like you're all clean. You can go."

Finally! Tommy stood from the bed, his cheap hospital gown scraping the rough sheets. He waited by the door while she unlocked it and fought back the urge to hug her when he finally stepped into the hallway. He didn't even know her name. They didn't wear name tags, and the nurses switched out every day. Still, he longed for human touch.

She led him along the hallway, through the chamber and into another enclosed room where a chubby cop stood holding a suit in one hand and a gun in another.

"Grabowski!" Tommy exclaimed. "Listen. I —"

"No need to apologize, sir." Grabowski pushed the suit out in front of him. "They told us that you weren't quite yourself."

Tommy left the hanger in Grabowski's hand, slipped off the pants, and shimmied them on under his hospital gown. "So, what's going on out there?"

"Release day," the young officer answered, helping Tommy to slip the shirt off. "Chief sent down a couple of squad cars to escort Bark and Newt back to jail. Asked me to tag along and bring you some clothes. And your gun."

Tommy chuckled. "She that eager to get me back on the job?"

Grabowski laughed. "I think she wants to shove you into a bunch of press conferences, honestly."

"Great. Sounds horrible."

When he slipped the jacket over his shoulders, Tommy felt like himself for the first time in days. He took the gun, slipped it into the holster along his side, and clapped Grabowski on the shoulder. "Thanks, Grabowski."

"No problem, detective. Just remember me when I apply for detective next year."

"You got it," he said, as the nurse motioned towards another slit in the plastic.

"Oh, Detective." Grabowski jogged to catch up beside him as the nurse opened the way. "You might want to prepare yourself."

The warning came too late. Tommy's eyes were already fixated on the bulk of the hangar floor taken up by a huge, dead monster. Its tentacles stretched out in eight different directions, each one pulled to its max. Evidence markers constellated the area around it, indicating bullet holes and abrasions.

Its sheer size overwhelmed his senses, but he didn't feel the same anguish for it that he had the day Miriam shot out its brain. Now it just looked like a comically over-sized octopus. Something he wouldn't want to contend with in the depths of the ocean, but no scarier than a whale or a shark.

Portable air conditioners lined the walls, pumping cold air into the hangar and keeping the humidity of Cape Madre at bay. That explained the incessant freezing of the past few days.

"Welcome back!" said a voice behind him.

Tommy spun to see Jess Gearhart. It felt like ages had passed since the two of them studied the severed leg down at the lab.

"What are you doing here?" Tommy asked.

"I'm the ME," he shrugged. "This is a dead thing."

Dead, maybe. But hardly human.

"It's just an octopus, man," Gearhart continued. "I mean, a new one. There are taxological differences from the little ones we already knew about, obviously. But it's not some inexplicable monster, really."

"Well, it carries a terrifying parasite," Tommy corrected, wondering how Gearhart could be so flippant in the presence of this thing.

"Oh yeah, that," Gearhart nodded. "Yeah. That's pretty special. The CDC are keeping that one a lot closer to the vest. Glad they found a cure, though. At least they think they did. You've got a lot of doctor's appointments ahead of you, Detective."

Tommy looked around the hangar, watching the dozens of people tending to the creature, busying themselves with clipboards and cameras. Tommy hardly recognized any of them. Spring Break was over by now, but it looked as if the circus would continue in Cape Madre.

"What about Miriam Brooks?" Tommy asked.

"Probably around here somewhere," Gearhart replied. "She was pretty adamant that they let her poke around. Sometimes, I think she's the one running the operation."

Tommy's stomach grumbled. He craved something unhealthier than the meals they'd been serving him in quarantine. Without Miriam in sight, he decided to look her up later, get out of the cold, and get back to his life. He pointed towards a small metal door, dwarfed next to the hangar doors.

"That my way out?" he asked.

"Yep," Grabowski said, jumping back into the conversation. "Easy to get out. Hard to get back in."

Tommy nodded, murmured his goodbyes to Gearhart, and crossed the expanse of the hangar floor with Grabowski in tow. He just wanted out, grateful for barely any inclination to gawk at the wonder of nature sprawled out beside him.

The sun hit his face as soon as he banged the bar on the exit door. Soaking in the warmth, he passed a line of guards, walked around a bank of metal detectors and out onto the tarmac of the quaint Cape Madre airport.

"I can give you a ride," Grabowski offered. "Your old Crown Vic is down at the station."

Tommy didn't hear the offer. His eyes were fixed on the long form of the woman leaning against her car just a few feet away. A smile graced her face, as it often did, but Tommy knew that this one was genuine. The first he'd seen in a long while.

"I'll take him," Stacy said.

"Yes, ma'am," Grabowski replied, quick to shuffle away to his squad car.

"So, you're back!" Stacy crossed the distance between them with her long legs, threw her thin arms around his neck, and pulled Tommy in for a hug. Not that different from the same hug he got every week when he left her house, but this one felt more important. More urgent. Less sad.

"So I am," Tommy said, releasing the hug and standing before her.

She looked him up and down, as if to take the measure of him. "You look the same. Thought maybe you'd be all heroic now."

Tommy didn't have the heart to tell her about what had happened after the ambulance whisked her away. Though he suspected that she already knew. He felt like he deserved some kind of blame — from her especially. For not taking Joe's condition more seriously. For not being able to fight against the parasite influencing his brain. For giving into his fears and not jumping into the water to save her when it mattered most. Yet Stacy stood before him, seemingly comfortable and, possibly, even happy.

"Thanks for saving me," she said quietly. "I thought Bark was going to kill me."

"Yeah. Me too," Tommy said. "I thought he was gonna kill us all."

Stacy looked into his eyes, regarding him for a minute, and making him uncomfortable with her intensity. "When he threw me off that boat. And I didn't know you were there. I thought I was gonna die. I thought I was going to drown just like Joe."

Tommy didn't know what to say, so he just stood there like an idiot, wanting to comfort her somehow. Her eyes finally tore away and scanned the pavement.

She continued, "I wanted to die. For months. Every day without Joe was a day that didn't feel like it was worth living. But alone in the water, something snapped, Tommy. I don't want to die. I want to start living again."

He didn't know how to take the confession or what it meant, but it felt significant. Shifting uncomfortably, he nodded and opened up his arms. She sank back into his hug again and he held her, not out of pity or guilt anymore. A forbidden topic crawled its way up from the purgatory he had pushed it to. He swallowed hard, unsure of what to do.

She broke away and eased the tension with a sharp laugh, "So yeah. Uh. Thanks for all the thrilling heroics and for saving the town from two monsters."

"Miriam Brooks had a little to do with it," he said.

"Yeah, I guess maybe she did a few things," Stacy said. "I don't know much about it, but they say maybe Bark isn't culpable for his actions?"

"I suppose that's for a jury to decide, but I can attest that whatever that parasite is, it does a number on your brain."

Stacy cocked her head towards the car. "Wanna grab some lunch? My treat."

Tommy's stomach grumbled again at the mere thought of food, goading him into practically sprinting towards Stacy's car. She followed behind, easily catching up and laughing that timeless laugh that Tommy thought she'd buried with Joe. Maybe something would happen between them. Maybe they could come to terms with what that would mean. But Tommy decided that they'd have to figure it out another day.

She slid into the car and laughed. "I'll take that as a yes. Calamari?"

Tommy winced. "Too soon, Stacy. Too soon."

CHAPTER 31

Miriam stared into brown eyes, the eyeliner in stark contrast to the pale face framed by wavy brown hair. A subtle glittery glow popped above the eyes, supported by rosy cheeks and a dark, all-business lipstick. She considered her reflection and wondered whether all the makeup meant that she'd sold out. Was this even Miriam Brooks anymore?

Macy stood behind her, biting her lower lip as she focused on her task of teasing Miriam's hair. The studio had provided a dressing table, but not so much a room, and certainly not a makeup artist. No matter, Macy seemed capable enough.

"I look weird," Miriam said to the stranger in the mirror.

Macy rolled her eyes. "*Pssh*. You look amazing. Like, seriously, Mir. I mean, I knew you were pretty, but wow."

Maybe. A little. It seemed more important that she was smart. Strong. Capable. But Miriam supposed she could take pretty, too.

On the table, her phone buzzed. She glanced at the screen, already certain of what it would say.

Dad.

"Are you ever gonna answer him?" Macy asked.

Miriam tapped the decline button. "Eventually, probably."

Skylar Brooks had gone almost two years after the death of Cornelius without trying to contact her. Now that she'd done the impossible, he suddenly wanted to reconnect. She'd managed to avoid it so far, but she knew that Tanner had already caved. It seemed like only a matter of time before Miriam and her father crossed paths, especially if she insisted on continuing this wild course that she'd been rocketed down since the discovery of not one, but two previously-unknown creatures. Most people wanted to focus on the kraken, but the mind-altering parasite interested her more.

"Knock, knock," Tanner said from behind. "This came for you."

Macy released Miriam's hair long enough for her to turn around and reach for the bouquet of happy daffodils. No one had ever sent her flowers before. With apprehension and curiosity, Miriam shuffled the card out of the envelope. She smiled when she read the note and signature scrawled along the bottom.

"They're from Tommy," she said, setting the bouquet on the table in front of her. "He says to break a leg."

"I don't recommend it," Tanner deadpanned, holding up one of his crutches. Just a few more weeks of the boot, the doctors said, and he'd be good as new.

A scrawny man with a headset and a clipboard strode towards them. "You're on in five, Ms. Brooks."

"Ok," she said. Macy frantically went back to work, as Miriam wondered why the back of her head mattered at all.

The rest of the five minutes went by like a blur: Macy finishing with her hair, a young woman snaking microphone wires through Miriam's shirt, then the clipboard man ushering her to the stage. Just offstage, the hulking cameras pointed towards a news desk, where two perfectly coifed anchors sat sipping coffee. They had teleprompters, but Miriam would have to think on her feet. She knew the gist of the interview, of course, but she didn't get to read her lines from a screen.

Her stomach fluttered. Miriam regretted ever agreeing to an on-air interview, but Macy and Tanner both thought it would be good for her and for the venture they'd all agreed to start. Her first order of business would be to hire a front man, or maybe turn Macy into one. She had the looks and personality for it.

And then Miriam was in the chair, sitting next to a woman hiding behind layers of makeup, the illusion of which made her quite beautiful, indeed.

The made-up lady watched a light go red, then went straight to work. "Here with us now is Miriam Brooks, the hero who saved Cape Madre from a giant octopus! Some are calling her the world's first micro-cryptozoologist. Welcome to the show, Ms. Brooks. May I call you Miriam?"

"Uh, sure," Miriam replied.

"Great!" the anchor said. "So, you are being credited with the discovery of two new species. That must be very exciting."

"Uh, yeah. It's pretty neat."

"The smaller of the two is a parasite that controls peoples' minds? Is that right?"

"Um. Not exactly," Miriam started. "It's more complicated than that. It's really about survival. The parasite infects other hosts and then compels those hosts to care for one another, and for the primary host. It's all just evolution, really. The parasite trying to stay alive."

"Uh huh," the anchor replied, clearly not paying any attention to the response. "And they've named this parasite after you, is that right?"

Miriam could feel the blood rushing to her cheeks, grateful for the makeup that Macy had slathered onto her face. "I guess so, yeah. *Diplomiriamus pseudopathaceum.* It's actually pretty closely related to some known parasites. This is just the first one to infect humans like this."

"Very impressive."

"Yeah. It's pretty neat. It only affects males, actually. The brain chemistry of human females is inhospitable to it, so it just dies out. I think maybe it might be the root of the Greek myths of the sirens."

Miriam could feel herself geeking out, but it felt more comfortable than awkwardly stammering through yes or no questions with diplomatic and public-friendly answers.

"Fascinating. And the other one? A giant octopus?"

Miriam nodded. "That's right. It's bigger than any we've known, of course. The specimen we obtained had been around a while. They live for a long time. Octopi in general are very smart, and we think that the size of this one made it particularly intelligent."

"Are there more of them?"

"Almost certainly. We don't know for sure, but it makes sense that there would be. We think they live deep underwater for the most part, hiding in a network of caverns under the ocean. Based on some paleontological evidence, there's a strong possibility these things have been around for millions of years."

The anchor's false veneer of awe evaporated, quickly replaced by one of concern and sympathy. "And that's the explanation for the remains of Hannah Huang that turned up in the waters of Nassau?"

"Right. I can't really speak to the specifics, but we think she was dragged down into the caves, and just surfaced there in The Bahamas. They're all connected."

"Our condolences go out to the families of those affected by this creature," the anchor responded. She twisted in her chair to face forward and away from Miriam, "Thank you, Miriam. Stay tuned after the break for this week's weather!"

The light turned off. The anchorwoman sank in her seat, instantly turning back into a normal human being. "Thanks, Miriam. You did great."

Miriam wasn't so sure.

Backstage, Macy gave Miriam a warm hug. "Good job!"

"You didn't mention the website," Tanner said, wrapping his arm around Macy's shoulder as she returned to his side. The coupling had begun, and, thus far, hadn't caused too many disruptions to their trio.

"Dammit. I knew I would forget something," Miriam said. She had completely forgotten to mention their hastily-constructed website. The plan to steal business away from Skylar Brooks wouldn't work if no one knew that Miriam was available for hire.

Sometimes, she wondered whether it was the right path for her. To follow in the footsteps of someone she hated so much. But fighting that thing, learning about it, participating in the autopsy — all of it invigorated her in a way that she couldn't deny.

Whether by choice or by happenstance, Miriam Brooks was a cryptozoologist to her core. She gave up trying to analyze it, fight it, or stop it. She decided to just embrace it. On her terms. With her own team.

She vowed to legitimize the entire profession.

Fighting monsters and finishing university.

No big deal, right?

EPILOGUE

Newt Goodreaux liked *Aunt Margie* well enough, though she would never mean to him what *Mama Jean* did. He sat out on the serene waters of Cape Madre, grateful to be free. Tommy had kept his word — it had all come down on Bark and, seeing how Ol' Newt didn't do anything except not stop it, the district attorney had agreed to a deal. The DA had gone pretty easy on Bark, all things considered. He'd be back out in the waters in just a few years, so Newt scrambled to fill the void of the best fisherman Cape Madre had ever known, hoping that he could keep his foothold once Bark returned.

Newt had been doing pretty well for himself, too, what with all the fish flocking back to the vortex. None of the others had thought to try it yet, so he enjoyed the easy pickins. He brought in massive hauls, sold it all off, then squirreled away the money. He never much cared for drinking or gambling or owning nice things, and now that he finally had some money, he couldn't think of anything to do with it.

Really, his favorite thing was doing just this — sitting out and enjoying the ocean breeze. All the craziness with the kraken seemed so far away now that he hardly thought about it, except sometimes in his dreams, but mostly he could deal with that. Not every man got to live through something so fantastical. Ol' Newt considered himself lucky, truth be told.

He felt a tug on his pole. While the nets brought in the bulk of it, Newt also enjoyed just dropping a line in from time to time. He pulled up hard, felt the hook lodge into its quarry, then started reeling. The fish put up a little fight, but he could tell it wouldn't be a big one. He'd probably just throw it back. Let it get a little fatter.

He reeled and reeled, pulling up and expertly guiding the fish to the surface alongside *Aunt Margie*. He reached down, grabbed the small thing, and worked the hook out of the roof of its mouth. He let it go. It sat there for a few seconds, then wriggled and started to descend.

Then something grabbed it, causing Newt to do a double take.

A small tentacle jerked the fish forward, just as the toothed beak of an octopus rose into view and slurped the fish down its gullet.

It surfaced right next to him, black inky eyes seeming to regard him with a kind of indeterminate purpose. Cute little thing, for sure, but Newt knew in an instant that it wasn't just an ordinary octopus. No, he recognized something in it. Something he knew intimately.

A splash caught his attention, dragging his eyes to the horizon where he saw another one pop up to the surface. To his right, another. Then another. More and more of them swarmed around *Aunt Margie* in numbers that he couldn't track. They were all small and unassuming. Surely no threat. Not yet.

Instinctively, he touched the scars along his midsection. Newt looked at each one in turn, looking into their eyes, nodding and reassuring them, certain that they'd understand his words.

"Don't you worry none, fellas. Ol' Newt won't tell a soul."

ACKNOWLEDGEMENTS

Hey, I wrote another one! *The Beast of Rose Valley* seemed easy because I was too naive to know how hard it was supposed to be, but *The Kraken of Cape Madre* made sure to remind me that writing a book is hard work with a lot of ups and downs. Like before, I have to first and foremost thank the team at Evolved Publishing for getting this out the door. Hats off again to Mike Robinson, Richard Tran, and Dave Lane (aka Lane Diamond).

I'd also like to thank my critique partner, Mistie. Her insight into the story every two weeks provided motivation for me soldier through to finish the book in record time. By the end, it felt like Mistie knew my characters as well as I did. There's nothing quite as humbling as the note "that doesn't sound like Miriam" and realizing it's right.

Thanks also to my beta readers: Amanda for her insightful critiques and genuine love of Miriam. Steve for making sure I didn't focus too much on inconsequential things (and for coining the term "squidnapping" which I desperately wanted to fit in the book somewhere, but never did). Also to Ben, who took his beta-reading assignment to the next level by actually printing out the entire manuscript, putting it in a binder, and painstakingly writing out his comments by hand. And to Rachael, whose keen eye fixed up a lot of easy-to-miss typos and missing words.

And, of course, I have to thank my wife, Akaemi. Without her, I wouldn't be chasing down this crazy dream. Not only has she been my stalwart champion, but she also reads everything I write and helps to make it better in every way.

It may have been harder to write *The Kraken of Cape Madre*, but it was also more rewarding, and I'm grateful every day that I've been given the opportunity to spend my time hunting beasts and chasing krakens.

ABOUT THE AUTHOR

J.P. Barnett grew up in a tiny Texas town where the list of possible vocations failed to include published author. In second grade, he worked harder than any other student to deliver a story about a tiger cub who singlehandedly saved the U.S. Military, earning him a shiny gold star and a lifelong appreciation of telling a good story.

Fast forwarding through decades of schooling and a career as a software engineer, J.P. Barnett stepped away from it all to get back to his first real passion. Years of sitting at a keyboard gifted him with some benefit, though, including blazing fast typing hands and a full tank of creativity.

As a child, J.P. consumed any book he could get his hands on. The likes of Stephen King, Michael Crichton, and Dean Koontz paved the bookshelves of his childhood, providing a plethora of fantastical and terrifying tales that he read way too early in life. Though the effect these books had on his psyche could be called into question, these masters of storytelling managed to warp his mind in just the perfect way to spin a fun yarn or two.

J.P. currently resides in San Antonio with his wife and hellion of a cat, both of whom look at him dubiously with some frequency.

For more, please visit J.P. Barnett online at:
Website: www.JPBarnett.com
Twitter: @JPBarnett
Facebook: JPBarnett.Author
Instagram: JPBarnett.Author

WHAT'S NEXT?

THE WITCH OF GRAY'S POINT
Lorestalker – 3
by
J.P. Barnett

*It hides in the shadows, waits in the desert,
ready to pounce on any who enter its domain.*

To Miriam Brooks, a solo study trip to an abandoned desert ranch house sounds like the perfect respite from the world, a way to unwind and center herself after a string of unbelievable encounters with terrifying monsters.

Yet the desert isn't devoid of life. Something lurks outside her window, changing its form to suit its mysterious needs. She's familiar with the stories, but legend becomes reality when she stands face-to-face with a soulless copy of herself.

Another day, another monster... but before she can act, Miriam is unexpectedly flanked by the father she's been trying to avoid, along with two cocky assistants who don't understand the threat they face. She's equipped to battle the shape-shifting terror hiding in the darkness, but being forced to finally confront her father might just kill her.

MORE FROM EVOLVED PUBLISHING

We offer great books across multiple genres,
featuring hiqh-quality editing (which we believe
is second-to-none) and fantastic covers.

As a hybrid small press, your support as loyal
readers is so important to us, and we have strived,
with tireless dedication and sheer determination,
to deliver on the promise of our motto:
QUALITY IS PRIORITY #1!

Please check out all of our great books,
which you can find at this link:
www.EvolvedPub.com/Catalog/

Thank you!